THE DIRECTIVE

THE DIRECTIVE
MATTHEW QUIRK

headline

Copyright © 2014 Rough Draft Inc.

The right of Matthew Quirk to be identified as the Author
of the Work has been asserted by him in accordance with the
Copyright, Designs and Patents Act 1988.

First published in Great Britain in 2014 by
HEADLINE PUBLISHING GROUP

1

Apart from any use permitted under UK copyright law, this publication
may only be reproduced, stored, or transmitted, in any form, or by any means,
with prior permission in writing of the publishers or, in the case of
reprographic production, in accordance with the terms of licences issued
by the Copyright Licensing Agency.

All characters in this publication are fictitious and any
resemblance to real persons, living or dead, is purely coincidental.

Cataloguing in Publication Data is available from the British Library

ISBN 978 0 7553 8745 8

Typeset in Palatino Lt Std by Palimpsest Book Production Limited,
Falkirk, Stirlingshire

Printed and bound in Great Britain by
CPI Group (UK) Ltd, Croydon CR0 4YY

Headline's policy is to use papers that are natural, renewable and
recyclable products and made from wood grown in sustainable forests.
The logging and manufacturing processes are expected to conform
to the environmental regulations of the country of origin.

HEADLINE PUBLISHING GROUP
An Hachette UK Company
338 Euston Road
London NW1 3BH

www.headline.co.uk
www.hachette.co.uk

For Ellen

The police closed in. I could feel his blood dry, tighten like scales on my skin. It marked me as the gunman. I knew I should raise my hands and surrender, trust my life to the laws I had sworn to uphold, the laws that had torn my family apart.

Or I could give myself to the killers. They waited in the black car beside me, my only escape. The rear door swung open. I was innocent, but I'd seen enough to know the truth no longer mattered.

A hand reached out for me.

The only way out was to go in deeper.

I stepped into the car.

Chapter One

Four days earlier

Never bet in another man's game. It's a simple rule I picked up from my father. So what was I doing walking down a Manhattan alley, fingering twelve hundred dollars in my pocket, heading toward a three-card-monte gang who looked like they'd decided to take a break from knifing people today to fling cards instead?

I had no idea. But if I had been thinking straight, I probably would have guessed it had something to do with the eight hours I'd spent that day looking over china patterns, bookended by my fiancée Annie and my future grandmother-in-law.

Bergdorf Goodman has a little playpen they call the Engagement Suite, where a salesman in a three-piece suit and a string of well-maintained women parade luxury goods past you until finally a $1,500 pitcher starts to seem reasonable.

The grandmother, Vanessa, had stepped in for wedding duty, since Annie's mother had passed away many years before. Our salesman had an accent that sounded Argentinean and walked us through every conceivable permutation of chargers, knives, forks, saucers, teacups, and bowls.

Annie didn't care much about material things – she'd never had to – but I could see the grandmother working on her with the weight of the Clark name, the family expectations.

Hour four became hour five. This was our second stop of the day.

'Mike?' Annie asked. She and her grandmother stared at me. The salesman and his harem frowned behind them like a jury. I'd zoned out.

'Did you hear me?' Vanessa asked. 'Flat cup and saucer, or footed?'

'Oh. I'd just go with something simple,' I said.

Vanessa offered me a smile that didn't touch her eyes, and said, 'Of course you would. Don't you think this one is a little more refined, or is this a bit more . . . elegant?'

Annie looked at me. I'd do anything to make her happy, but after four days in New York in dude-on-wheels mode, getting dragged from store to overpriced store, I was running out of steam.

'Exactly,' I said.

Annie looked troubled, Vanessa angry.

'Well, which is it?' her grandmother asked. 'It was a question.'

A couple of years ago Annie's father had sent debarked German shepherds to kill me, but he was starting to look pretty good compared to Vanessa.

Annie looked from her grandmother to me. 'Mike?'

The Argentine twisted his watch chain. Vanessa pulled a 600-thread-count napkin tight as a garrote. My eyes were so dry from the endless staring and overbright glare of the department store lights I could almost feel the lids scrape as I shut them.

Flipping out – maybe clearing the table with a sweep of the arm – was growing in appeal, but probably not my best move.

I stood and clicked my tongue. 'Sorry,' I said. 'Will you excuse me? I just remembered that I have to get a call in to my accountant by the close of business.'

It was a lie, but an effective one. If there was one thing Annie's family held sacred, it was money. This would spring me.

I fast-walked for the exits. The Argentine waved me back – maybe they had some emergency recovery area with rib-eye and ESPN for overwhelmed fiancés – but I needed air and the streets.

Chapter Two

I had caught the monte game out of the corner of my eye on our way to Bergdorf's. It was down a side street piled high with garbage, about halfway between the marble showrooms of Fifth Avenue and the Middle American mall that Times Square had become.

Making my way through the crowded sidewalks, I saw the swindlers at work among the tourists. A pickpocket plied the crowd that had gathered around a Chinese portrait-sketcher. Across the street a few aspiring rappers roped in passersby, writing their names on a ten-dollar CD and then using unsubtle threats to complete the sale. Being around all that noise and mischief did me good after hours of forced manners and conditioned air.

With no real thought about where I was going, I soon found myself turning toward the monte game I had seen earlier. I was surprised to see it was still going on, though they'd moved it to the other end of the street.

The operator throwing the cards was a lanky white guy with a wiry, desperate strength to him. He wore an oversized Yankees cap pulled down over his eyes, and jeans hanging around the middle of his ass.

For a table, he had three milk crates stacked vertically with a newspaper on top. The cards and the patter flew: 'Twos lose and the ace gets paid. Find the honey, find the honey, find the honey.'

He glanced at me, but pretended not to notice as I approached. With the slightest rise of an eyebrow, he indicated to the rest of the crew that the game was on. There were four players.

As I moved in, he signaled them subtly, and they made just enough room for me to get close to the action. They played four rounds as I stood there: cards dancing, money falling and flying in the operator's hands between winners and losers. Not that it mattered. They were all working on the same team, all pooling the same money, all on the operator's side. That's how the monte con worked.

And that's why it was so stupid to risk a dime in it. Even if I knew their tricks, I'd have to beat them at their own rigged game.

I should have stopped and thought for a second about what the hell I was doing, then walked away, back to Bergdorf's and the sterling-silver sorbet spoons.

But instead I stepped into the game. The operator started working me: 'Money or walk. *The Lion King*'s down the street if you wanna gawk at something. This is players only.'

I ignored him, acted a little scared, a little tough, like your typical mark putting up a front of sophistication. Jesus, I looked the part. I'd been so busy working that week that I told Annie to throw some clothes into a bag for me for the trip. I had on a V-neck sweater under a blue blazer, some kind of moleskin pants, and boat shoes – I guess she was trying to yacht-club me up for the meeting with grandma. I looked like stupid money. I would have mugged myself.

The crew closed in behind me, pushed me closer to the game. 'Shutting the gates,' it was called, part of hooking the mark, the first stage of the short con. There was only one woman playing, and she'd just won twice. The stakes were up to forty-dollar bets. After the operator threw the cards around, you placed your bet in front of the card you thought was the ace of spades. Someone could outbid you by doubling your bet on another card. The highest bet played, leaving only one player and one bet per round. That was key to the hustle.

'He's not taking my bets anymore,' she whispered to me. 'I'm too good. I got this figured out.'

She was about five feet four, pale and blond, a city creature with a fierce look in her eyes and a body that was hard to ignore. 'Help me out,' she said with a knowing look. She slipped me eighty dollars in worn twenties as she pressed against me. 'Lay that down, on the left.'

Some pasty, mouth-breathing kid put forty in the center. I took her money and laid it down on the left. 'Eighty,' I said. The operator looked down at the bet, seemed pissed, then flipped the ace of spades next to my bet and handed me $160.

The monte con has its classic roles. The love interest to my left was 'the booster,' and her job was to give me a risk-free taste of the action, to make me believe that the operator was beatable, to convince me to get my own money in the mix. I pushed the cash I'd just won across the newspaper to her. As she went to scoop it up, the operator grabbed her wrist. 'What the fuck?' he said. 'My man here won. Beginner's luck.'

'It's her money,' I said. 'I put a bet down for her.'

He wheeled on me. 'Don't pull that Wall Street bullshit up here, Thurston Howell. You want to play? Money up. Or you spend it all on your little sailor suit?'

Berate the mark. That usually wrapped up the hooking portion of the show. I was insulted, angry, and eager for revenge – ripe for a rip-off.

'The corner's bent on the ace,' the woman whispered in my ear. She was hanging on to me like a Bond girl now, pumping up my confidence. The corner was bent back, but a skilled operator can crimp and uncrimp at will. It was another way to draw me in, convince me I couldn't lose. I took out my wallet and pulled out a twenty.

I watched him throw the cards, picking up two at a time and tossing one. Everyone assumes you drop the bottom card, but you actually throw the top with a sleight-of-hand move called a hype. This guy wasn't very good at it, but it's a convincing technique even when poorly done.

The cards fell. The ace was obvious with the crimp. I put my twenty down. Then the mouth-breather did his part. He was a 'capper.' If you ever hit the right card, his role was to immediately double the bet so you couldn't win. When you bet wrong, the capper just stands back and lets the dealer take your money. The game is hopeless.

And so it went. The capper's bet played. He lost, and then the dealer flipped over the ace where I had bet.

'You would have won, see,' the girl whispered in my ear.

I took out a few more twenties from my wallet. The operator's eyes lit up. By now we had a decent crowd going. To my right stood a few well-dressed, well-built guys who I gathered were in town for some kind of black fraternity event. To my left was an older Chinese woman carrying a big woven plastic shopping bag.

She ventured a ten-dollar bet, correctly, on the center. Maybe the capper, who seemed a little slow, missed what was happening, because he forgot to double the bet, and the lady's ten bucks stood.

It didn't matter. The operator slid the right-hand card – which I had followed and knew was a two – under her winning ace in the middle to flip it over. Somehow, as it landed, the winning ace became a losing deuce. The operator had swapped them during the turnover. That's why, even with all the money in the world to outbid the capper, you can never win.

I knew everything I needed to know to beat these guys. I pulled all of my money out of my pocket, about $900 minus what I had spent today, and palmed it. I tend to keep a lot of cash on hand: old habits.

'Ace pays and deuces lose. Follow the honey, honey's in the hive, money with the honey.'

The operator threw the cards and kept up the patter. The crimp disappeared from the card as the operator shuffled. He didn't need it now that my money was out and my trust in Pussy Galore was absolute. I followed the ace. The cards fell.

'Left,' the woman clinging to me whispered, leading me wrong. I laid ten on the center where the ace had landed. They wouldn't let me win, so the capper laid twenty on the right. All according to plan. I double him to forty on my ace. We went back and forth, 80, 160, 320 . . .

'Six hundred forty,' I said and laid it on the newspaper next to the ace. The beauty of a bet that big is that when you lay it down, the bundle of cash is wide enough to cover the cards for a split second.

The capper looked at me, dumbfounded, then at his roll – there were maybe six twenties left over. He couldn't double my bet. He licked his lips, then turned to the dealer for help.

I'd been watching them as they went for their money. I knew they didn't have me covered. The dealer didn't seem fazed.

'Gekko's greedy. Greed is good! Six hundred and forty's the bet.' All he needed to do was swap the center ace I had correctly picked with one of the deuces on the side, and the whole stack was his. He should have pretended he was a little concerned, but the guy was beaming. I was having second thoughts myself. I wasn't looking forward to explaining to Vanessa and Annie that we'd be eating at Wendy's because I got rooked at three-card monte.

I watched as he lifted the right-hand deuce and used it to flip over the ace I'd bet my money on. He switched them in the process, of course, and laid down what he was sure was the losing card.

10

'Twos lose,' he began, triumphantly. But then he bothered to actually look down at the cards, and saw the ace of spades staring up at him next to my $640 in cash. His eyes bugged out.

The spectators who weren't in on the con whooped with joy. One guy grabbed me around the shoulders.

I hadn't messed around with cards for years. Still, it wasn't too much trouble, especially with a sloppy operator like this one, to switch the cards myself with my pinky and ring finger as I laid my money down. I knew what his next move would be, so when he switched them later, he actually ended up giving me the winning card.

I'd won fair and square. And crooked.

'Cops!' the capper shouted.

I should have expected it. If the game goes south, or he takes a mark for enough money, the lookout shouts 'Police!' and everyone scrambles. It's the last resort of the short con. Even if the mark wins, he loses. The gang bolted. In one swipe of his hand the operator pocketed the money and the cards, and tried to dart away. My new friends from Alpha Phi Alpha looked like they might lend some muscle to the principle of fair play, and blocked him on two sides. As a result, he had to come through me, with a right hook to my kidneys as he knocked me out of the way and his milk crates tumbled to the ground.

The other guys shouted some very inventive threats after him. I just watched him go.

'You going to let that punk rob you like that?' one of the spectators shouted. 'You won straight up, man. I'd find that dude, and I would get my money back.'

'Never bet in another man's game,' I said, shrugged, and walked away. As I turned out of the alley, I realized I was smiling. I hadn't had that much fun in a long time. After surviving my run-in with the grifters of New York, I could certainly face down my 120-pound fiancée, her grandmother, and a footed teacup.

The whole incident took twenty minutes. Soon I was back in Bergdorf's, between Annie and Vanessa. The pain under my ribs had mellowed to a dull throb. Arturo was demonstrating the merits of different fish forks.

'Mike,' Annie said, and looked at me sweetly. 'You doing okay? Are you weddinged out for the day?'

In my lap, out of sight of the rest of the party, I examined what I had lifted from the dealer as he crashed past me. When your target is wearing pants that baggy, picking someone's pocket is easy.

He'd run off with nothing. I walked away with my $640, plus another $800 or so for my troubles and a knife unlike any I'd ever seen. It was slim, with a beautifully grained rosewood handle and brass bolsters. It must have been eighty years old, Spanish or Italian. It wasn't a switchblade, but it flicked open with such speed and ease it might as well have been. I had a feeling the kid had ripped it off from someone. That knife was one of the more lethal-looking items I'd ever held. I closed it carefully, then put it and the money away.

As I rested my hand on the cash in my pocket, I smiled. 'I'm having the time of my life,' I said, then turned to Annie's grandmother. 'You're right about the gravy boat, Vanessa. Limoges all the way. And Arturo,' I said, rubbing my hands together, 'do you still have those Haviland catalogs?'

That was the moment, flanked by my fiancée and her grandma in the Engagement Suite, fingering the six-inch blade in my pocket and the grimy roll of twenties I'd lifted off a street hustler, when I realized maybe something wasn't quite right with me, and with this dream I'd been chasing for years of a quiet, respectable life.

Chapter Three

We met Annie's father a half hour later for dinner at a French place with three Michelin stars. He was drinking champagne and talking on his cell phone at the center of an empty banquette. He ended the call, then greeted Annie and Vanessa. Finally, he looked at me, then Annie, and said, 'You still wasting your time with this guy?'

No one responded.

Then he barked a laugh and crushed my hand with his. 'Joking! Sit!'

Larry Clark, actually Sir Lawrence Clark, is an English ex-rugby star who now works in high finance, running a hedge fund. He radiates aggression and good health, and favors the sort of humor that involves putting you on the spot or lying and then laughing at you when you believe him.

He'd maintained his dense rugger's build into middle age and shaved his bald head daily into that gleaming pink power orb a lot of chief execs are going for these days. It went well with the scowl he always wore when looking my way.

I was still so wound up from my close call with the card-sharps that I didn't mind breaking bread and trading a few jabs with Clark. After the second course, I excused myself and tracked our waiter down in the labyrinth of wine racks. I intercepted the bill before Clark had a chance. It took a bit of coaxing, but I managed to get our server to let me pay.

The pleasure of outplaying the hustlers that afternoon was nothing compared to seeing Larry's face at the end of the meal, when the waiter explained, with a look in my direction, that 'the gentleman has taken care of it.'

As we walked back toward the park after dinner, Vanessa said that she was tired and asked Annie to walk her back to the hotel. Clark asked if he could 'borrow me for a moment.'

I smelled a setup. Annie lifted her shoulders.

'I'll get him back in one piece,' Clark said, but after my move at dinner and his barely concealed rage, I wasn't so sure. I went along with it. This wedding was a done deal. Maybe he finally wanted to make peace.

We strode toward a section of Fifth Avenue that was lined with McKim, Mead and White behemoths, Gilded Age hotels and robber barons' clubs.

Clark turned the knob and led us through the heavy wooden door of a town house. I didn't see a sign. Maybe it was his club, and we would hammer out a peace treaty over brandy and cigars. I didn't particularly look forward to club talk, though I'd learned to have fun playacting it over the past couple of years – laughing along with guys as they complain about being 'horse poor' and what a hassle their sixty-foot steel-hulled yachts are. But if it meant ending my troubles with Lawrence, I was all for it.

He led me into a library, and we sat down on a pair of leather chesterfields. There was no small talk. He leaned forward on the couch and started in.

'I know your family, Mike. I know the kind of people you are. It's out of my hands. Annie has made her decision, and there's nothing I can do about it.'

This is what I get after those years of hard work: the navy, then putting myself through college and Harvard Law, nights so broke and hungry I just went to bed at eight. It could have been that I was having trouble adjusting to this world, but as

14

I sat and endured Clark's glare, I realized that some part of it was due to the fact that this decent life was having trouble with me. He thought I was some delinquent, my whole life one long con.

'Larry,' I said. I knew he hated the familiar tone. 'Your daughter and I love each other. We look out for each other. We take care of each other. It's a sweet thing, and rare. I really wish you and I could start over and find a way to get along. It'd make everything easier and make Annie happy. What do you say?'

He didn't respond, just knocked his heavy ring against the marble table beside him twice. The door opened. Two men joined us. 'These are my attorneys,' Clark said as he introduced them.

So much for brandy and cigars. What bothered Clark most was that he and I were so similar. He came from nothing, and started his fortune with some very shady real estate deals in London. When he first tried to scare me away from Annie, I had hinted that I knew about the dirt in his past. That bought me some breathing room, but it also earned me an enemy. He's always resented me for outmaneuvering him.

If you hustle long enough, you can buy all the stage dressing you need to look legit, even the manners. But Clark, I feared, had finally convinced himself. That sort of hypocrisy is dangerous, and I – by who I was and what I knew and who loved me – threatened him deeply. No matter how much he talked me down to Annie, I tried to stay above it. I didn't tell her about his past. It would just look petty.

'There's some business to settle, Mike,' he said. 'I'm heading to Dubai tomorrow, so unfortunately I have to fit it in this evening.'

One lawyer handed Clark a sheaf of papers. Another held a thick leather-bound binder that looked like a corporate checkbook.

'Are there any incentives that might make you rethink this relationship? To see that it's in your and my daughter's best interest to take separate paths?'

'You're kidding,' I said.

He stared back at me. He was totally serious.

I rubbed my chin for a second, took in the mahogany bookshelves and my three inquisitors.

In my jacket pocket, I had a white card that the check had come in back at the restaurant. It was nice linen paper, blank and folded once down the middle. I took it out, along with a pen, then leaned forward and jotted something down inside. I slid it across the table, sat back, and crossed my arms.

For a moment, Clark seemed pleased that I was on board, that he could play his favorite game: haggling over money. Then he read the note.

He breathed hard through his nose in anger, and dropped it on the table.

I could see what I had written: *There's a seed in your teeth.*

I saw his tongue working behind his lips to extract it as he glowered at me. After I left my last job, a lot of firms had sought me out to come work for them. So I had a fair amount of practice shooting people down when they tried to buy me. Clark placed the sheaf of papers on the table in front of me.

I was angry, of course. I could feel the heft of the knife in my pocket, and for a moment I had a surreal image in my mind: if I poked one of these beautifully upholstered counselors, only wool stuffing would come out. But the truly infuriating issue was that I couldn't show how furious I was. That would play into his hand, his belief that I was some hood. No, I had to be Bruce Banner. *Calm. Stay calm.*

'You may be aware that we have considerable family business interests,' Clark said. 'Annie is involved with several trusts and holding companies, and there's some housekeeping – legal, financial, tax – that needs to be squared away before . . .' he trailed off in a pained breath.

I started leafing through the stack. It was a half inch thick and as complicated as a merger agreement, but it was, in essence, a prenup, in case I was trying to gold-dig the lovely Annie Clark for however many tens of millions she was due as Sir Larry's sole heir.

'This is a legal document,' attorney two began.

Thanks. Clark tended to forget that I had a JD/MPP from Harvard. I let his attorney ramble on while I finished reading through and marked the contract in a few places.

'This is just a draft,' he said. 'A starting point. I'm confident we can work something out. You're free to seek independent counsel, of course. Do you see any problem with that?'

I tossed the papers on the table. 'I do, actually.'

They exchanged glances. Attorney one's nostrils flared slightly. I could see their excitement grow. Legal battles were better than sex to these people. The whole contract was a slap in my face, of course, and I'm sure what Clark wanted was a fight. But I wasn't going to indulge him.

'There's a mistake on page nineteen. You were probably thinking of New York. Virginia goes with the Uniform Legal Code on family law,' I said. 'But that's no big deal.'

'It's a draft,' Clark's lawyer stammered.

'It's fine. Who wants to witness?'

'Sorry?' Clark said.

'I couldn't care less about money, Larry. If this will get you out of the way, I'll sign on the spot. It's fine.'

'We could work up another draft.'

'That's okay,' I said. 'I already corrected it.' I signed three times on the last pages, stood, and handed it back.

'If you need to do it with a notary, just let me know,' I said. 'Have a good night.'

If getting rid of that prick only cost me a few million and my signature, I'd gotten off easy. I walked out.

When I made it back to our hotel room, I found Annie sitting up in bed, working on her laptop.

'How did it go with Dad?' she asked. 'Looks like you survived. Olive branch?'

'Prenup.'

'What? He never even talked about it with me. He just ambushed you with it?'

'And two lawyers.'

'Oh God. What did you do?'

'What did *I* do? Nothing. I signed it. It's up to you, of course, but I'd be fine if you did, too. Just get him out of the way.'

I don't know what she expected. That I would throttle the guy?

She put her laptop down, shaking her head and fuming. 'I'm going to go down there and—' she threw the covers back.

'Don't even worry about him,' I said. 'Though this means that if things go south for us, you won't be able to get your hands on my Jeep.' The car in question was a twenty-year-old Cherokee, with fading paint and no shocks, that I couldn't bring myself to get rid of.

Even Clark's rude awakening couldn't completely burn off the pleasant haze surrounding my brain after four courses and a bottle and a half of Chave Hermitage Burgundy that made me finally understand how people could be so obsessed with wine.

I lay down next to her on the bed.

'You'd still love me if it meant having nothing?' I asked.

'What kind of question is that?' She asked it with sympathy, mainly, and a little offense thrown in. After a moment, she softened. 'Come on, Mike. Of course,' she said. 'Of course,' she whispered in my ear, then moved down to kiss my neck.

Chapter Four

I don't have very sophisticated opinions about pairings: which wine goes with this or that. But I do have one matchup I feel strongly about. If tonight's menu involves breaking and entering, life-and-death sprints from the police, or any sort of manic violence, you really can't go wrong with Steel Reserve in a twenty-four-ounce can and a shot of Old Crow.

Both of those potables were sloshing along on the Metro seat beside me on my way to my brother's house. They certainly looked out of place in Annie's cloth tote bag, which read Tranquil Heart Yoga on the side, over some sort of mandala earth-mother logo. I hadn't tasted them in years, though they were once the go-to for me and my brother, Jack. You'd drink the top two ounces out of the can of Steel Reserve, pour in the equivalent volume of bourbon, seal the can's mouth with your thumb, invert once, then sip. Typically this was done while driving (holding and turning the wheel with your knee), very often to the scene of a crime about to be committed. The beer is 8 percent alcohol, but there's more to it than that, some special alchemy from the combo of cheap bourbon and the medicinal tang of the high-gravity lager. Together they went down like a swallow of burning regret. Within minutes they trashed every restraining impulse in your body and left you an amped-up object of imminent destruction, a teenage hand grenade.

Tonight was a special night. I needed a best man. I was letting the past back in, no matter how awful it tasted. For a long time my father had been urging me to get back in touch with Jack. He said he had gone straight. Years before, I'd cut my big brother, my only sibling, my old hero, out of my life. However much Jack deserved it, it still broke my heart. I'd been dead wrong about my father's sins, so maybe Jack deserved another chance, too.

I missed him. No one knew me like he did. And, for all his faults, Jack had looked out for me when I was young and my father was inside. Annie and I had a great crew of friends, but there was a part of my past I couldn't really talk about with them. I needed someone I could drop my guard around and joke about the old days with. I needed a way to vent without doing something stupid like I had at that monte game in New York; I still had the bruise on my ribs. If people like Lawrence Clark were going to hold my past against me, why bother hiding it? Jack was back in town now. Maybe I could use this wedding to pull us all together. After New York, I called him to meet up, and after a few awkward messages and calls back, we'd decided on dinner tonight.

When I had looked up his address on the fringes of Takoma Park, just outside the District boundary, all that showed up on Google was a vacant lot with a lady pushing a cart full of junk along the sidewalk. As I neared his house, I passed auto body and pawn shops and storefront churches. This was everything I had pictured for our reunion. It was a mistake. He must have still been running cons. Though I guessed I'd made the right call on what to bring to this dinner party.

I turned the corner. After a few blocks, the neighborhood changed. The liquor stores became wine shops, the cars rose in price, and then I found myself in front of a row of brand-new town houses, 'Starting in the 600s!' a banner exclaimed.

The shot of the vacant lot must have been out of date, from before they started construction. And the bag lady was long gone, replaced by a very attractive young mother in yoga pants pushing a double stroller the size of a Zamboni.

Jack's place was number 108, a three-story house on the corner, the prime spot in the development. As I climbed the stoop, I wondered how Jack had got his hands on that slice of real estate. This cute spread with the marigolds out front actually made me a lot more nervous about what Jack was up to than if I had found him living in a dive next to a vacant lot.

I rang the buzzer.

Thirty seconds later a man I barely recognized opened the door. He had brown hair trimmed short, with salt-and-pepper gray just beginning to show around the sideburns. He smiled, showing the lean cheeks and jawline of a dedicated runner. He was wearing a Patagonia vest, chinos, and a newish-looking pair of $130 New Balance running shoes in dull gray. This was not the brother I knew. Jack's style was disposable flash all the way. This guy reeked of quiet, dignified affluence.

'You didn't have to bring anything,' he said, and took the bag of booze as he led me back toward the dining area. 'But thank you.'

A delicious smell drifted over from the kitchen, which was kitted out with high-end culinary toys: Shun knives, a stand mixer, a half-dozen different Le Creuset pots. I was lucky I'd had my crash course in conspicuous consumption at Bergdorf's.

'I'm glad you could make it,' he said. 'I've been wanting to try this Thai recipe, but I haven't had a good reason to go for it until now.'

A clipping from the *Times* lay on the counter. I looked out the rear window at the driveway: Audi A6, in gray. A corporate lawyer's car. Jack always preferred American muscle. When we were younger, he had a '69 GTO he'd taken two years to restore himself. I felt like we built the damn thing one piece at a time from parts snatched from junkyards, leaping fences and outpacing Rottweilers.

I turned back to the kitchen to find Jack frowning at the six-pack and the plastic bottle of whiskey I'd brought.

'Would you like me to pour you one of these?' he asked. He had pulled a crystal pilsner glass from the cupboard and was not doing a great job of hiding his distaste.

'Are you drinking?'

'I don't really drink much anymore,' he said. 'But feel free.'

'I'm sorry,' I said. 'If it's a recovery thing, I can get rid of those. It was sort of a joke.'

'No. No cold turkey or anything like that. Just not during the week. I'm so busy with work is all. Don't bounce back like I used to.'

'That's great,' I said, then looked around the first floor – marble counters, stainless-steel appliances, new flat-screen – silently tabulating his overhead.

'You have a full-time thing going?' I asked. 'Machine shop?'

'No,' he said with a chuckle, as if I must have been joking. 'Nine to five. Actually more like eight to eight, you know how it goes. Just another wingtipper now.'

'Good for you. What sort of work?'

'Security consulting,' he said. 'Stuff like that.'

It was a curious posting for Jack. In the old days, if you wanted to manage risk, step one was to not let a guy like him through the front door.

'Really?' I said, letting more surprise than I had intended creep into my voice.

He smiled. 'I know what you're getting at, Mike. Wolves and the henhouse. But I'm all clean these days, and some of my past . . .' he searched for the right word '. . . experiences actually prove pretty useful. I do some courier work, contracts

for law enforcement, investigations, running things to informants. I'm comfortable in that world. Though for the most part
I spend my days sitting on my can in front of a computer,
running background checks.'

'Who do you work for?' I knew a few names in that
industry.

'My own company,' he said. 'Just a one-man S corporation,
sort of a tax dodge.' He reached inside the refrigerator and
pulled out a green glass bottle of sparkling water.

'And who does your company work for?'

'No can do, Mike. You wouldn't believe the NDAs I have
to sign,' he said. 'You probably know what it's like, right?'

'Sure.' I wanted to call bullshit, but he seemed so at ease in
this habitat. If I had gone white picket fence, why couldn't he?
God. It was almost a letdown. Jack Ford, one of the all-time
great con men, had finally been taken by the squares.

'So Dad told me you're between things now, or working for
yourself,' Jack said.

'Yeah. My own firm.'

'If you ever need any work or help, just let me know. I
haven't forgotten all the times you bailed me out. I owe you
big, Mike. It's the least I can do.'

That almost sounded like charity, which galled me. But I
kept my temper in check. All Jack knew was that I was drinking
malt liquor and rotgut whiskey and taking public transporta-
tion. To someone who didn't know the world I'd come from
– learning at the knee of DC's most powerful fixer – the idea
of a thirty-year-old having a nice little political shop where his
only job was to pull strings sounded pretty far-fetched. Jack
hadn't seen me since I was a navy recruit with a fresh arrest
who'd only barely avoided prison. God. He might have thought
I had come here to shake *him* down.

'Thanks. I'm all set.'

'And this girl. Annie? She sounds amazing from what Dad told me. Where'd you get engaged?'

'Tuscany.'

He whistled.

'It was the least I could do,' I said. 'She's great. Hilarious. Crazy smart. Calls me on my bullshit. Makes me a much better guy. I'm nuts about her, man. So I don't mess around when it comes to the romance stuff.'

'I'm so happy for you, Mike.' He looked at me for a moment as if he really meant it, then turned and checked his recipe. He had laid out a dozen ingredients in small glass bowls.

The dining room table was set for two at the opposite ends. There was a charger under each dinner plate. It looked like a spread from *Gourmet*, except for the can of Steel Reserve beside my wineglass. Waste not, want not: I cracked the beer and topped it off with a splash of Old Crow.

'To brothers,' I said, and lifted my drink. Jack looked at his sparkling water in distaste.

'Actually,' he said, 'pour me one of those.'

'You sure?' I asked.

'Oh yeah. It can't be as bad as I remember.'

I walked over to the counter, fixed him a drink, then handed it to him. We raised our cans and sipped. He came up with eyes shut tight and mouth in a grimace.

'Jesus. It's worse,' he gasped, knocking his fist against his chest. We both started laughing. I was glad we were feeling so chummy. It would give me a chance to go behind his back before he could go behind mine. Trust, but verify: it was due diligence time.

Chapter Five

I'd checked out his recipe, and the last fifteen minutes looked slightly less complicated than a mitral valve replacement. That was my chance. As Jack started toasting peanuts, I pressed the volume control on my phone down until the ringer switched to vibrate and it buzzed in my pocket. I pulled it out and apologized to Jack. Bent over the pan, he barely noticed. I answered it with a 'Hi, sweetheart' and headed upstairs to take the call.

I had one advantage when it came to scoping out Jack. I'd spent the better part of my youth tagging along with, eavesdropping, and spying on the guy, so I had a good sense of his hiding habits. How else would I have kept myself stocked through adolescence with high-powered fireworks and old *Playboys*? I checked under the mattress in his bedroom, mostly for old times' sake, and found nothing.

I tapped on the closet walls: no false panels. That left the dresser. It was solid oak, very heavy, but I managed to pivot it eighteen inches away from the wall without making much noise. In high school Jack had used a hole punched in the sheetrock behind his dresser to hide his contraband. He would put the goods into a bundle, tie a string to it, lower it into the space between the walls, then tape the string just inside the hole. There were probably still a half-dozen M-80s sealed up in the walls of the apartment building where we'd grown up.

His setup these days was a fancier variation on the theme. There was a section of sheetrock behind the dresser that pulled away to reveal two high-end biometric safes. The top one had a powder-gray steel door about four feet wide and two feet tall. That usually meant guns. It was big, too; he could have fit a squad automatic in there. But there was no way I had time to get into either right now.

As I searched, I kept up my end of the imaginary wedding conversation I was using as a cover. 'Sure. Whatever color chairs you want . . .'

It made for a nice juxtaposition as I took stock of the dangers Jack was concealing in this cozy house. The safe on the bottom was smaller, with an eighteen-inch-square door, a Group 2 combination lock and relocker. It probably cost about $1,200. In my experience you didn't buy equipment like that to keep your birth certificate dry. It usually meant a lot of jewelry, money, or drugs. Or maybe the guy was just a security freak. We'd grown up around enough thieves that the habits were ingrained.

I managed to get the dresser back in place, then went to the closet and started checking his belts. In his teens, Jack carried a piece-of-shit Raven Arms .25, one of the classic Saturday night specials. He mostly used it for plinking cans but wasn't above sticking it under someone's jaw if things got hairy. He always carried inside-the-waistband on his strong side, so I knew what to look for.

The closet kept up the same story as the rest of the house. A half-dozen suits hung there, nice stuff: Zegna, Brooks Brothers, and so on. The wider belts, the ones you'd wear with jeans, were about two inches shorter than the thin ones you'd wear with a suit. And on most of those thin belts, I found what I was looking for about six inches to the right of the buckle: a contour worn into the leather from a holster, a decent size, maybe a .40. Jack had moved up to a bigger caliber, and whatever work he was involved in, it meant wearing a good suit over a concealed weapon. He sure as hell wasn't just punching investors' names into Accurint to see if they'd been kiting checks.

I heard a phone ringing downstairs. I rifled the desk drawers, going through the usual office detritus, until I found a black card, the shape of a regular credit card but three times thicker, with copper contacts on the bottom and four glassy rectangles on the front.

It was electronic, but I couldn't fathom what it did. As I turned it over in my hands, I accidentally pressed one of the rectangles with my thumb. An LED in the card began flashing, tinting the dark room red in a complex pattern.

After a moment it stopped, and as I tried to figure out what I had just done, Jack's laptop screen blinked on with a similar pattern of white flashes. A command line appeared, code scrolled down the screen, and then, across the middle of the display, a message appeared: 'Fingerprint not recognized.'

I stepped in front of the computer and started to sweat. I didn't want there to be a record of me poking around up here. A second later a light turned on beside the webcam built into the top of the display. My face appeared on the screen.

The computer let out three loud beeps.

Scanning . . . authentication failed, the display read.

Please wait while we contact a representative.

My heart pounded. I dropped the card back in the drawer and slid it shut.

Jack probably heard it. And now *I* would look like the thief. I waited for the knock on the door, the totally justified accusations. None came.

It was odd. The food should have been done. He should be looking for me by now. I heard the sounds of blinds dropping downstairs, of furniture moving.

I walked to the top of the stairs.

'You should just stay up there,' Jack said.

I took a step down, looked across the living room, and discovered where that Glock .40 had gone. Jack held it raised in his right hand. 'Don't come any closer!'

Now *that* was the brother I remembered.

Chapter Six

Annie had done a good job hiding her concern when I told her I was going to meet up with Jack tonight. I knew she had a few worries about my old life, but I think she understood that it would be good for me to reconnect with him, have someone I could talk to, square things from the past.

'Go, see your brother,' she'd said.

She and I had moved in together four months before, though we'd barely spent a night apart over the past year. We lived in a quaint neighborhood in Alexandria called Del Ray, all 1940s bungalows and throwback main street shops. It was just across the river from the capital, and I was glad, after the scandal, to have put a little distance between me and Washington. We'd thought about trying a new town, but it was nice to be near my father now that he was out. My family had fallen apart when I was a kid, and I finally had a few pieces of it back. That was part of what drew me to Jack.

Annie gardened. I mowed the lawn. There were always some folks stopping by to chat with us as we sat on our porch. I would have the neighbors over for barbecues – an orthodontist on our left and a tax attorney on the right – nice enough people, if a little dry. They liked to talk about QuickBooks and bond funds.

Some nights Annie and I would open a bottle of wine, climb through a dormer window, and watch the stars and lunar eclipses from our roof. We'd hide notes in each other's bags. I'd get to court, face down a federal judge, and open my case to find 'Thanks for last night, counselor' scrawled on a Post-it.

But something wasn't right. Ever since the madness at my last job, ever since that one awful moment at the end, there had been a distance between me and Annie. It's one thing when your fiancée hears you, after fifteen minutes on hold with Comcast, groan 'Jesus, I could kill somebody.' But things take on a much different cast when you say that in front of a woman who has actually seen you standing over the body of a man after you took his life. She told me she understood that I had no other choice, but she never quite forgot. I'd catch her watching me sometimes with something like suspicion, and I knew it was still on her mind, maybe feeding those doubts about me that her dad had planted.

She wasn't the only one who didn't like to think about the day I was forced to face down our former boss, Henry Davies. I felt fine enough, for the most part, but every so often – when I was trying to sleep, or riding home on the Metro – I would remember his face, like it was right in front of me, or picture the photos of his grandkids on his desk, or feel his fingers clawing at my wrists.

From the work I had done at our old firm, even after all the bloodshed and the hard work of cleaning up the scandal, I had a reputation around DC as a competent political fixer. I was glad to leave behind the hard-core black bag stuff I'd learned at my last job. I could afford to pick and choose clients, for now at least, to take only the cases that let me sleep well at night and still cover my overhead. It was nothing like the money I was used to, but it was enough. You don't find much better bargains than the ones you make with the devil. And if I really believed in the cause, occasionally I might use a trick I'd picked up from my old mentor: only a light touch, a little leverage, or perhaps absentmindedly failing to correct the impression that I knew someone's secrets.

With her mother gone, Annie's grandmother – with her posh accent and coin-purse lips – had stepped in and was driving Annie crazy in the run-up to the wedding. It was the Clarks' chance to show off their class and wealth to the wider world. The perfect day. The perfect daughter. The perfect life. And if the wedding and the need to make me a proper, respectable man with no sharp edges was starting to get to me, it wasn't Annie's fault.

At the house, some nights I would watch the red glow of the numbers on the alarm clock, listen to the sleepless dark. Eventually I'd step out of bed, careful not to wake Annie, and leave the warmth of that body I loved so well. I'd walk down to the porch or just stand in the backyard, watching the sky, ignoring the bite of the cold spring air. I was afraid there was something out there, as basic as gravity, pulling me out of this peaceful home into the night.

I hoped Jack would understand, that we could help each other out. That's what had brought me out to his house tonight.

But this was not what I had bargained for.

I laughed and shook my head as I came down the stairs at Jack's house. I'd been dragging my feet on choosing a best man, and Annie must have known it was because a little part of me hoped to have my brother up there beside me, the past forgotten, everything in its place. Jack would just have to stand there and hand me a little box. How badly could he screw that up?

Here was my answer: Jack had pushed an armchair up against the front door. He stood to the side of the front window, peeking out the blinds, a bead of sweat running down his temple. I could see into the open kitchen, where the noodles were congealing in the pan. It was a nice interior scene, carefully arranged and suggesting a title like: 'Waiting for someone to come kill me.'

I ignored Jack, walked over to the range, and tried some of the pad thai.

'This is great,' I said.

'Thanks,' he replied, without looking away from the street.

I sat on the couch and placed two bowls of noodles on his coffee table. I offered Jack one. He looked at me blankly, didn't say anything. I twisted some onto my fork.

'I'm in trouble, Mike.'

'Really?' I said with mock surprise.

He nodded, then glanced at the pistol.

'Oh yeah,' I said, looking at the gun. 'I was going to ask about that. I hope it's not for me.'

'No.' He went on in a monotone. 'I was working a job as a courier, and I started to wonder if maybe this wasn't just about security, if someone was playing both sides. I was worried I'd end up taking the fall for something big, someone getting hurt, you know? So I started looking into the people who'd hired me.'

'Were you maybe thinking of fleecing them?'

'Just covering my ass. And it *was* big. These guys are serious. I got scared, tried to beg off a job. The people behind it, maybe they found out I was digging. Whatever it is, they're after me now.'

'So the gun,' I said, nodding. 'Any chance these bad guys are due to stop by tonight?'

'Maybe. They just called. They could come for me any second. They're saying I owe them. They're setting me up—'

'How much?'

Jack looked up at me, startled. 'What?'

'How much did they say you took?'

'I didn't take it, Mike. They're setting me up.'

'I know. But how much?'

'It's not about the money, Mike, they said I messed up some plan. They said I had to make it right or they'd hurt me.'

'Get to the point. How much do you need?'

He took a drink from a bottle of water he'd placed on the shelves. 'The payment was sixty-five thousand,' he said. 'But I gave it back to them. That didn't settle it. They said it was too late, that I botched everything and I'd have to do the job myself now. But I'm trying to stay straight. I swear I didn't take anything, Mike. I didn't want to tell you about it, get you involved. They jumped me yesterday on my way from the Metro. Worked me over in the stomach. It was bad. They said if I didn't give them what they wanted, they were going to really mess me up, send me to the hospital.'

'Huh,' I said. 'So they beat you in the one spot that doesn't bruise much.' It's a handy technique for enforcers who don't want to leave marks, and for liars who don't have any. 'Go to the cops.'

'I wanted to. I tried asking around. They must have found out somehow. They said they'd kill me if I did.'

'Of course,' I said, and had another bite of pad thai.

'I think they're just trying to scare me off for what I know, make me disappear.'

'So why don't you?'

'Mike,' he looked hurt. 'I don't want to run anymore. I just want to live my life. I haven't done anything wrong.'

'So what, you need to buy your way out? Pay them for the job you messed up?'

'I'm not asking you for anything, Mike. I just need somebody to talk to. I need a way out of this, and I'm so goddamned scared I can't think straight. Maybe you could help me expose what they're up to. Outthink them somehow. I mean *maybe* I could make up what they lost on the job. I'm not sure if they'd go for that, or how much it'd cost.'

The soft sell. Jack still had his touch.

'Who would I make the check out to? Or I guess cash is better with shadowy types like this.' I patted my pockets, looking for a checkbook or wallet.

'Seriously?' Jack asked.

'Of course not,' I said, and put my bowl down. 'You're not getting any money out of me, man.'

I couldn't believe I'd given him a second chance and he was pulling something like this.

'You know, Jack—'

Bright lights shone through the blinds. Then came the chirp of tires. The slamming of doors. Loud voices. All the stage dressing for an old-fashioned shakedown. It sounded like three men. Jack had really gone all out.

'Right on time,' I said.

'Mike, you should get out of here. Do you have a gun?'

'I don't need a gun, Jack.'

I stepped toward him so I could get a good look at his eyes, the size of his pupils, to see if he was using.

'So what's this massive plot you stumbled across?' I asked.

A fist pounded on the door.

'Get away from the window,' Jack said. He retreated to the kitchen and took cover behind the counter that separated it from the living room.

I watched the doorknob shake, then heard the rattle of metal scraping inside the deadbolt: someone raking the lock. Any self-respecting arm-breaker would have just knocked the door in, but these fellows happened to be interested in preserving property. Interesting.

I went to open the door.

'What are you doing, Mike? These guys don't joke around.'

'You've done this before, Jack,' I said, shaking my head. 'You've literally done this same setup before, where the bad guys come to beat you up for doing the right thing, and I have to pay them off. Tampa, I think. Do you even remember? I gave them eight hundred bucks.'

'Mike. You've got to believe me.'

I was about to lay out a whole heartbreaking speech about how I'd given him another chance, come here to ask him to be my best man, and now this. But I was too disappointed and angry to even get into it.

'Forget it,' I said, then muttered a few curses under my breath as I shoved the armchair to the side and pulled open the front door.

Chapter Seven

A guy with a build that in the navy was usually called 'brick shithouse' knelt in front of the door. He looked awfully pissed as his lock pick and tension wrench were yanked out of his fingers. Behind the lockpicker stood a bone-thin man with very small teeth. To his right was a hulking fellow wearing glasses so thick they looked like submarine windows. They were all well tailored except for the guy with the glasses, who looked like Mr Magoo, but I'm sure he had his strong points.

'Come on in,' I said, and walked back toward the living room. 'I imagine you're here to do some grisly violence unless I make right for Jack's mistakes.'

The thin man looked at his associates. This wasn't in the script. 'That's the general idea,' he said.

Jack tried to warn me off again. I ignored him.

'I'm Mike,' I said and shook the hand of the thin man, who seemed like the group's leader. 'Your name?'

He looked at me for a moment, trying to figure out what was wrong with me, and then glanced around the room.

'I don't know,' he said. 'Mr Lynch.'

'What's the plan, Lynch? Break my fingers, one at a time? Beat me with a sock full of batteries?'

He considered it. 'That seems a bit much. We'll just get you out of the way and deal with your brother.'

'Let me save you some time. It's a great performance and all, but I'm not buying it, so—'

Lynch nodded toward the guy with glasses, who stepped forward and clamped his hands on my biceps. 'He doesn't understand!' my brother yelled from the kitchen. 'He thinks it's a joke. Don't hurt him. He had nothing to do with this.'

As I was pulled away, I turned my head toward Jack. He stood there, absolutely ruined with sadness. At first I thought it was shame, for betraying me after I'd let him back in.

'God, Mike,' he said. 'I'm sorry. I guess you had every right to think it was a setup, but this is for real.'

As the man with glasses held me to one side, I saw my brother struggle with the other one, who barked at Jack in an Irish accent as he wrestled his arms under control. Lynch walked over and struck Jack across the face with a pistol. He groaned and fell to one knee. He hit Jack with the gun again, in the temple, and Jack crumpled.

I peeled away the hand of the man holding me and lunged at Lynch, shouting 'Leave him the fuck alone!' before I could even think about what I was doing. I knocked him against the counter. The two other men took hold of me. Jack lay facedown on the ground, blood trickling from a cut over his eyebrow.

Lynch walked over to me, took me in with a clinical look, then smashed the clip of his pistol into my cheekbone, under the eye. The world turned black for a second. Sparks of light shot through my vision, and I felt pressure bloom through my sinuses. I groaned. As I blinked back the pain, Lynch reached into my pocket and pulled out my wallet.

'Michael Ford,' he said, then looked at Jack. 'I see. It's a family act. And you live on Howell Ave. Del Ray, right? That's a cute neighborhood. You ever go to the Dairy Godmother?'

'What?' I asked.

He sighed, like the whole thing was out of his hands. 'So

what's wrong with you? Martyr complex? Why would you involve yourself in this kind of shitshow?' He pointed to Jack with the pistol. 'Congrats,' he said to me. 'This is on you now, too. You seem like a pretty together guy, so pay attention. Your brother makes things right, or next time we kill him. You understand me?'

'You can't pull this kind of shit.'

He leaned over, reached down with his finger on the trigger, and pressed the pistol against Jack's hand.

'Do you understand?' he asked.

'Yes,' I said.

He kept my license, tucked my wallet back into my pocket, then started out the front door. His associates slammed me hard against the bookshelves, knocking the wind out of me. As I picked myself off the ground, searching for breath, they walked out.

I staggered toward the door to try to get the plates, then stopped and turned back to Jack. I heard the car outside peel away. Jack had rolled onto his back. I sat beside him on the floor, my back against the wall, and lifted his head up.

'I'm sorry, Mike,' he said, looking up at me. 'I didn't mean for this to get to you. I told you to stay upstairs. I just can't get away from this shit.'

'It's all right, Jack,' I said, and thumbed the blood away from his eye. 'Don't worry about that now. It's going to be okay.'

I didn't believe it, but what else could I say? All I could think about was the fact that Lynch had my address. He was coming for me now.

I spent the night in the emergency room with Jack, six hours for ten stitches. I wanted answers, but he was asleep or out of it most of the night. After he came to early the next morning, I pulled my chair up beside his bed.

'We're going to the police, Jack.'

'I tried. They have informants with the cops. That's why they came after me.'

'Who are they?'

'I don't know.'

'Don't bullshit me, Jack. You were working for them.'

He reached onto the tray beside his bed for a plastic tub of juice and pulled the foil back. 'I just have a number, no names.'

'And where did you meet them?'

Jack strained to remember: a Metro station, a library, a sandwich shop. All public, all anonymous.

'Here,' he said. 'My phone's in my pants. The number's in there.'

I leaned over, then stopped myself.

'Forget it,' I said, and fell back in my seat. 'I don't want any part of it. Every time I get my life sorted out, you always try to drag me into something like this. That guy took my license. He has my address, where I sleep, where Annie sleeps. They said it's on me. What does that mean?'

'Could you just back off?' he said. He shut his eyes and winced, hiding in the pain.

'I swear to God, Jack,' I said, rising out of my chair and standing over him. 'If this comes down on me, I will—'

The curtain drew back. The physician assistant came in. No matter how righteous your position, you never look good shouting down a guy as he lies in a hospital bed wearing his own blood.

Jack had a slight concussion, but no serious injury. The PA handed Jack a few prescriptions and a bill for two thousand dollars, and we were done. I drove back, stopped to fill Jack's meds, then dropped him at home.

'You going to be okay?' I asked as he walked up his steps.

'Yeah,' he said. 'And I'm sorry I got you dragged into it. I'll take care of this, Mike. It's probably what I deserve for trying to do the right thing. Go home and don't worry about it. I mean it.'

The good guy in me wanted to tell Jack I had his back. Growing up with a dad in prison, Salvation Army clothes, and free lunch tickets, I had every bully in town gunning for me, and Jack had taken more than his share of beatings to protect me. But I had bailed him out plenty of times since, more than my share. This was a different level. I had too much to lose. What could I say? I didn't know, and after a night in the hospital, I was too exhausted to think about it. I told him to get some sleep, then headed back to the Metro to catch the first, predawn train back home.

I stepped through my front door, sat down on the couch, and shut my eyes.

'Are you just getting home now?' Annie asked as she came downstairs. 'Jesus, Mike. It's the middle of the week.'

'I'm sorry. Every day is Saturday when you're with Jack Ford.'

She inhaled sharply as she saw the bruise on my cheek. 'Did you get in a bar fight?'

'Collateral damage. Some guys jumped Jack.'

'Where were you?'

I'm sure she assumed it was some sort of roadhouse, which was less scary than the truth. I stood up. 'Nowhere good,' I said. I wasn't lying. I was just leaving a few things out.

'You didn't even text me until after midnight. I thought—'

She could have rolled right into a proper harangue. I deserved it. But she stopped there.

'Just make me a deal. Give me a heads-up next time,' she said. 'You okay?'

'Yeah.'

'And Jack?'

'Mostly.'

'Head hurt?' she asked.

I nodded. The pain was due to blunt force, fatigue, and worry, not alcohol, as Annie suspected. She watched me suffer for a while, then decided to commute my sentence.

'You poor idiot,' she said, and ran her hand through my hair. 'I'm glad you got it out of your system. If one night of acting like an ass is what it took to find some peace with Jack, I'm happy you're done with it. Couldn't you just talk about this stuff, have some tea?'

'Doesn't work like that.'

'It *is* out of your system, right?'

'Sure thing. A cup of coffee and I'll be all squared away.'

'Good,' she said, and picked up her briefcase. 'I have to run.'

I walked her out and kissed her goodbye. Annie paused at the bottom of the porch steps. 'And no more trouble with Jack, huh?' she said.

I didn't answer. I was distracted by a car I saw parked up the street. I thought I recognized the man inside.

'Mike?'

'Absolutely,' I said. 'Lesson learned.'

She started off.

Parked half a block up from my house in a black Chrysler 300, not caring if he was seen, sat Lynch. I watched him watch my fiancée walk away.

Chapter Eight

I stepped outside and glared at Lynch as I approached his car. He looked back, seemed bored. He made no effort to hide himself. It wasn't surveillance. It was intimidation.

He rolled the window up and started the car. I ran inside to get my keys. When I returned, my neighbor across the street, a Korean War vet, was backing his car out of his driveway. That usually took about three minutes. I scanned the cross streets both ways. The Jefferson Davis Highway was two minutes away on my left, and 395 five minutes away on my right. Lynch was long gone.

I drove into the city for a meeting with some election lawyers I was working with on a dark-money case. Special interests from both ends of the political spectrum dump hundreds of millions into 'social welfare' nonprofits, then spend it to buy elections. It's all anonymous, all tax free, hidden by shuffling the cash among a web of shell organizations. We were trying to untangle it all and bring the people behind it into the sunlight.

I loved the case. We were close to exposing the major funders behind these shells and getting some political buy-in to go after them. Their lawyers and lobbyists were fighting back hard. It was just starting to get fun, but I could barely pay attention to anything that was said during the next two hours. All I could think about was Lynch, who he was and why he was after me.

I kept going over what Jack had said about his meetings with him.

'Mike? Where do you land on this?' one of the other attorneys asked.

'Very interesting,' I said, and chewed my pen. I had completely lost track of what we were talking about.

Jack and Lynch had only repeated a single meeting site: a lunch spot ten minutes away. As soon as my appointment wrapped, I headed for Jack and Lynch's meet-up. Just for some coffee, I told myself. The sign said Euro Café. It was a small, Korean-run buffet place. I ducked in and filled a Styrofoam cup. The teenager at the register put a textbook down, and I paid for the coffee.

'Thanks,' I said. 'And can I ask you something? Do you ever see a guy in here, tall, thin, pale, narrow teeth?'

She looked at me blankly.

'I see lots of people in here.'

She picked her book back up. I asked her a few more questions, with no success. I don't know what I expected. Name and address? I didn't even have a photo. I walked around the block, wondering what would bring Lynch here. It seemed like the kind of spot you would frequent if it was the only option near your office. Maybe he'd lowered his guard as he grew more comfortable with Jack.

I stopped. In the lot behind an office building, I saw a black Chrysler. I circled the building, keeping to the sidewalk on the far side of the street. There was no one around. Five cars were crammed into the lot behind it, including one that I recognized as Lynch's from the extra antenna on the trunk. I walked out front and scanned the entrance. There were no signs for any businesses. After a glance both ways, I started toward his car.

I saw some papers on the back seat, leaned in, and tried to make out the letterhead. I'd managed to read 'Draft – Confidential' on the top of a piece of paper sticking out of a folder when I heard footsteps to my right. I looked up to see Lynch. That instant, a large hand shoved my head sideways into the car window.

I reeled back. Someone twisted both arms up behind my back and pressed me against the hood of the car. I turned my head far enough to see that it was the guy in the glasses from Jack's house. He locked my legs in a wide stance in a confident impression of a police restraint and shoved my cheek against the cold sheet metal.

Lynch stood near the hood, then tsk-tsked me. With his right hand, he drew a lockback knife and flicked it open. 'Okay,' he said, and the man stood me up.

'It's bad enough we have to deal with your brother,' Lynch said. 'What's with you? It's like you want more trouble.'

He pressed his finger once into the bruise on my cheekbone. 'Michael Ford of Howell Avenue. I did some homework last night, and I'm impressed. You extracted yourself from a very complicated situation a while back. We're going to need that,' he said. 'Because I don't think your brother can manage this on his own. This job is now your baby.'

'What? What happened? Did he steal some money from you? A handoff? How much was it?'

'No. We got that back. This is about opportunity costs. It was a simple job. He didn't deliver the payment to our guy on time. He started asking questions. Jack grew a conscience all of a sudden. He spooked our inside man. There was a nice easy way to do this, but now that's gone. So you and your brother need to figure out another way to get us what we need.'

'I'm a lawyer,' I said. 'I don't know who you think I am or what sort of job you want me to help with, but I'm not good for much more than filing briefs and padding bills. I can't help you.'

'Come on,' he said. 'Breaking into the DOJ. Taking down your old employer. Word gets around, Mike. You're going to enjoy this one.'

'I don't know anything about that. And I've barely talked to my brother in years.'

'This will give you and Jack a chance to catch up. He owes us. And you seem to have inserted yourself into the situation, so you're in my ledger, too. All you need to do is help us finish what Jack fucked up. Then I'll forget you exist.'

'What are you talking about?' I asked.

'The job.'

'What job?'

'A bank.'

'You want me to rob a fucking bank? This is ridiculous.'

'Jack didn't tell you?'

'What bank?'

'All of them, really.'

'This is a joke?'

'No,' Lynch said. 'But it's not as bad as it sounds. You're thinking of guns, stopwatches, rubber masks. This is different. This job you could do in a suit and tie without breaking a sweat. That's the beauty of it. It could get bad—' he waved the knife '—but that's entirely up to you. A respectable guy like you is always handy. I don't think you'll have much—'

'That's good,' someone said behind him. 'Right there.'

Lynch turned, and the newest member of our party came into view: a blond woman wearing a field jacket over a sweater, and jeans tucked into leather riding boots.

Lynch looked amused until she eased her jacket back with her right hand and rested it on the butt of a gun in a hip holster. Great. Were Lynch and Glasses now the better of my options?

'Put the knife down,' she said. 'Don't make this complicated. Just let him go, and step back.'

45

'You don't understand—' Lynch started to say. She drew the gun.

'Drop the knife and let him go,' she said in a commanding tone.

Lynch looked to the man holding me and nodded. He released my arms.

'Send him over here,' she went on. They stepped back.

Enemy of my enemy and all that, I walked toward her.

'Thanks,' I said as I neared her. 'Who the hell are you?'

'Emily.'

'Nice to meet you. I'm Mike.'

'Likewise,' she said, and glanced around. 'Could you do me a favor there, Mike?'

'Sure.'

'Grab those trash bags.'

There were two black ones lying beside a dumpster. She'd saved my life. The least I could do was haul her garbage.

'Head out and to the right,' she said. 'The old Land Cruiser. Get it going. Toss the bags in the back.'

She handed me the keys. I stepped out of the lot, threw the bags into her car, and started it. She walked backwards out of the lot while watching the two men, then ran to the car and jumped into the passenger seat.

'Go go go!' she said.

I pulled away fast. She called someone on her cell phone, described the two men who had cornered me, then told the other party to 'send some guys down.'

Her truck was a vintage Land Cruiser from the 1960s or '70s. As we barreled toward Rock Creek, I grew increasingly certain that a five- to seven-liter modern truck engine had been dropped into it. I looked in the rearview at the trash bags.

'What line of work are you in, Emily?' I asked.

'Investigator,' she said. 'We can stop by my office and get you cleaned up.'

I wasn't all that interested in cleaning the grime off my face in the office of some PI. I'd met a few. I pictured her working out of a 350-square-foot office in a seedy building on 15th Street, where you needed a key tied to a stick to access the shared bathroom in the hallway.

I appreciated her help, but something wasn't right. I needed to know why she was behind that building at the same time I was jumped.

Chapter Nine

We drove across the bridge into Georgetown and turned down toward the canal, where the old factories and mills had been converted into luxury offices and condos. The Ritz-Carlton had a smokestack.

She directed me off Water Street into a garage under a brick warehouse that had been redone as lofts, then had me park in a reserved spot beside the entrance. We carried the trash bags in through a basement corridor and then stepped into an elevator.

That neighborhood is lousy with well-dressed, casually rich types, and the elevator accumulated a half dozen or so as we rose. Several gave Emily looks. I assumed it was because she was hauling garbage through their creative-class high-design Eden.

We exited on the sixth floor. It looked like an architecture firm or ad agency: lots of exposed brick, open space, funky lighting, and modern furniture.

'You're back soon,' a guy in a suit and no tie said to Emily.

'My shootout didn't take very long.'

The man chuckled, waved his finger as if to say *Good one*, and walked away. This was starting to make more sense. With her vaguely equestrian duds, classic wheels, and loose bun, Emily looked like old money that knew how to have a good time, not the kind of woman who'd be lugging around Glad bags.

Given the squash-court dimensions of the offices and the allure of the assistants, I figured we were on an executive corridor.

She walked straight to the end of the floor, to an office with floor-to-ceiling windows and a view along the Potomac from Georgetown University to the Capitol. It probably had three-quarters the square footage of our house in Del Ray.

She pretended to be embarrassed by the size. 'I didn't realize it'd be this over the top when we were drawing up the plans. Don't think I've got a personality cult going. We use it for meetings, too.'

'So this is yours?'

'Make yourself at home.'

She threw her trash bag on the twenty-foot-long hardwood conference table and started rifling through it.

'Thanks for helping me out back there,' I said. 'I hate to seem ungrateful, but maybe you can tell me what you were doing behind that building?'

She looked up. 'We've been watching that office for a week. There was a chance we'd finally get a break on this investigation, and then you came along and nearly got yourself killed, so I had to come out. Meanwhile, everyone at that address is probably spooked, and we're back to square one.'

No wonder she'd seemed annoyed with me on the ride in. I looked at some of the papers on the desk.

'What did you say your name was?'

'Emily.'

'Emily?'

'Bloom.'

'As in Bloom Security?' I asked.

'That's me,' she said. 'You can toss that bag up here, too.'

I put it on the table. I knew about Bloom Security. It was hard not to. It was the largest corporate intelligence firm in the world. They worked the high-end market in DC and had offices in every major capital. Think of a modern Pinkertons, or a private CIA. The firm was more than a century old and had started as private guards for the railroad, steel, and mining barons of the Gilded Age.

They'd tracked down the hidden assets of the world's worst dictators and war criminals, and for a price they could do anything: snatch a kidnapped chief executive back from the FARC or muster up a full sea-air-land military force and quash a coup.

I couldn't believe that this woman dusting coffee grounds from shredded paper was Emily Bloom, Georgetown's most unattainable young woman.

'I'm Mike Ford, Tuck Straus's friend.'

She thought about it for a second. 'Oh, sure. I think he's mentioned you.'

Tuck was *very* fond of her. He was one of my best friends in DC, and talked a lot about Bloom. She was the heir to this corporate security fortune, and Tuck had been pining for her since undergrad. I began to see why.

'You mind telling me how you're associated with those gentlemen?' she said. Bloom Security had a good reason to be on the tail of a guy like Lynch. I didn't.

She rolled over to her desk and typed something into her computer. Reflected in the window, I could see my face on the screen. She was checking my record.

'My brother may be in trouble with those guys,' I said. 'I was trying to find out their story, to see if I could help him.'

She chewed her lower lip while she looked over the text on the screen.

'What kind of trouble?' she asked. She seemed only half interested. It may have been genuine, but I suspected it was an information-gathering tactic.

'I don't really know anything about it,' I said, 'only that they're threatening him.'

Bloom Security was very tight with law enforcement, and I was starting to get an interrogation vibe, so I left out most of the details.

'Do you know who they are?' I asked. 'Anything about what goes on in that office building?'

I guess whatever file she'd called up told her most of what she needed to know about me. She relaxed a little, returned to the table, and started going through the shredded papers idly, like someone might sit back at their desk with a crossword puzzle. Apparently I checked out.

'If I knew the full story, I wouldn't be digging through trash,' she said. 'It was a contract job for law enforcement, surveillance, all compartmented. I'm not fully read-in. Something about financial crimes. Frankly, I don't think anyone knows anything that matters about that crew.'

She slid another piece of paper into place. 'What aren't you telling me, Mike?'

'That's all I know,' I said.

She appraised me coldly.

'What's with the trash?' I asked. Anything to get out from under that stare.

'I figured the whole place was blown, so I grabbed whatever I could.'

'But why are *you* doing street stuff?'

'Oh. Just acting out. That job was the most interesting thing going on in town today. It's a lot more fun than PowerPoint decks and earnings projections, and it's good to remember that despite the Gulfstreams and ex-senators and the Saarinen coffee tables, at the end of the day people are paying us to go through garbage, literally.'

'Is that legal?'

'Legal enough. As long as it's on a public right-of-way.'

One of Bloom's colleagues, a good-looking guy in his mid-twenties, popped his head in and handed her a note.

'You need anything?' he asked.

'Yeah,' she said. 'Something to clean up my friend here.'

From his manner I figured him for an assistant. I checked out my reflection in Bloom's office window. I was a mess, with a gray smear down my face from Lynch's hood and a swollen bruise from last night. He came back with a warm towel – so nice and thick I checked the label to put it on our registry.

'The deputy director is here,' the assistant said. Bloom checked her watch, then cursed under her breath. 'Send him up in five,' she said. 'Thanks, Sebastian.'

'I gather there are some other things you could be doing right now,' I said.

'Rainmaking. Business breakfast, business lunch, and business dinner seven days a week. False smiles, shitty jokes, and pleas to stuffed suits to give us more work. Half of them refuse to believe I'm actually in charge around here. For the other half, I'm just a last name and a handshake so the big contracts can feel like they went straight to the top. But I shouldn't complain. The nice thing about having your name on the building and a hundred percent of the A shares is that I can get away with pretty much anything.' She lifted a piece of paper. 'You sure you don't know anything else about those guys?'

'Positive.'

'That's a shame,' she said. 'I thought maybe we could help each other out.'

Information was currency, and I would have to trade to get anywhere.

She looked down among the papers and discarded trash. 'There you go,' she said.

'Is that a clue?' I asked, and pulled closer.

'This?' she said. 'No. This is worthless. I think it's a P&L for a law firm. From what I know, this outfit never makes a single mistake. We didn't have the men or go-ahead to take them.

They burn everything, and have probably already cleared out of that office.

'This, however—' she pulled an extra-large black binder clip from the bag, stepped over to her desk, and clamped it on a stack of papers – 'is exactly what I needed. We're all out.'

The phone rang. Bloom glanced at the display on her desk. 'I've got to press the flesh. But if you think of anything else you maybe forgot to mention and want to compare notes, just give me a call. Then maybe I'll have some more for you.' She wrote her cell phone number on the back of a business card and handed it to me. There it was, nicely played and subtly stated: the quid pro quo.

'Sure thing,' I said.

'And be careful, Mike. I don't know much about these guys, but I do know they're no joke. Tread lightly.'

I could have used someone to talk to about this Jack mess, but as I weighed her offer, I looked through the glass door of the office and saw the deputy director of the FBI, one of the most senior lawmen in the country, striding down the hall. Jack had warned me about talking to the police. And there was another element I didn't want to think too hard about. I wasn't going to throw in with the law until I understood just how dirty I would have to play to get out of this.

I walked out just as the deputy director was walking in. He gave me a long, distasteful inspection as I passed, which, considering that I'd just been dragged down an alley and signed on to rob a bank, I probably deserved.

Chapter Ten

Annie was already home when I pulled up the street. Her car filled our short driveway. I found a spot around the corner. As I neared our house, I saw the light was on in the bay window, and then saw Annie walk across the room in a runner's tank top. There was no sign of Lynch's car, just the usual Del Ray crowd: stroller gridlock, a few people eating ice cream. Maybe his threats were all bluster. I let myself relax from outright panic to simple dread.

I was halfway up the block when I recognized the ice cream eaters.

'What the fuck are you doing here?' I shouted down the street.

The stroller dads looked at me, shocked. I didn't care. My main focus was on Lynch. He was leaning against a tree across the street from my home. The squat Irish guy from Jack's house stood beside him. Lynch divided his attention between hunting for peanut butter cups in his sundae and staring into my house.

As I came closer, I could see he'd caught just the right angle to peep into the living room, where Annie was folded in half at the waist, stretching.

'To answer your question,' Lynch said, 'the custard place was closed this morning, so I swung back.' He looked at the window, then licked his spoon. 'Very tasty.'

I started toward him. The dads had retreated around the corner and were watching me with growing alarm.

'Easy, Mike, easy,' Lynch said.

'I swear to God—'

'You can't kill me, and you certainly can't kill me here.'

'Get away from my house.'

'Just enjoying the evening, Mike. I'm glad I happened to run into you, though. We didn't get to finish our talk.'

'I'm calling the police,' I said, and took out my phone.

'Please,' Lynch said.

I lifted it, let my thumb hover over the dial pad.

'It's nine-one-one, if you forgot,' Lynch said.

I dialed.

Lynch dropped his spoon into his empty paper cup. 'Though it may not be the best idea to have the police come here asking questions after you ran down the street screaming obscenities. And what exactly are you going to say? There are a couple of nicely dressed guys blowing their diets across the street from your house? There's some vague plot going on you barely understand? And you have the whole story from your ex-con brother, who can't open his mouth without telling a lie?'

'Alexandria Police Department,' the voice came out of my phone. 'What is your emergency?'

Lynch went on: 'I'm sure local PD will have this all cracked wide open by bedtime. You're making things harder for yourself and your brother, Mike. You're prolonging this unpleasantness. But if you want the extra challenge, go ahead.'

'Are you there?' the dispatcher said. 'What is your emergency?'

I waited, ground my teeth together. Lynch looked on.

'I'm sorry,' I said. 'I misdialed. No emergency.'

'Okay. Have a good night, sir. And please be more careful in the future.'

'I think we got started on the wrong foot,' Lynch said. He reached into his pants pocket and handed me back my license.

'I'm a reasonable guy. I protect my interests like anyone else. If I pay someone to do something, I expect it to be done. And if they don't do it, I expect them to make it right. That's only fair.'

I took back my ID. 'Or else you send them to the hospital? Kill them?'

He tossed his cup into a neighbor's garbage can. 'I'm more about carrots than sticks. You're a very competent operator. You have no record. You're clean. You've got this whole respectable lawyer thing nailed. I think you can figure out how to get this done with a minimum of fuss or danger to yourself. After that, you never see me again. And you return to your lovely girl and picking out doilies for your wedding.'

How did he know so much already?

'Your brother has nothing to lose, Mike. But you have everything. It's unfortunate I have to put the screws to you, but that's the way it is.'

'So you want me to rob a bank?'

'That would be more fun, but no. This operation was all very neat and clean before your brother decided, against all evidence, that he was one of the good guys. It's not a break-in, Mike. It's inside information, tipping.'

I was worried they wanted me for some ugly crime. But insider trading, like Martha Stewart? What could be more country club than that?

'We had an economist lined up to give us some market-moving information. Your brother flubbed the payment. The economist bolted. Now we need to find another way to get our data.'

'What sort of tips? What's the target?'

'I'd hate to ruin the surprise.'

'Why aren't you leaning on your inside man instead of on me?'

'Who says I'm not?'

'You seem to be spending most of your time up my ass.'

He nodded as if I had a point. 'He's a tricky case. Can't find him presently. And it's probably best not to poke that hive at the moment, unless he does something rash. We'll get to him eventually.' He looked down the street. Annie had stepped onto our porch. She was walking toward us. I needed Lynch gone.

How scary could an economist be? I would just talk to him. It was a small price to pay to keep this away from my home. 'What if I brought him back on board?' I asked.

Lynch smiled and looked down the street at Annie. 'So you're in,' he said.

'No. I'm out. I'll just talk to this guy in order to remain out.'

'Great. You're in. Bear in mind, if you fuck this up or spook him or bring more heat down, it's only going to make your job harder.'

Annie was about thirty feet away. I could see Lynch savoring my distress as she moved closer and closer.

He waited another second, until she was almost within earshot.

'His name is Jonathan Sacks. You have twenty-four hours.' With that, he walked away.

'Hey, hon,' Annie said. 'Who was that?'

My new boss.

'Nobody,' I said.

Chapter Eleven

My first day on the job as a criminal co-conspirator was turning out to be pretty boring. I parked across the street from Sacks's town house, one of a dozen in the complex. It had its own entrance, which made surveillance easier. It was 7:30 a.m., a good time to catch people going to work. After a half hour with no sign of activity inside, my impatience turned to boldness, and I headed toward his stoop.

I noticed flyers for pizza places sticking out under his door. He had a drop-in mailbox hanging on the siding. I tapped on it. The metal returned a muted clank. It was half full.

Sacks hadn't been around for a few days in the middle of the week. I guessed he had run. I peered down through the blinds. No sign of a hasty packing job, probably planning on coming back. I didn't have days to wait him out, though. I was supposed to be prepping a deposition for the dark-money case, but between this stakeout nonsense and a bar association lunch that Annie had reminded me about this morning, I didn't know when I'd be able to take care of it.

Sacks was an economist at the Federal Reserve. The Fed regulates a lot of banks, so I guessed he had access to some sort of inside data. I pulled up my laptop, which had a broadband card, and checked for a directory on the Fed website. Nothing jumped out at me. The 'Contact Us' page had a few numbers, most of which I assumed were just dumped to voicemail. Several shared the same area code and first four digits of the number.

That usually meant that by dialing those first four numbers followed by 000 you could reach the switchboard.

So now I had a number to call, but who was I?

I had done an Accurint search on Sacks last night. That's one of the big data-mining sources. If there's a piece of information about you floating in a commercial or government database anywhere in the world, they buy it, pull it into one place, and make it all searchable. Once you learn how to read those reports, those few pages will tell you someone's life story and a good portion of their secrets. I had Sacks's addresses from his childhood home on, and lists of his relatives, associates, co-workers, neighbors, anyone he lived with, as well as their phone numbers, employment histories, criminal records, and most of their Social Security numbers.

From the last names and birthdays, I could see that Sacks had two daughters and a wife, and a single-family home in Falls Church. Then last summer he started living alone in a new luxury town house in Southwest DC. That sounded like divorce, which would explain financial motives.

Work is a good first place to look for a workaholic. I went to LinkedIn, and they spun off a list of a dozen of Sacks's colleagues and associates. I picked a guy who worked at the Treasury in the same policy area and could have had a good reason to be getting in touch with my man.

I was now Andrew Schaefer. I hesitated for a moment before I made the call. It felt like crossing a line, my first action for Lynch. I Googled a few more terms and found an actual org chart of the Fed staff, with phone numbers.

That cinched it. I had no good excuse and plenty of ways to work this. I dialed the main switchboard. 'Monetary Policy,' said the man who answered the phone.

'Laurie Stevens, please.' She was the admin in Sacks's office.

'One minute.'

'This is Laurie.'

'Hi, Laurie,' I said. Being transferred from the main switchboard meant my number would show up as an internal extension on her phone, which made it more trustworthy. 'This is Andrew Schaefer at OEP. I was wondering if I could get some time on Jonathan Sacks's schedule today.'

'Did you try e-mailing him?'

Clearly I had no idea how things were done in this office.

'Yeah. I haven't heard back. Having trouble getting ahold of him. Sort of need to get this squared away today for the CPI.'

'He's been out for a few days. Flu or something. E-mail's probably your best bet.'

'Do you have his cell phone number?'

'His cell phone? I don't think so. You can talk to the deputy director if it's urgent.'

I'd overstepped. Time to throw it into reverse.

'No. I'm all set. Just double-checking something with Jonathan. I'll wait for him to get back on e-mail.'

'Okay.'

'Thanks.'

He'd bailed on work. Sacks really was hiding out. I looked at my list of his family and associates in the area. With fewer than twenty-four hours, I didn't have time for door-to-door or even trying them out one at a time over the phone.

I had hoped to turn Jonathan Sacks slowly and deliberately, the way I'd been taught, a gradual closing of a trap he couldn't escape. But that was too bad. I was on deadline. I just had to reach out and rattle his cage.

After I'd made some calls and broken the ice, I was on a roll. There was a sliver of something else, too. Fun wasn't the right word; it was more the pleasure of giving in to one of your weaknesses.

I looked over at the property manager's office and thought for a minute. Then I dialed Sacks's ex-wife's number.

'Hello?'

'Hello. I'm sorry to bother you. This is Stephen at River Park Homes. You're listed as Jonathan Sacks's emergency contact.'

'Is everything okay?'

'Oh yes. We had a pretty major leak over here, and we only have his office number. We need to access his unit and were trying to get in touch with him.'

'You tried his cell? Do you have the new number?'

'We only have his home and office.'

'He just changed it,' she said, and read out his new number.

Now I could get in touch with him, but what would I say? I had a vague sense of my pitch in my mind, trying to be on his side, to be the good guy to Lynch's bad, but I didn't know what the ask was, what the terms were.

Jack had given me some background on Sacks the night before, along with Lynch's number. I took a walk up and down the block and called it.

'Who's this?' Lynch said.

'Mike Ford,' but I didn't get much further than that. A Prius rounded the corner, and I recognized a man who looked like Jonathan Sacks if he'd just finished a three-day bender.

'Shit. He's here,' I said. 'I'll call you back.' I ducked behind my Jeep.

From what I could see, Sacks's car was a mess. A rubber plant in the back seat wobbled back and forth as he stopped in front of the complex and marched toward his town house in a dark blue sweater, khakis, and running shoes.

He entered his house for a quick inspection, then walked over to the property manager's office. I could see him through the window as he gestured back toward his unit. His ex-wife must have called him about the leak. This was moving far faster than I'd planned.

I watched as his confusion gave way to suspicion and he peered out the windows of the office.

He emerged, started up the Prius, and took off. I jumped in my car and followed, hoping to at least find out where he was staying so I could contrive a way to talk to him.

I kept my distance, but it hardly mattered. Sacks was in his own world. In his mirrors, I could see him talking to himself at the stoplights. From Southwest he drove along the Mall, then crossed to the Navy Memorial and parked with half his car in a bus zone.

He walked up Pennsylvania Avenue, then turned toward Indiana. The cold realization hit me. He was heading toward Judiciary Square, my least favorite place in DC.

The whole area is a palace of nightmares for the criminally inclined. On my left the FBI building hung over the street, a brutalist concrete fortress. On my right stood the Department of Justice, where I'd had the pleasure of nearly being incinerated a while back. Ahead were the main headquarters of the Metropolitan Police and the Superior and District Courts for the District of Columbia. I did a lot of pro bono work there, so you'd think I'd have gotten used to the place, but they never failed to unnerve me.

The Superior Court was where, when I was twelve, I'd spent weeks sitting on hard plastic chairs, waiting outside as my father navigated a labyrinth of pretrial meetings with DAs and prosecutors, all false smiles as they rushed past me and my brother. It was where I'd had to sit, wearing my church clothes, and watch as a jury foreman announced that my father was guilty, where I'd listened to the judge give him twenty-four years, where I'd watched the bailiff pull him out of my mother's arms. For most of my life he'd been gone.

And it was where Sacks was headed. A perfect spot to do my first work for my new criminal confederates.

Cops filled the sidewalks and wide steps in front of the courthouses. I counted four uniformed marshals as I walked, and who knows how many plainclothes.

Sacks stopped in front of an ugly 1970s-era building of water-stained concrete and black glass. He stood out front and stared at the entrance, one hand deep in his pocket, the other compulsively picking at something on his neck. I was twenty feet away.

My phone rang.

Sacks turned as I silenced it and pretended I'd been casually walking by.

It was Annie's number. I checked the time. Damn it. If I didn't wrap this up soon, I was going to be late.

Sacks was still staring at the building. He looked as if he might start crying. Finally, he took a deep breath and walked back the way he'd come. He passed a sports bar, considered it for a moment, then ducked into the gloom. I found a spot on the sidewalk where I could see him through the door.

My phone rang again. I looked down, half wincing, expecting Annie. It was Jack.

'What's up?'

'Where are you?'

'Judiciary Square. I found Sacks.'

'What's he doing?'

'Moping around like it's the last day of summer vacation.'

'What do you think he's after?'

'I don't—' I looked back toward the building he'd approached, then backed away from. I couldn't believe I hadn't figured it out before. It was Judiciary Center, home to the top prosecutor in the District. 'US Attorney.'

'Oh shit,' Jack said.

'Lynch said he'd leave him alone unless he did something rash.'

'Snitching seems pretty rash, given what we know about Lynch. You can't let him go in. They'll kill him. I just wrapped a meeting. I'm not far. I'll head over.'

I told myself that I was doing a good deed in all this. Lynch might be watching me and Sacks right now. If he saw his inside man walk into the US Attorney's office, Lynch was liable to do anything. There was another reason I had to stop him: if Sacks talked, my only easy way out of this – luring him back into crime – would disappear.

Sacks didn't order anything at the bar. After five minutes, he gave up. He stepped out onto the sidewalk in front of the fountains at the Navy Memorial. He looked up Indiana toward the courts, then back to his car.

Just go, I willed him.

He picked up his cell phone. I moved closer.

It was a short call, but I was able to catch the end: 'I'm coming in. I'm right across the square. Okay.'

He started walking toward the courthouse, with a head start on me.

My phone buzzed again. A text from Annie. 'Where are you?'

I didn't have time to reply. As I followed Sacks back across the square, I could have sworn I saw a black Chrysler cruise down Fourth Street.

I didn't have time to try to turn Sacks inch by inch. I had to wrangle him in on the fly, in the heart of the criminal justice system.

I walked fast after him as he neared the intersection. He

caught a break in the traffic. I had to pause and finally just go for it. I played chicken with a US Marshal's Escalade that braked and blared its horn as I ran across the street.

I watched as Sacks reached the front door of the courthouse. I ran after him, but I was too late. Sacks was already going through the metal detectors, and I was at the back of the queue. Eight police officers stood between us, and it didn't seem like a good place to shout an invitation to a criminal conspiracy.

I waited, sweating, as they cleared me through security. I scooped up my cell phone and keys, and ran down the hallway after Sacks.

He heard me coming, turned, and faced me with a startled look.

Two more uniformed marshals passed us.

'Jonathan Sacks?' I said.

My cheeks were red from running. A bruise lingered near my right eye. I knew I looked crazy.

'Yes,' he said, inching away as he glanced toward the nearest cops.

'My name is Michael Ford. I'm an attorney. And I have reason to believe your life is in danger. I'm sorry to surprise you like this.'

'Who do you work for?'

'No one. I've learned some information recently. I had to warn you.'

He started backing away.

'Listen. If you cooperate with a prosecutor or give information right now, you're putting yourself at risk. If I can find out what you're doing, so can they. Please, give me five minutes of your time.'

'This is some kind of threat?' he said.

'The opposite. I'm here to help.'

'Go on,' he said.

'Not here,' I said. 'I can't tell you how dangerous it is for you, and for me, to be in this building. They have informants. If you talk, they'll know.'

'And how do you know all this?'

I stepped closer. 'My brother tried talking. They found out. I watched the men behind this beat him until he was unconscious. His life is in danger, too. So please, hear me out.'

His eyes were fixed on the nearest marshals. One shout and I was done.

Families stood near the courtroom doors, wearing looks of shock or quiet distress. Dozens of prosecutors, judges, and police strode by. I saw the hard plastic chairs where I'd spent so much time, saw a grandmother waiting, a kid swinging legs too short to touch the ground. Through an open door, I saw a judge taking her seat. In that moment I relived my own arrest and trial ten years before, remembered the judge staring down, the night my whole life fell apart.

With every step, I expected to feel the hand on my shoulder, the steel on my wrists.

Chapter Twelve

'You have five minutes,' Sacks said.

I couldn't believe he'd gone for it. 'Follow me,' I said. 'A public place. Just not here.'

He nodded.

Before he could think twice, I led him out of the courthouse and across Constitution to a stand of trees at the very end of the National Mall. We were across from the fountains in front of the Capitol.

'Talk,' he said.

I had to seduce this man into a conspiracy that I knew almost nothing about. I had to get inside his head, to know his motivations in order to bring him around. My brother had given me what he had learned, the rough outlines. Sacks was a typical DC workaholic, so single-mindedly focused on saving the world that he'd lost his wife. I read a lot of his speeches and white papers, all very dry and technical, but they were what passed for muckraking in his circle: arguments for raising bank capitalization requirements, reining in derivatives and prop trading.

Jack filled in the rest. After the divorce, when Sacks actually needed money – alimony, child support – none of the banks would hire him. He'd burned his bridges trying to do the right thing. The revolving door was jammed. He played the part of humble bureaucrat, but he couldn't stand having a roommate, a basement apartment. He thought handling billions in T-bills meant he could handle his own money in the markets. He couldn't. And from there it was an easy fall into being checkmated by Lynch.

What deluded me into thinking I could turn him? The guy comes to DC to try to live a decent life and do some good among seemingly respectable people, then gets lured into a crime he can barely understand, and is presently scared shitless.

I could relate.

'These men you're running from,' I said. 'They have sources everywhere.' I had heard as much from my brother, and it was in my interest to believe it now. 'If you talk, they will find out, and they will get to you.'

'The prosecutors can protect me.'

'For a financial crimes case? You think they have the resources for that? This isn't the Five Families. You regulate the banks. You know how these white-collar deals go. Six years from now, whoever's behind all this *may* face a fine that amounts to a few percent of the interest they've made off the profits. They sign a deferred prosecution agreement, and it all goes under the rug. Are you going to hide out that whole time?'

'How do you know all this?'

'I'm just a boring grind, like you. My brother is another story. He was involved, facilitating. He came to me for help. He tried to go to the police. The men he was working for found out. And now they're going to kill him, unless . . .'

'Unless I go along with it.'

I nodded. 'Have they threatened you, too?' I asked.

He didn't answer, just gazed at the Lincoln Memorial in the distance.

'You came to Washington to do good,' I said. 'I understand. It's what brought me here. And you work every waking hour trying to stop the everyday graft. And what do you get?'

He looked down at the bare dirt of the Mall.

'They grind you down,' I went on. 'You try doing the right thing, and you end up losing everything you've worked for.'

'What do you know about it?'

'I've got my own story. That doesn't matter right now. I know about paying the price for your principles. I know about being cornered. If all these hedge funds are trading on expert networks and inside info, what's one more tip? What's the difference? Why should you be the only one to suffer when everyone is rigging the game? You just send them the information. Two seconds and this all goes away. There will be no long, ugly interrogations, no grand juries, no rows of cameras, no black mark on your résumé, with everyone you meet for the rest of your life knowing what they drove you to.'

I scared myself with how easily these dark promises slipped out. I wasn't only trying to convince Sacks to sell his soul. I was trying to convince myself.

'Like you care what happens to me,' he said.

'I do. My brother's brought me nothing but trouble my whole life. But you're a decent guy. What happened to you is terrible. Just pass them the information. It will be untraceable. And then you get your life back. None of this ever happened.'

He took a deep breath and looked toward the reflecting pool as it rippled under a cold wind. I was more interested in what he was doing with his hand in his right pocket. If I hadn't just watched him clear the metal detectors at the courthouse, I might have been worried about a gun.

'Okay,' he said. 'Where do we go from here?'

I had given a decent speech, perhaps too familiar too early. Maybe I was just that good, and I really had turned Sacks. But flattering myself was dangerous, especially when talking to a man who a few moments ago was doing his damnedest to cooperate with the US Attorney. I never really thought I'd be asking someone, 'Are you wearing a wire?' but then again, it was a day for firsts.

I didn't know what the next steps were. He saw my hesitation, seized on it.

'You're in the dark on this,' he said. 'Do you even know the target? The stakes they're playing for?'

He laughed, like I was the biggest sap in the world. My father's advice came back to me: Never bet in another man's game. I turned slightly and saw, parked two hundred feet away, Lynch's Chrysler. A gray cylinder was sticking out of the rear window.

My instincts told me to drop to the ground or run like hell, but I realized that the object wasn't a gun. It was some kind of microphone. Lynch could hear every word.

Sacks followed my gaze, and as he turned, I stepped forward and looked down into his jacket pocket, held open by his hand inside it. The top of a digital recorder stood out from his fist. A red light glowed. He'd been taping me. He was going to give me up to the prosecutors.

'They're after the directive,' he said.

Chapter Thirteen

I wasn't going to turn him. At least he hadn't been wearing a live wire, broadcasting back to the US Attorneys as I made my pitch. There was no easy way out of this. I should have just walked away.

I started to, and Sacks lifted his cell phone and dialed.

I stopped and turned. 'Don't call the prosecutor,' I said. Lynch was listening. Sacks was going to get himself killed.

'Don't move,' he replied.

'You don't understand.'

'I understand perfectly,' he said, then lifted his phone. 'I've got one of them here. No. Right around the corner.'

He started walking toward the courts, walking directly toward Lynch while diming him out. He was ordering his own execution.

I ran and grabbed his arm.

'They're listening,' I said, seething in his ear. He shoved me away. I held on, pulled him closer. 'They'll kill you. You've got to run.'

He stumbled toward me. I caught him under the arms and kept him from hitting the ground.

Something was wrong. He groaned and his whole body went tight. I held him up for a second, but all the strength went out of him as he crumpled.

It was just a little spot at first. I could barely notice it through the blue of his sweater, but it was growing fast.

I tried to keep him from falling. I bear-hugged him, held him up. The warmth spread. I felt it leach through my shirt.

I eased him down to one knee, then to the ground, and laid him on his back. I took off my jacket, tore the sleeve off my dress shirt and balled it into a compress. He'd been shot in the chest.

Half a dozen people walked by as he lay bleeding on the dirt. Lynch's car had disappeared.

My phone rang.

Sacks stared at the sky, unbelieving. He mouthed the words 'Oh my God' over and over, but with the hole in his lung he had no breath to speak with. Thanks to the traffic, the wind, and the idling tour buses, I hadn't even heard a shot. Maybe they'd used a suppressor. I knew Sacks had told the police where to find me. I had to run. I might have time to get away, but that would mean letting this guy bleed out on the Mall.

I held the compress tight. 'What's the directive?' I asked.

He was too far gone to hear me, to give any sign.

Four Capitol Police walked toward me across Madison. I lifted my hand off the balled-up cotton, saw blood pool and spill down his chest, then pressed it back down.

'What's going on here?' the lead cop shouted.

'This guy's hurt,' I said as they gathered around. 'I don't know what happened. Here,' I took one by the arm and guided his hand to the compress.

'I'm an EMT,' I said. 'I've got my kit in my car.'

I jogged toward the rows of parked cars, picked out an Escalade, and circled around it. Once out of sight behind the SUV, I ducked down and sprinted across the street toward the trees surrounding the National Gallery.

'Hey!' I heard the police yelling behind me. I kept moving

toward Constitution. As I wiped the sweat from my forehead, I succeeded in painting my face with my bloody hand.

The police must have put the word out. Soon I had company: Metro PD drove past on Pennsylvania, then pulled a U-turn and came back at me with the siren screaming and some ground-shaking *whoomp* emanating from the bottom of the cruiser.

I wheeled toward the Metro entrance. One escalator was out of order, the other two clogged with the lunch rush. Washingtonians can be a little cranky about the rules for the Metro escalator. It's stand right, walk left. I needed something faster, so I jumped onto the sheet metal between the escalators, eased myself down on two hands, and turned sideways onto my hip as I slid. I hadn't noticed them as I sized up the slide, but as I shot down the incline, little steel discs bolted onto the metal slammed hard into my tailbone every eight feet. I shot off at the end, lost my footing, crashed face-first into the filthy red tiles, and came up running.

Metro police spread out from the other end of the station. The only thing I had going for me was that we were at a stop on the stepchild Yellow/Green line, which serves some of the poorer parts of DC. It only comes every fifteen minutes, and the cars and stations are always packed.

The flash of the red lights along the platform and a cold rush of air announced that a train was coming. I worked my way toward the front, and waited until the last minute. As the crowd surged toward the doors, I pushed back and darted into a dark corner past the escalators, where an elevator entrance was framed in greasy sheet metal.

The police held the train, and as I rose in the elevator I watched them begin to search the cars, barking orders into radios. The elevator doors opened aboveground. I expected a wall of blue. But the police were still arriving, and had only covered the escalators, fifty feet away. I stepped out.

I had seen my reflection in the wired glass of the elevator car, blood streaked across my face. I needed to get myself cleaned up. As I sprinted away from where the sirens wailed the loudest, I ducked between two of the street vendors' trucks that worked the tourists around the Mall. I took a deep toke of generator smoke as I passed through, grabbed a sweatshirt and a bottle of water, then darted through traffic across Constitution and threw myself under the thickest shrubs I could find.

I emerged a minute later, my head wet but no longer smeared with blood, wearing a too-small sweatshirt that read 'You Don't Know Me' across the front. Underneath, my dress shirt was damp, lukewarm with Sacks's blood. The entrance to the Sculpture Garden was fifteen feet away. Soon I was just another tourist puzzling over Louise Bourgeois's spider.

My car was parked back near the courthouse, but returning there wasn't an option. Soon enough the police would realize I hadn't taken the Metro, and the dragnet would spread.

I peered through the gates and saw a patrol car parked on the opposite corner. I circled the Garden to the other side, waited for some Park Police on bikes to pass, then exited onto Madison. More cops were coming, motorcycles from one direction, cars from the other, men on foot fanning out between the museums. I was trapped.

A hand closed on my arm.

I turned. It was my brother.

The black Chrysler idled a few feet away. Jack moved toward it. Lynch sat in the driver's seat. 'I can get you out of here,' he said.

The police closed in. I could feel Sacks's blood dry, tighten like scales on my skin. To all the world, I was the gunman. I knew I should raise my hands and surrender, trust my life to the laws I had sworn to uphold, the laws that had torn my family apart.

Or I could give myself to the killers who had just framed me. The black car waited, my only escape. The rear door swung open. I was innocent, but I'd seen enough to know that the truth no longer mattered.

Cops circled the block.

Jack jumped in and stretched out his hand to me.

The only way out was to go in deeper.

I stepped into the car.

Chapter Fourteen

Lynch pulled away, and I ducked low behind the tinted windows.

'You fucking shot him?' I said to Lynch.

'It's more complicated than it seems,' Lynch said.

I turned on Jack. 'And what are you doing with them?'

'I was right there, Mike. They picked me up. They can get us out of here.' He looked over to Lynch. I could see the black-and-purple bruise under the bandage on Jack's temple, see the fear in him. 'They're here to help.'

'We'll get you someplace safe,' Lynch said.

'Dupont.'

'What?'

'Take me to Dupont Circle,' I said, looking over the missed calls and texts from Annie. 'Or else my fiancée will kill me herself and deprive you of the pleasure.'

I had to talk to her before the news hit, to explain things before every network painted me as a murderer. But there was more to it than that. If I was going to run, I wasn't going to do it without her.

'There's a lot of heat,' Jack said.

'Dupont,' I said, and tried to think of a place where I could shower in the middle of the day.

Lynch looked at me as if he was humoring a seven-year-old, then said, 'Fine.'

At the cross street with Florida, I stepped out at the red light. Jack started to open his door after me, but Lynch stopped him and let me go.

'We'll get you through this, Mike,' Lynch said to me as I walked away. 'Don't worry. Just remember: Don't do anything rash. It never ends well.'

I made it to the Hilton. I'd bought some clothes at the first store I saw, some trendy urban-style skate-shop boutique, then showered and changed at the community pool behind Marie Reed Elementary.

As I crossed the lobby, I realized that my outfit of khakis and a plaid shirt looked less casual Friday and more rapper going mainstream. In the main ballroom, busboys cleared dessert plates and knots of judges and lawyers stood around talking.

I waved to Annie on the other side of the room. She was carrying a heavy piece of engraved crystal and holding court in a small circle of prosecutors and judges. As the other people she was talking to saw me approach, I could see the concern grow in their faces, as if they were witnessing a car crash. I gathered they understood the significance of my bailing on what looked like Annie's big moment.

'Michael,' said an older intellectual-property lawyer I was friendly with. 'You finally made it. You're looking at the newest Copeland Pro Bono Service Award winner.' He raised his glass to Annie.

'Congratulations,' I said. 'I'm so sorry I'm late. It was an emergency.'

I leaned in to kiss her on the cheek. She was as receptive as a cedar shingle.

'You okay?' she murmured.

'Yeah.'

77

'What the hell are you wearing?' she whispered through a false smile that reminded me, awfully, of her grandmother's.

'I'll explain.'

On a TV at the end of the bar, the news played. An army of cops and EMTs had converged on the spot where I'd left Sacks.

Before I could get away, I was being introduced around. I shook the hands of the other men and women.

'—and this is Judge Gustafson. Only one in DC who actually writes his own opinions.'

They laughed. I noticed the blood still under my nails. I was about to shake hands with a judge from the court where I'd met Sacks. I stood there like an idiot, staring at my hand, then reached out for his. For the life of me, I don't know what we talked about or how long we stood there. My mind was filled only with sirens and the image of Sacks as he bled on the ground.

I expected my face to be on the news any minute.

'I have to go,' I said, cutting off someone's anecdote.

Annie looked at me: *What are you doing?*

'I'll walk you out,' she said. 'Excuse me for one minute.'

We walked into the lobby.

'Where were you?' she asked. 'I was stood up by my own fiancé. Do you know what that looks like? I've had it with whatever's going on with you all of a sudden. And why are you dressed like that?'

'I'm sorry. You're right. Jack's in real trouble.'

'What's going on?'

'Some guys are after him. They're threatening him.'

I hadn't had time to think this through. My instinct was to run. But could I ask her to leave her whole life behind at a moment's notice? Could I tell her everything?

No. She was strong, a fighter, and even if I tried to keep her out of this, she wouldn't let me face it alone. I couldn't tempt her. I had to protect her from this.

'Is he hurt?' she asked. 'Are you part of it? You need to go to the police.'

But Jack had tried to go to the police. Sacks had tried to go to the police. I looked at her, here in her element. I was so damn proud of her. What was I thinking? That we'd run? Live in motels? Holed up somewhere like Whitey Bulger and his girl, wearing bad dye jobs, counting down to our last dollars, blinds down and fighting over the remote for the rest of our lives?

My hand in my pocket, I felt the digital recorder I'd pulled out of Sacks's pocket as he lay dying. Dried flakes of blood crumbled off it. Sacks could have handed me over to the US Attorney. Lynch had protected me. It made me sick. My mind ran in circles, all the ways I could escape, all the lies I could tell myself.

But there was no comfort in them. There was only one conclusion, however much I fought it. There was no way out. Lynch owned me. That's why he had let me walk away from the car. He knew I had no choice. I couldn't ask her to run. I had a life here. Annie had a life here. I had too much to lose.

'You're right. I'll take care of it. It's all going to be fine,' I said, and kissed her. 'I'm so proud of you. Go celebrate. You deserve it. I'm going to make sure Jack's okay, give him some counsel, and that will be the end of it.'

She pressed her lips together. 'You'd tell me if you needed help?'

'Yes.'

'Fine,' she said. 'And no more trouble. I'm going to head back. Our managing partner invited me over to the Cosmos Club, one-on-one. He's probably going to fire me for doing so much pro bono work.'

'I doubt that,' I said. 'You're a machine. Just keep doing your thing. Are we cool?'

'Give me a little time,' she said.

I kissed her on the cheek. She turned back toward the ballroom.

I walked through the café area and pocketed a steak knife. As I passed the entrance to the business center, a woman stepped out. I let her pass, then stuck my foot into the door just before it closed.

I sat down at a computer. I knew that one phrase – the directive – and I knew where Sacks worked. With those two facts it didn't take long to find out what Lynch wanted. If you're after the biggest score in the world, forget the banks. Go to the source of all the money, the banks' bank, the Federal Reserve.

Every eight weeks or so, a committee gathers near the National Mall in a marble citadel known as the Board of Governors of the Federal Reserve. Twenty-five men and women sit at a long wooden table with an inset of black stone shined to a high gloss. By noon they decide the fate of the American economy. They don't announce their plan publicly until 2:15 p.m.

The Fed decides, but it doesn't dictate. The newspapers always talk about it setting the interest rates, but it can't just issue edicts to the banks or force them to make cheap loans.

So, at the end of the meeting, that committee in DC issues a directive to the trading desk at the Federal Reserve Bank of New York. That one desk is the Fed's gas and brake for the entire economy. The traders buy and sell to steer the markets according to Washington's orders. Known on Wall Street simply as 'the desk,' it has a four-trillion-dollar balance sheet, backing the value of all US currency and bank accounts, and trades billions of dollars' worth of securities a day.

I looked at a photo of the most recent committee meeting. And there, in a chair against the back wall, half hidden behind a column, sat Jonathan Sacks, looking like the most junior guy in the room.

The directive was the playbook for the American economy. The committee had been flooding the country with easy money, hoping to kick-start growth. But at some point, that would have to end. And knowing when the music would stop could earn you billions.

Lynch didn't want a sneak peek at some bank's earnings report. He was after the crown jewels of the Federal Reserve, and he wanted me to steal them.

I couldn't run. I knew what I had to do.

Chapter Fifteen

I stood in the woods at Fort Totten park, freezing my ass off. Old beer cans and condom wrappers littered the ground. A ten-foot-tall dirt berm ran in a perfect circle, with a wide ditch around it. I stood at the top.

You find them on random walks around DC: the old forts, Civil War earthworks once armed with cannons to hold back the Confederates. They're desolate, hidden in the back of urban parks, overgrown with thorns, frequented mostly by horny teens and the homeless.

Jack had called. I needed to get my car away from the crime scene. It had been at Sacks's that morning, and I had my dossier on the guy inside, as well as my laptop. Both would connect me to the murder. Jack and I had agreed to meet here after he picked it up.

As I stamped my feet in the moldering leaves, I heard footsteps on the trail: more than one man.

They came, flanking Jack.

'Mike,' I heard my brother say.

'Don't try anything,' I heard someone call out to me. I recognized Lynch's voice.

'What the hell is he doing here?'

'It's cool, Mike,' Jack said. 'He's with me. He's here to help. I went to get your Jeep but the police had it all cordoned off. I nearly got picked up. They helped me get your car back.'

'We're going to come up,' Lynch said. 'We just want to talk. All right?'

I wished I had the pistol from my lockbox at home. All I had to protect myself was the steak knife. I pulled it out, felt the wood handle warm inside my fist.

'Come on,' I said.

Jack and Lynch picked their way through the trees toward the fort. There was only one route over the dry moat, a dirt ramp. In the fading light, I made out one figure to my left. I guessed there were more in the woods, covering me.

'He helped me out, Mike,' Jack said. They stood about thirty feet away. 'The police were watching the area. I couldn't have gotten the car out without them. He just wants to talk.'

I carefully slid the knife into my back pocket with the handle out, ready to draw. Lynch moved closer.

'What happened to Sacks?' I asked.

'He died a half hour ago,' Lynch said. 'And for that I'm sorry. No one likes bloodshed. But it was a complex situation.'

'It's really not. He was going to talk, so you killed him.'

'He was about to take you down with him, too, Mike. Don't forget.'

He walked up the dirt ramp and held out an envelope.

'Here,' he said.

I took it. There was a recordable CD inside and a few pages of printer paper.

I fanned them out: still photos of me with Sacks, just before he was killed.

'Shots of you on the scene. And those are the only copies. We destroyed the originals.'

Those photos could end my life. It was like holding a live grenade.

He offered me a lighter. I slid the papers and the disc back inside the envelope, then sparked the flame near the corner. Red and yellow tendrils climbed the paper. I dropped it, and let it burn at my feet. The plastic disc blackened and warped in the ashes.

'A peace offering?' I asked.

'Just trying to be helpful,' he said. He took the lighter back, tapped out a Winston cigarette, and lit it.

'You can stop with the hand-holding,' I said. 'I understand what's happening.'

It was my worst fear, that every prejudice against me would be confirmed. Lynch had everything he would need to make me a fugitive, a lowlife killer, to make Annie's concerns, and her family's whispers, true.

I would do anything to prevent it. He had me cold. The only thing that would make it worse would be to lie to myself, to welcome his patronizing, to pretend this wasn't base extortion.

'I'm listening,' he said.

'You win. You've got me. So what do you want?'

I had to keep him off-guard. I had started to see a way out of this. I didn't have the whole picture, but the traces were there, like a great idea that comes as you fall asleep and is forgotten the next morning.

'Finish the job,' Lynch said.

'You want the directive,' I said. 'And how exactly am I supposed to steal the most closely held secret in capitalism?'

'I didn't say it was going to be easy.'

'I can find another man inside that room when the decision is made. When's the next meeting?'

'Tuesday.'

'Next Tuesday?'

'That's right.'

'I'll find a way. And you leave me and Jack and my family alone. And this murder doesn't touch me. Deal?'

He took on a pained expression. 'There is one small complication. People know who Sacks is. They know he had access to that decision. He didn't tell the prosecutors everything, but they know enough. They're locking down everything in DC. They're watching everyone with access to that room. There's no way. Not after today, not after you were seen on the Mall.'

'So you'll kill me if I don't make the impossible possible.'

'New York.'

'No no no,' I said. 'That's the hardest vault in the world.'

'It's no Fort Knox,' he said.

'It has more gold than Fort Knox.'

Lynch smiled. I gathered that was his idea of a joke. 'But you're not going for the vault,' he said. 'There's only a few hundred billion in it. The real money's upstairs. The desk.'

'The police probably have my house surrounded by now.'

'You'll be fine. They don't have anything to ID you beyond a few very hazy sketches from the first cops on the scene. Painting yourself in blood is a little Apache for my taste, but it got the job done.'

Let him think I was that crazy. I needed all the leverage I could find.

Jack licked his lips. I stalled, but there was nothing to decide, no choice in Lynch's questions. They were commands. I felt the knife once more, then stepped forward, within arm's length of Lynch.

'I get you the directive,' I said. 'Then we're done. I never see you again. All debts paid in full.'

'That's the deal,' he said.

The only thing that felt right was burying that knife in Lynch's throat. But he had serious resources behind him, and that would only get me killed. I had to play along, to buy time.

'Done,' I said.

'So what's the plan?' he asked.

'My plan for the impossible task you first mentioned twenty seconds ago?'

'Yes.'

'See if you can find me a 2004 World Series baseball, Red Sox, signed.'

'Seriously?'

'Yeah. I have a few ideas.'

He nodded. He seemed to like my resolve.

'I'll check around,' he said, and patted me on the shoulder. 'Couldn't have done it without you, Mike. Here's something for your troubles.'

He lifted a dime from his pocket and held it out to me. Dimes are used as messages, left on dead men as a warning against informers.

'Go fuck yourself,' I said, and walked past him.

Lynch wanted to rope me in? Fine. His mistake. Because I was going to get to the heart of these sons of bitches' operation, then blow it up from the inside.

I had six days.

Chapter Sixteen

I sneezed. A few crumbles of hashish flew off the plastic evidence bag and came to rest in a dusty corner of the room. I was in Metro PD's evidence warehouse, a former factory in Anacostia surrounded by drug dealers' fiefdoms. It was Aladdin's cave: stolen goods everywhere, piled in the loading dock and spilling into the street. The drug vault was constructed of plywood, and periodically some PCP would combust in the stifling heat. The warehouse was like a forensic wheel of fortune, great for public defenders. Evidence would always get lost, and the defendants would walk.

It was the last place I wanted to be, but I had a pro bono client I couldn't let down. He was a good kid from Stronghold, headed for college, who'd been busted with the hash. They'd reformed the pot laws, but they didn't apply to hash. He had been a tenth of a gram over the limit, which would bring him serious time. I checked the evidence bag.

The police hadn't weighed it yet, typical dysfunction. The less said about that the better. My allergies had just saved this kid eight years of his life.

As I walked out, I was reminded of another case, one that might offer another way into the Fed. I needed to get back to Virginia. I headed for the Pentagon City Mall. I picked up some tux studs while I was there, but my real target was the Apple Store.

I saw him before he saw me. He looked about seventeen, but he was three years older. Derek had an afro fade with a part shaved in and wore Buddy Holly glasses and the standard Apple employee T-shirt over a dress shirt buttoned all the way up to his throat. He'd grown up over in Barry Farms. It seemed like a hard place to be a nerd, but at least the computer stuff kept him indoors and safe.

He smiled when he recognized me, but it was an uneasy look. Last time I'd seen him, we'd been facing down the prosecutor as I worked out a deal.

He sidled over to me. 'Hi, were you interested in the iMac?'

'You doing good?' I asked quietly.

'Great. Anything wrong?'

'No. Don't worry. Keeping out of trouble?'

'Yeah. They extended my internship.'

He started to sound more like a kid from Southeast as he relaxed and code-switched back. Derek was a great mimic. That was part of his problem.

'John hooked you up?'

'He did. Thanks. They don't mind the brush with the law. Actually think it's a badge of honor.'

I'd represented Derek at the District Court. The kid had hacked Tajikistan's embassy – apparently it wasn't too hard – and somehow placed himself on a list to receive plates from the Diplomatic Motor Vehicle Program. He put them on his little souped-up Acura, thinking he could drag race around the city and park wherever he wanted. They caught him after a day.

I thought the whole thing was hilarious. I did a lot of pro bono stuff for DC kids. The little hustlers reminded me of myself at that age. With some decent representation, I could help them avoid being chewed up by the legal system and maybe get them to stop acting like morons. The prosecutor wanted to go after Derek for cyberterrorism and a laundry list of other charges. We managed it down to a misdemeanor, expunged after two years. I was impressed with how much trouble he could get away with from the comfort and safety of his bedroom.

'I was wondering if you can help me with something,' I said as I checked out the computer. 'I have a case, can't talk too much about it, that involves some malware. The program takes over the computer and reports everything on it back to the hacker. The state expert is a little behind the times, so I was wondering if you could help me out.'

'Sure,' he said. 'What does it do?'

'We're not totally sure yet. What's the worst thing out there?'

'There's some nasty stuff written in Python and C++. Records everything typed. Takes screenshots. Remote access. Remote disable. They can even record audio and video.'

'From the webcam? What about the little light?'

'They turn it off.'

'Holy shit,' I said.

His supervisor strolled by in forced-casual mode.

'That's one of the advantages of the Mac,' he said, a little louder for his boss to hear.

'Can you write one of those?'

'Hell no. You just download them.'

He walked me over to the little bar for tech help and pulled up a website on a laptop. Ads bordered the page: pop-ups for some Russian-language shoot-'em-up game, credit card machines, teenage girls in their underwear pouting at cameras. This looked like the sketchiest neighborhood on the Internet.

'Does it root into BIOS and Recovery?' he asked.

'I think so.'

'Survives a clean wipe?'

'Absolutely.'

'Here you go,' he said, pointing to the page. 'It's probably one of these.'

'But what do you do with it?'

'E-mail it. Load it up on pirate software. A lot of ways to get the payload in.'

'How about this?' I said, and pulled a USB flash drive from my bag.

'Sure,' he said. 'But you've got to be careful with them. You just stick that in the computer and it is going to be diseased beyond curing. And tell everyone you give the drive to. They need to sandbox it in a virtual machine.'

'I will. You think you could make a few? We're in discovery, so everybody needs a copy.'

I had a couple of old flash drives in my bag, and pulled them out.

He gave me a suspicious look. 'These are for evidence?'

'That's right.'

I held the drives out to him, then waited.

'What, you think I'm going to do it here?' he asked.

'Wherever.'

'This is the genius bar, man. Have some respect. Do you *see* that?' He pointed to the web page. 'I'm not touching anything from there at work. I'll get fired. I can probably do it tonight, though. Is there any money in this for me? Consulting fees?'

'You're a man of the world now, Derek. It's about giving back.'

He shook his head, muttered 'Pro bono,' then took the drives.

Chapter Seventeen

The USB keys didn't even have to work. They just had to be good enough to satisfy Lynch. He wanted my plan by that night, so I dug in on casing the New York Fed. The executive suite had been renovated in 2010, and all the bidding and contracting records were public. From the request for proposal documentation, I was able to find everything from the hardware in the president's office down to the manufacturers of their toilets and doors.

I spent the day making phone calls, trying to trace exactly how the directive went from DC to New York and who had their hands on it. I posed as a reporter, then a low-level researcher at the Government Accountability Office, and then a security analyst with Booz Allen Hamilton, which does a lot of government work. I said I was looking for best practices on information security, and wanted to compare notes with other agencies.

Spoofing phone numbers is crucial, and easy. There are plenty of pay websites that will let you change your caller ID to whatever you like. Match something close to the main switchboard, and people assume you're in-house. Hold music helps, too. I spent a lot of time on hold, and I would always record the music or the droning voices telling me my call was important. When I had someone on the line, I would say I had another call and ask them to hold, then play back the hold music from the appropriate agency. No one doubted me after that.

During the first phone call you invariably sound like an idiot, messing up names and jargon. But if you say it's your first day, or you're an intern, they'll usually guide you toward what you need to know.

'That sounds like Form 2110. You mean the operations group?'

'Oh, yeah,' I would say. 'Do you know the direct line?'

Maybe people at the FBI and CIA are cagey enough to challenge people outright. They will hang up and call back through the main switchboard to confirm identities. But the fact is, most people are too easily embarrassed and conflict averse to confront you directly.

Soon enough I was calling Mary direct for a 2110 Reg E-Claim reauthorization, like I'd been working for the federal government for a decade. There's a certain dialect I started to pick up, a tone of dark and weary humor, that identifies you as a Fed lifer.

It was during Derek's case that I had first heard the phrase 'social engineering.' That's the term, among tech nerds and hackers, for these methods of talking your way past security measures. It involves a lot of calling around to learn the lingo, rules, and bureaucratic structure of your target, and then using this against them. It was really just con games practiced against institutions from a safe distance, over phone and e-mail. You take the cold, irrational, infuriating rules of a bureaucracy – 'This is the wrong line. You'll have to fill out form 660-S. Come back on Tuesday. We're open from ten until four' – and you turn it back on them. There was no trust, no familiarity among the different cogs, and that was their weakness. If you learned the procedures, the right number to call, the right name to drop, and the right phrasing for your requests, you could get away with anything.

Working the phones was the easy part. I also needed to find some supplies that honest men don't sell, so that afternoon I stopped by a den of thieves I'd sworn off a long time ago: Ted's Roadhouse, longtime haunt of my father's crooked friends and the delinquents I used to run with.

I drove past it the first time. The Ted's I remembered was a windowless shack by the side of the highway. It had been so weathered by age the color was hard to identify. Maybe it had been blue at some point, but when I knew it, the paint had faded to a Rothko wash of green and gray.

But now in Ted's place there was a halfway-decent-looking joint called Ted's Bar and Grille, with new wood trim around real-life, non-boarded-up windows.

Had Ted's closed down? Had some restaurant group taken it over and kept the name? I parked in the gravel and stepped inside. Gloom filled the place, and it took a moment for my eyes to adjust. Wood paneling, an enormous fish tank, a cigar store Indian, a twelve-foot jukebox – the décor made my heart sink. The only adornment in the old Ted's had been a blue tarp where the roof leaked. The institution I knew and loved was dead.

But then I heard my name in a chorus of voices from the bar. A half-dozen heads turned my way, and a few figures came toward me out of the shadows like ghosts.

Luis and Smiles and Licks: Jack's and my old crew. Their age showed, in their bellies rounding over their belts and the used-up looks on their faces. They put their arms around my shoulders, punched me affectionately, and called for shots of Old Crow.

'What happened to this place?' I asked.

'Oh,' Smiles said, looking around. 'Ted went in on something with Cartwright, wouldn't say what, came into some money, fixed the place up.'

'Is Cartwright around?' I asked.

'In the back probably,' Luis said.

I noticed a guy at the end of the bar staring at me, his face washed in wavering green light from the fish tank. When he saw me looking, he returned his attention to his beer.

'Hey,' Licks said. 'You and Jack into something? You got a piece for us? You just say the word.'

'What'd you hear we were into?'

'Well, my cousin heard from a guy who saw Jack downtown, very high-class stuff—'

'You should talk to Cartwright,' Luis said, cutting him off. He looked like his patience with his drinking partners had run out several years ago. 'These guys are just fucking up some rumors they picked up secondhand.' He nodded his head toward the back door.

'Thanks,' I said, and walked past the bathrooms, then through the kitchen. The guy who'd been checking me out headed for the front door, his hand in his pocket.

At the door to the back office, I pulled the knob to the right, clearing the latch. I'd bar-backed at Ted's in high school, and the lock on the door was so old and loose that the trick always worked. Ted kept everything that mattered in a safe.

Coming into the back office, I was just about to make a joke about how, after twelve years, he still hadn't fixed it, but any mirth I was feeling dried up when I saw two guns brandished: a shotgun in Ted's hand and a pistol from the guy sitting across from Cartwright.

They lowered the weapons once they recognized me. Ted calmed everyone down, then came over and clapped me on the shoulder. He had a gaunt face with a gray scruff of a beard and a nose crooked as lightning.

'Michael Ford,' he said. 'God. What's it been? Ten years?'

'More or less,' I said.

'Your father's out?'

'He is.'

'He never came by to see us.'

'That's just the terms of his probation. No association with felons unless he's doing reentry work.' Ted seemed to take it in stride.

Cartwright only nodded at me and said, 'With you in a minute, Mike.' He sat at a card table with a Danny DeVito look-alike playing checkers. There was a good-sized stack of money lying beside the board. Cartwright watched a basketball game on a TV in the corner while he waited for his opponent to take a turn. He was drinking whiskey neat instead of old-fashioneds, which was usually a good sign he was losing money, either on the board or on the games.

The other guy made his move, hesitantly, and then smiled. Cartwright smiled back, jumped a king backwards, and held out his hand to get paid. His opponent looked confused for a minute, and then his defeat sank in. He slid the money across. Cartwright scooped it up, then joined me near a dartboard they had set up in the back.

'Good to see you, Mike. What's up?'

'I was looking for a camera.'

'You'll get a better deal at the mall.'

'I'd rather go through you. A small one. Pinhole, hopefully smaller than a deck of cards.'

'They make them smaller than the button on your shirt now. I can do that.'

'And something that runs off a battery. Almost like a baby monitor, so I can pick up the signal and see what's up inside.'

'I could work that out. Battery lasts about a week. You can set it to send in bursts. Just need a repeater nearby with a power supply.'

'How close?'

'A city block.'

'Cool. What do you think that'll set me back?'

'All together? This sounds pretty fucking dodgy, so I'll have to charge the I-don't-know-nothing tax. Say six hundred. Why aren't you just buying this off the web?'

'I'd rather it not be connected to my name.'

Cartwright took a deep breath, looked to the basketball game for solace, then cursed as the spread got away from him. He motioned for another whiskey.

'If this is a domestic matter, Mike, let me volunteer something. The answer to suspicions isn't more sneaking around. That never ends well. It's being straight-up.'

'It's not that.'

'You came all the way out here for some spy shop stuff?'

'Well . . . that was just breaking the ice. I could use a couple of wallets, too.'

'Uh-huh,' he said, his suspicions confirmed. 'Social Security cards?'

'No. Just drivers' licenses, a few credit cards, just in case. I don't need them to work. Just to make the licenses look more legit.'

When I was seventeen, I stole Jack's birth certificate and went to the local DMV to get a duplicate of his license with my picture on it. It was the best fake you could find, because it was real. I thought they'd grown a little more sophisticated since then.

Cartwright took a sip and looked pained. 'I hate to even mention this, Mike, because your family and I go way back, but you wouldn't happen to be doing this on behalf of any law enforcement types?'

A snitch? I guess I could have been offended, but I was only a few years out of Harvard Law and knew a lot of prosecutors. I was a hard person for a criminal to trust, so I actually took it as a compliment of sorts that Cartwright didn't shut me down completely.

'I'm not working with any cops,' I said.

'Good,' he said. 'Because then I'd have to kill you. And I'd hate to do that.'

He laughed. I joined him.

'Seriously,' he said. 'I knew you as a little kid. It'd break my heart.'

I swallowed. 'Understood.'

'Good. So much for that. The price has gone way up on all that stuff, Mike. "Interesting times."'

'How much?' I asked. 'I might need a few. A couple for me. One for Jack.'

'I'll get a quote,' he said.

'I'm in the market for some practice locks, too,' I went on. I had a good sense of the hardware they were using at the Fed. 'Up-to-date Medecos, some of those card-and-codes. And the whole kit: picks, shims, bypass, files, bump keys, decoders.'

'I have some here,' he said. 'Some's in storage.'

'And you wouldn't have a lead on a Red Sox World Series baseball?'

'Like a collector's item?'

'That's right.'

In my briefcase I had a photo I'd found while doing my homework on the Federal Reserve. It showed the number-two guy on the trading desk at the New York Fed. A Boston native, he was an economist and therefore a stats geek. Those guys have a weakness for baseball, for endless inky rows of numbers. The photo was a head shot, fairly close-in. He was in his office, standing beside his desk. And behind him stood a row of baseballs on wooden bases. I could read some of the plaques. There was Carl Yastrzemski and Bobby Doerr. Nothing had more than one signature. A Red Sox fan: that made it easy to find my Trojan horse, a trophy he couldn't resist. I'd gathered everything I could about this man's background to figure out how to get to him.

'I'll make some calls,' Cartwright said, and walked toward the end of the room. He opened a locked door and led me in to a storeroom. From a shelf he pulled down a door handle with a keypad. 'These are the new Department of Homeland Security spec card-and-codes. Swiss. Thirteen hundred dollars. Eight-digit PINs and 256-bit encryption. They're certified to withstand pick attempts for up to six hours.'

'Jesus,' I said.

'That's only if you pick them the way the government labs expect you to. The electronics they're cramming into hardware these days create a lot of weak links. It's sloppy work.'

He entered 12345678 on the pad. The red LED flashed for an incorrect entry. As it did, Cartwright jammed a pick into the housing beside the flashing light. The whole thing went dark, and he swung the handle down.

'You ground the board and it opens. My fucking grand-daughter could do it,' he said. 'Have you been practicing?'

'Not in years.'

'Start here,' he said, pointing to the door we'd just entered. He reached onto a shelf and handed me a hook pick and tension wrench.

The lock was a six-pin Schlage. I got down on one knee in front of it, placed the wrench in, and slid the pick inside. A thrill ran through me. It felt like I was getting high for the first time in years.

With tension on the wrench, I started in on the first pins to bind. I pushed them up until I felt the slightest give in the cylinder, at the shear line, then felt the lower half of the pin go loose, no binding, no more pushback from the tiny spring above it. That meant I had a good set.

There was some commotion out front, but I was too absorbed by the lock, these old puzzles I had spent years learning to crack.

As I eased up the last pin, the cylinder spun free. The lock was open. I laughed. God, it felt good.

'Cartwright!' Someone shouted. 'Cartwright!'

I turned, but it was too late. Someone grabbed me by the collar and threw me against the wall.

Chapter Eighteen

A man stood over me, glaring, the veins in his neck and forehead plump with anger.

'Hey, Dad,' I said.

I deserved it. He'd caught me in the act with a pick and wrench, the sort of thing that had ruined his life and nearly ruined mine.

I looked around the room. 'Some of these guys, Dad – you'll break parole.'

'You're worried about *me* getting in trouble?'

'I don't do soaps,' Cartwright said before he walked back toward the main room. He did, actually. All those guys had been sitting around card tables in the backs of restaurants and delis, hatching plots all day every day for about forty years with the TV on in the background. They would break your wrist if you tried to switch off *The Young and the Restless*.

My dad let me go, stepped back, and took a deep breath.

'What the hell are you doing here?' he asked.

'How'd you know where I was?' I asked as I stood up.

'A friend called, said you were looking for trouble.'

'It's not like that.'

'Then what is it?' he asked and stepped closer, as if to tower over me. He'd been away a long time, and always seemed to forget that I was bigger than he was.

'It's Jack. He's in trouble.'

'Bad?'

'It could be. I'm just giving him technical advice, nothing heavy.'

'I have to ask: is he scamming you?'

'I thought so at first, then I watched these guys work him over. He's on the level. They told him – You know what? Don't worry about it. He's got it under control.'

'What'd they say?' he asked.

I knew he'd get it out of me eventually. 'That they would kill him. He needs to steal some inside info. Tipping.'

'*Kill* him?'

'They're serious, Dad. Trust me.'

Since the shooting on the Mall, every time I shut my eyes to think or to sleep I saw the same image: Sacks trying to speak but no words coming, just a sucking hole in his lung. I didn't feel like explaining why I was so sure, so I left it at that.

'What's the job?'

'White collar. Nothing too crazy. Financial.'

'I've worked a lot of paper. Who are you after?'

'You're not going within a mile of this. I went through hell to get you out. I'm not going to get you tossed back in.'

'Technical advice, huh?' he said, looking down at the pick in my hand. 'I don't think so. What's the target?'

'The Federal Reserve Bank in New York. They're going to steal the directive, get the committee decision before it's public.'

'The New York Fed? That's impossible. They've got the heaviest vault in the world.'

'We don't want the gold. We want the desk.'

'We?' he said. He rocked back on his heels. 'Mike, come on.'

He looked at me closely, searching me out. You can never lie to a con man. It made being his kid particularly tough.

'What aren't you telling me?' he asked.

'They're after me, too. It comes back on me if Jack bolts. Or we don't pull it off. They know about Annie.'

He swung. It came out of nowhere. I thought he was going to knock me out, but he pivoted on his toe and sent a tight right hook into the stacked bags of flour next to my head. They wheezed white dust out of the corners.

'If *they* don't kill him,' he said, 'I will.'

'You can get in line behind me. Except he says he was trying to stay straight. That's why they're after him. He wouldn't play ball.'

'So what are you doing? You're not going to break into the goddamn Fed.'

'No. Just rope-a-dope long enough to figure out how to make the whole thing blow back on the guys who are threatening us.'

'Who?'

'He told me to call him Lynch, though I'm sure that's not his real name. Drives a black Chrysler. He's got vampire teeth, real thin, about six one.'

My dad shook his head. 'Why didn't you ask me for help before?'

'I'm not getting you involved, Dad. I'm keeping the whole thing at arm's length. I'm just doing surveillance at this point, getting eyes inside the target, very low risk.'

'Break-in?'

'No. Everything has a camera on it these days, so I'm trying a few things to get a look inside the suite. Actually . . .' I said, and thought about it for a second. 'Can you do some milling for me?'

My dad had a decent shop set up in his garage. I knew this because whenever I went to his house, he dragooned me into a several-hours-long home improvement project. The last time

I'd ended up on my back in an eighteen-inch crawl space holding a hot copper pipe as he worked the blowtorch and dripped molten solder onto my forearm.

'Depends on what you need done,' he said.

'A display stand for a baseball. I'll show you a photo. I need you to hollow out the wooden base.'

'That's no problem. What for?'

'You're better off not knowing. I'm going to go up soon, sort out the perimeter and access control. If these cameras work out, we'll have some images of the interior layout to figure out the target setup.'

'You're not going in, though?'

'No. If anyone goes, it'll be Jack. But no one's going to go.'

'How hard did these guys come at you?'

'Hell-bent.'

'I don't like it. Why are they so particular about you? For all they know, you're a citizen, an amateur.'

'I guess they heard about what I did to get out of the last mess.'

'Still, what's their endgame? You think they'll let you just pull the job and be done with it? Does that make any sense? After they threaten your family? You don't piss off someone like that and expect to cool them out by the end.'

'You think it's a setup?' I said. I'd been wondering the same thing myself, going through the angles. I'd made an enemy with every case I took on. I went after the money, the corruption. I had systematically pissed off the most powerful people in Washington. It was easier to figure out who *didn't* have a reason to screw me.

'It could be,' my father said. 'You always have to know who you're working for. That's rule number one. Or else you could be walking right into a trap. Never bet in another man's game.'

'That's why I'm hoping to turn it back on them.'

'They'll get the committee decision early?'

'That's their plan.'

'But how much do stocks even pop on that? It's not like a merger, where one company will jump a hundred percent.'

'It's going to move markets for sure. This meeting is a big one. The analysts are all mixed on what the Fed will do. The regional presidents are divided. No one knows if they're going to hold the gas down or slam on the brakes.'

'Still, that wouldn't account for more than a single-digit jump. Is it worth the risk?' he asked.

'Things have changed. Any idiot with a 401k and a Schwab account can buy a triple-leveraged ETF and short the Dow with a single click. There are derivatives on everything.'

Dad had done some white-collar cons before he went away, only going after people who deserved it, but they were nothing compared to the everyday mischief that passes for finance today.

'So they must be leveraged like crazy,' I said. 'It's smart. You go all-in, leverage it all five-or tenfold, even more. The markets don't have to move all that much, and there is so much activity you're not going to get hit for insider trading. Everyone has an opinion on inflation and interest rates.'

My dad squinted a little, thinking hard. 'Which means if they bet wrong, you can blow them up.'

'I just give them the wrong numbers,' I said.

He shook his head. 'Sounds great. But you have to steal them before you can switch them, and that's suicide. And you just told me you're not going in. This is fun to throw around in a backroom with the other bullshit artists, but think about your life, think about Annie. Just go to the police.'

'They have the police wired.'

'The DC cops?'

'I don't know, exactly, but I know they've killed whistle-blowers before. These guys are very professional and very well financed. Jack was thinking of talking. That's why they went after him. I have a few leads on people I know who might be safe to talk to.' I thought of Emily Bloom again.

'That's all you should be doing right now. I love your brother. I'd trade my life for his, but I'm an old man. And family's family, sure, but Annie's your family now, too. You busted your ass to tear yourself away from all this no-class garbage. Don't get involved. Don't throw your life away for him.'

'They're threatening everything I have, Dad. I'm doing this to keep that life.'

'Jesus Christ,' he said. 'You think if you can figure out in five minutes how to turn the tables on them, to rewire this so it blows up in their faces, that they haven't seen it, too? Something stinks here, Mike. Don't go near this thing. And don't even think of dabbling until you know who's behind it. Until you know how they're trying to fuck you over. That was my mistake. And it cost me sixteen years of my life.'

'Switch the numbers,' I said. 'You shifty old bastard. I love you.'

'Don't even think about it, Mike.'

I was trapped. Lynch had left me with the choice between losing everything or undertaking a suicide mission. Even if I somehow managed to pull it off, they'd probably let me take the fall or just kill me outright. But now I saw a way out. All I would have to do is break into the Federal Reserve Bank of New York, steal the best-protected piece of economic data in the world, and outgun Lynch at his own game, under his nose.

'Seriously,' my father said, 'if you don't know who you're working for, you've already lost.'

'I'll find out,' I said, then dragged my hand back through my hair. 'God. How does this stuff always find us?'

He lifted a tool that looked like a small chisel from Cartwright's cache. It was an antique graver, used for making printing plates, and also for forging currency and bonds.

'Don't think you play pretend with this, just go through the motions and find an easy way out,' he said. 'It finds us because we love it, Mike. That's what scares me. It's in your blood.'

Chapter Nineteen

Back in my car, I picked up my phone to call Lynch. I was up against my deadline. He could come by my house any minute. I needed to keep him happy to keep my name away from that murder.

I lifted my prepaid, but my legit cell phone next to it was impossible to ignore. The LED was flashing, and there were a dozen notifications on the status bar. Before I could check them, it started ringing.

It was Annie.

'Hey, sweetheart,' she said. 'The photographer just called. Are you on your way? You didn't forget, did you?'

'No. Just stuck in traffic.'

I had forgotten the deposit, which meant I would have to mow through sixteen miles of traffic. As I sped along the Beltway, my phone lit up with messages from one of my clients, the man who covered a decent chunk of my overhead.

He was in town, and suggested, in an increasingly insistent series of texts and e-mails, that I meet him at a cocktail spot near Mount Vernon Square. I'd already blown him off, and I couldn't afford to anger this guy. He was temperamental enough as it was.

After I dropped off the check at the photographer's, I tried Lynch on the way downtown. No answer.

*   *   *

My client Mark was upstairs, waiting for me at a table, wearing a power suit, breaking the first rule of 'new, hip' DC. You can't afford any of the new places – the craft cocktails, the reclaimed wood furniture, the farm-to-table restaurants – unless you're fully in hock to the corporate world, but you're supposed to at least change into some hipster garb before you go out.

I sat down. Mark had no inside voice, and soon he was upstaging the bartender's long speech on the history of punch.

Mark had cashed out of some dot-com thing, and now split his time between Los Gatos and New York. He'd grown bored as a tech investor and was trying to buy his way into politics. I steered him to where he could do the most good, getting to the root of corruption, stemming the money that led politicians to worry more about their next fund-raising check than their constituents' needs. He supported some of the dark-money work, but there wasn't enough glamour in it for him. He was always pushing back. He wanted easy wins, headlines, scalps.

He couldn't understand why the causes he and his friends all agreed on were not getting traction in Middle America. Was it bad faith among the voters? Republican brainwashing? It never occurred to him that he was just out of touch, or that people might reasonably disagree. His new thing was giving out quotes to the press where he would say he couldn't believe no one had drafted him to run for Congress or thrown him an ambassadorship.

'If only you could force people to vote their interests, you know?' he said.

I was thinking of telling Mark that that approach hadn't worked out so well for my friend Robespierre, but I refrained. My phone buzzed in my pocket.

I glanced at the prepaid. It was a message from Lynch: 'Time's up. What have you got for me?'

'Could you excuse me for a second?' I asked Mark. He didn't

like that one bit, but I cut away before he could voice it. I called Lynch back from near the entryway.

'You forgetting your deadlines?' Lynch asked.

'I've been working my ass off. I've got something for you. Can we meet later?'

'I'm right by your house. You need to give that side yard some attention. People are going to figure out that deep down you're trash.'

'It's on my list,' I said. 'I'm not home.'

'Pity. Annie's back from her run. She looks lonely.'

'Don't you dare,' I said. 'I'm on my way.'

Mark looked furious as I walked back to my seat. The bar was tiny, and quite a few people were giving me dirty looks. It was as if I had taken a phone call while waiting in line for communion.

'I have to go,' I told him.

'We've only had one drink.'

'It's an emergency. I'm sorry.'

'You have seemed sort of distracted recently, Michael. I don't know if I'm getting one hundred percent from you.'

'Can we talk about this later?'

'No, we can't. I don't think you're giving me the amount of respect I am due. I might have to reevaluate our relationship.'

Jesus, he never gave a straight answer.

'Are you firing me?'

'If you walk out now, I fear it may come to that.'

I felt relief more than any angst about being done with this guy.

'I'm leaving,' I said, and laid a twenty down on the bar. 'So thanks for your business.'

Chapter Twenty

I raced home and found Lynch in his car, parked around the corner from my house, reading the newspaper. The man with glasses was in the passenger seat. I tapped on the window. He rolled it down.

'What's your sign?' Lynch asked.

'What?'

'Come on.'

'Capricorn.'

He lifted the paper. '"Today's new moon may mark the beginning of a grand adventure. Many will be traveling to exciting places, which could ultimately change their life." Sounds auspicious,' he said. 'Get in.'

'Where are we going?'

'I found your baseball.'

I stepped into the car. We crossed the river and headed south as Lynch peppered me with questions. I told him about getting eyes in the suite first, and everything I had learned about the procedures for getting the directive from DC to New York on Fed Day.

He didn't say anything, just nodded slowly as he judged my progress. We drove past Bolling Air Force Base to a desolate part of Southeast. He pulled into a large yard of gravel and sand surrounded by marsh. A few commercial fishing boats rusted out on jack stands or lay on their sides.

'Follow me,' Lynch said as he stepped out of the driver's seat.

'I'm not getting a sports memorabilia vibe from this place,' I said.

'First things first,' Lynch said, and led me toward a two-story building with an observation deck on top, some kind of decommissioned yard office. His partner stayed with the car, watching over us.

Lynch stopped at the front door, pulled out his pistol, and cocked the hammer back.

He pointed to the door. 'The Fed uses the same lock,' he said, and checked his watch. 'You have four minutes.'

I knelt down and looked at the lock, a Medeco. I had the picks from Cartwright, but this lock, while an older design, was one of the most difficult ever made.

To open it, I had to raise six high-security pins, designed with serrations and false sets to throw off lockpickers, to the correct height. That was the easy part. Medecos are such bears because once you have picked the pins to the correct height, you then have to *rotate* them around a vertical axis to the correct orientation. The pins have notches on their sides that, when lined up, allow a piece of brass called a sidebar to retract and let the cylinder turn freely.

'That's impossible,' I said, and turned back. 'I need a—'

Lynch held it: a thin wire with a ninety-degree bend at the end. In theory it would let me rotate the pins.

'So this is a tryout?' I asked.

'We can't send an amateur in.'

'By all means, don't. I *am* an amateur,' I said. 'And I don't want the job. You're not giving me a lot of incentives here.'

'You're ours either way. Do your best. If you don't check out, you become expendable.'

'I'd need ten minutes even under the best of—'

He raised his pistol. The flare from the muzzle blinded me. The gunshot was deafening that close. My ears rang. I took a stumbling step to one side. Gravel rained against the cement walls of the office. Lynch lowered the gun.

'Three minutes and thirty seconds,' he said. 'Don't waste my time.'

'Forced entry?'

'Strictly bypass. No damage. No trace.'

The picks were top-of-the-line Southern Ordnance models with comfy plastic handles. I hated expensive picks. They were like driving a Mercury Sable. I didn't have the second-skin touch I needed for a lock like this. I'd never picked anything this hard, not even close. This was like going from flag football to the NFL.

I placed a tension wrench in the keyway and put some pressure on as I felt around with the hook pick. It took a while to get the basic layout.

'Two minutes thirty seconds.'

To deal with the security pins, I overset them deliberately, eased way off on the tension wrench, and began to lower them one at a time.

'Two minutes.'

I worked it back to front and thought I had three pins set, but it was impossible to know for sure with a lock that complex.

'One minute,' Lynch said. He stepped behind me and held the gun to his side.

Expendable, like Sacks, I thought, and remembered the scene on the Mall. That didn't help. Sweat soaked my shirt despite the cold air. My heart pounded, too hard, distracting me from the feel in my fingers.

There was no give, that subtle movement of the cylinder to tell me I had the pins at the right height and could move on to work the sidebar. Something was wrong. I kept the tension on and started over.

It was the fifth pin.

'Thirty seconds,' Lynch said.

I worked on it but I was lost, groping blind, unable to tell the real shear line from all the misdirection. There was no time. I had to start with the rotations and pray I had the heights right. I put the wire in.

'Twenty,' Lynch said. I heard the gravel crunch behind me. He was standing over me where I knelt.

'Ten seconds,' he said.

My hands started shaking. I could feel the lock seizing, the sets falling, all my work lost.

'Five.' He pressed the muzzle to the back of my head. I fumbled with the wire. My hands were trembling too much to do anything.

'Zero.'

I felt the muzzle of the gun dig into the back of my skull. He tightened his grip.

'Click.'

He didn't fire. He reached his hand forward and rested it on mine on the tension wrench. Then he moved to the side, the gun aimed at my eye.

'Step back,' he said.

He seemed to know what he was doing with that wrench. I stood up and moved a few feet away, my eyes fixed on the gun.

Slowly he let the pressure off the wrench. I could see the focus in his eyes as he felt the pins fall back into place. A skilled hand could tell how many I'd set. Those pins would decide my fate like a jury.

He pressed his lips together as he considered my work. His hand tightened up on the gun. His thumb slid up and engaged the safety.

'Five, maybe six pins,' he said. 'No way to tell on the sidebar.'

He holstered the gun. 'You need it under four minutes or you're a dead man on Fed Day.'

I shoved him. 'You point a gun at me again and I'll kill you, I swear.'

His sidekick moved closer. Lynch waved him back. 'You think this is scary?' he said. 'Wait until the real job. This is tough love, Mike. The Federal Reserve Police won't give you a second chance. They'll put two bullets in your brain.'

The fear left a taste in my mouth like I was sucking on a penny. I took a minute to calm down. As much as it infuriated me, Lynch was right. This wasn't a game. That lock had beaten me. And if I failed when it mattered, I would end up dead or in prison.

'So I walk?' I said.

'For now,' he said. 'You need a practice lock?'

'I'm set.'

'Keep me happy, Mike. Then you and your people will be fine.'

'I'm going to case the Fed.'

'When?'

'Tomorrow,' I said. 'With Jack.'

'Good,' he said. He gestured to his partner, who came over with a thick roll of cash. Lynch counted out a stack of fifty-dollar bills and placed it in an envelope.

'Any supplies you need?'

'It's taken care of.'

'How's your little law practice going?'

'Just great,' I lied.

'What did I pay you last time?'

'Ten cents. But I didn't take it, and I'm not taking that.'

He held the money out. 'I don't want you to think this is extortion,' he said.

'Yeah. God forbid I think you're some kind of criminal. Keep your money.'

'I pay my men. I pay them well. You're taking it,' he said, and held it touching my chest. 'I'm not going to let you fuck this up by doing it on the cheap.'

'No,' I said.

'I don't trust men I don't own.' The other man took out his pistol. Lynch folded the envelope over once and tucked it in my jacket pocket.

'Tomorrow, after New York, you tell me how you're going to get the directive.'

So much for rope-a-dope. There would be no stalling him, no games. The minute he lost faith in me was the minute he came after everything I loved.

He left me with the man in glasses and stepped away to check his phone. He carried two on his belt. Right now he was on a basic flip model like my prepaid. I'd seen him use it before, and it always seemed to be for orders about this job.

'Time to go,' he said.

Chapter Twenty-One

When I arrived home, Annie was on the cordless phone in the living room.

'Dad. Dad . . .' She was talking loud, trying to get a word in and failing. 'It's a little late for that. The wedding is only a few weeks away.' Clark had been doing a lot of international travel recently, back-to-back trips to the Middle East and South America.

The wedding planning was getting tense. It was becoming clear that the Ford and Clark clans would explode when mixed. Annie and I had had a two-day standoff over the hotels. I wanted to be near my father and family, but they couldn't afford the hotel Annie's grandmother picked out. And the Clarks wouldn't set foot in a place that offered a free breakfast.

My father's enthusiasm was another issue. He had just given me a couple more names for last-minute invites. After all that time inside, he was eager to get the family back together. Unfortunately, half his guests were deceased or incarcerated. He seemed to think that his share of the guest list was gross, not net, so he kept tacking on names when his first tries couldn't come, which was driving both me and Annie nuts. 'I think there may be a cousin . . .' he would say, and ransack a drawer looking for one of my mom's old address books.

No wonder this call from Clark had her on edge. 'Fine,' Annie said into the handset, not bothering to hide her anger. 'I'll have them send it to the lawyers.'

She hung up without saying goodbye. As I approached the living room, I expected her to be upset. What I didn't expect was to see her hurl the phone against the couch as hard as she could. I caught it as it ricocheted toward the hardwood floor.

'God,' she said. 'Have you ever felt like you could kill somebody?'

I leaned my head to the side. I had, actually, and then some. It was an odd question considering everything Annie and I had been through.

'Sorry,' she said. 'It's my fucking father.'

I considered the option. 'If we killed him it'd save us a meal, but we'd probably have to fit somebody else for a tux. So call it a toss-up. I'll leave it to you. What'd he do this time?'

'It's him and my grandmother. They're changing everything. It's so over the top. I think they want to make it so expensive that I'll feel indebted, over a barrel. I just don't have time to deal with it anymore. And now I have to go to Palo Alto for work.'

'When?'

'Flight's in an hour.'

She'd just won a major intellectual-property case. That's what the managing partner had taken her to the Cosmos Club to talk about. He wanted her to take the strategy national.

There was an invoice from Oscar de la Renta on the desk in front of her: the wedding dress. Thank God I couldn't see the price.

'Next time he gives you a hard time, tell him you don't need his money.'

'Hon,' she said, 'this is getting pretty expensive. Are you sure?'

I had an envelope from Lynch in my pants pocket so thick with cash it was hard to sit down.

'Absolutely,' I said. 'I'll take care of it. Is there something else, though? Your dad's been pulling that move for a while.' She had said something on the phone about lawyers.

'He's giving the vendors a hard time.'

117

'Is he trying to change the terms?'

'Don't worry about it,' she said.

I looked at the table and saw marked-up contracts. 'The refunds?' I asked.

She let out a long breath. I guess I'd found her out.

I started laughing. 'In case you call it off?' I said, and shook my head. 'Hedging his trades.'

He could have just been worried about it getting rained out. The last time we were at his place, Clark had actually toned down his open contempt for me to more of a simmering disdain. He dumped me off with the dog trainer, and I'd spent the afternoon hanging out with the hounds. Maybe he'd given up. He must have known that the wedding was going to happen either way. I liked to think that I had earned some respect by rejecting his money in New York.

'It's his job,' Annie said.

'Fine. I'll take the other side of that bet.' I said. 'You?'

'Absolutely,' she said, and hugged me around the waist. 'I shouldn't be so hard on him.'

'I think you're actually going easy on the guy.'

'Not that. I'm starting to wonder if he's sick or something. Last time I was home, he just didn't seem right. He was really down, low-energy. And when we were at the country place, he was in his office on the phone, and when he came out, he looked like all the life had gone out of him.'

'Maybe he got some bad news in the markets.'

'No,' she said. 'He thrives on that stuff, loves fighting back, doubling down, going to war.' She walked to her suitcase and started throwing clothes into the laundry basket and restocking clean ones. The case was always packed these days.

'My dad has a few more tack-ons,' I told her.

'How many?' she asked.

'Four,' I said. 'Down in Floyd County.'

'God. Who can we sit them near?'

I looked over the seating plan on the side table as if it was a map of a minefield, then back at Annie. 'No one,' I said.

She shook her head. 'See if you can figure it out,' she said. 'I have to get to Reagan.'

'I'll give you a ride.'

'You were out late,' she said. 'Jack?'

'No. Work. I'm in the weeds, and then Mark Phillips kidnapped me for drinks.'

'How'd that go?'

I thought about it. 'I think we're finally moving in the right direction.'

'Great,' she said. 'You're in a good mood.'

'Really?'

'Yes. You seem very, I don't know, vital.'

'Thanks.'

I thought I was a wreck after my run-in with Lynch, but who knows? One of the upsides of Annie moving up at work was that she was almost too busy to pay attention to my comings and goings. And when wedding planning grew to be too stressful, I could soothe my nerves with my new hobby: robbing banks with a gun to my head.

I had some suspicions about why I might seem so full of pep, but I didn't want to examine too closely the idea that some part of me was actually enjoying this stuff. And with a main client gone and a thick stack of dirty money in my pocket, it seemed more and more that I was, as Larry Clark liked to claim, nothing but a criminal.

I thought back to when I had left the boatyard with Lynch. He had told me I was doing good work. 'Take a breath, Mike,' he said. 'I think you're actually going to pull this off. You're a natural.'

That's what I was afraid of.

Chapter Twenty-Two

Before I headed up to the Fed the next morning, I needed to round up my tools. I stopped by my dad's first, then went to see Cartwright. He was known for being resourceful, but still I was impressed when he presented me with a 2004 World Series Red Sox ball signed by most of the team. I decided not to ask how he'd gotten it, since it seemed too good to be honest.

I collected my flash drives from Derek, and after getting a short course in sketchy Internet anonymity and confirming that there was nothing on the drives that might ID him, gave him a few hundred bucks for his work.

On my way to New York, I stopped at Jack's house to pick him up.

'You drive,' I said. 'I've got to work the phone.'

He climbed into the car. His coffee steamed the window. 'Weather's perfect,' he said.

It was thirty-eight degrees. Drizzle streaked the windshield. Criminals love bad weather: fewer witnesses.

Jack put the car in reverse and started backing out the driveway. Then he stopped and put it back in park.

'No.'

'What?'

'I can't.'

'You're backing out?'

'You are. I can't let you risk it. I'll take care of it. Go home.'

'I can't let you do this on your own,' I said.

'I've got this, Mike. It's my fault. We didn't really talk, so I never got a chance to tell you, but I'm so goddamned proud of you, everything Dad told me about. I never shut up about it. My brother graduating from college, then going to Harvard, for Christ's sake. My buddies probably thought it was part of some con.' He laughed and leaned forward, his left forearm on the wheel.

'But when I was down it gave me hope, Mike. That I could change. That I could straighten myself out. So thank you. You've got a great girl. You've got a good life, a decent life. I can't let whatever's wrong with me fuck that up. So go home.'

I took a sip of coffee, listened to the mechanical whine of the wipers flicking back and forth. 'Thanks, Jack. But that's why I'm doing all this. Everything I have worked for is on the line. I can't stand back and let you take the lead on fixing it. No offense or anything. I hear you, and I appreciate it. I played my part in screwing this up, too. And now it's on me. I'm going to take care of these guys. I'm going to keep the life I earned. Sometimes you have to get your hands a little dirty to stay clean. Let's go.'

We headed for New York. I needed to know exactly what happened on Fed Days – when the committee in DC makes its decision – and who gets their hands on the directive between DC and New York, so I started dialing the follow-ups from my social engineering calls.

The answer, I learned, is precious few. The directive was the best-protected piece of government information outside of national security. That made sense. A quarter of a percentage point change in a single number from the directive, the Fed's target interest rate, could turn the global economy on a dime.

Designated 'Class I FOMC – Restricted Controlled,' it was limited to a handful of people outside the Fed boardroom on a strict need-to-know basis. The senior vice president, my Red Sox fan, was one of them. Despite everything I learned, I couldn't figure out what means they used to transmit the information from DC to New York.

Jack had been working on his own schemes. 'I think New York's a mistake, Mike. They must get the directive over to Treasury down in DC, right?'

'They walk it over,' I said.

'That's what I was thinking,' he said. 'So what if we posed as the recipients, like a dummy office or something?'

'So we just have to break into the Treasury and set up a fake office without anyone noticing?'

'Not that exactly, but *like that*. Or if we get the real courier in trouble, plant a gun on him before security or something, and we pose as *another courier* and they give it to us to protect it.'

'That is some awful *Gilligan's Island*–caliber shit you're coming up with right now.'

He rubbed his forehead. 'I know. It's terrible. I'm all blocked up.'

Jack was off. He'd never played for stakes this high.

We arrived in Manhattan a little after noon and parked in a garage on Pearl Street. Jack pulled the hood on his raincoat up and cinched it down over his face, then pulled a newspaper from his bag.

I stepped out of the car. We'd driven straight through. My legs were so stiff from the ride I walked like I'd been at sea for two weeks.

'You have anything sketchy in your bag?' I asked.

'Sure.'

'Leave it here. Anything you wouldn't want a cop to find on you.'

He emptied it into the glove box: a set of picks, pepper spray, a blackjack, and an automatic knife.

'That's everything?'

'Yeah,' he said.

As we headed toward Maiden Lane, we walked under construction scaffolding. I started making an inventory of the trucks and normal inhabitants of this neighborhood – the movers and mechanical contractors, the deliverymen and bankers.

We turned toward Ground Zero, the Federal Reserve, and the New York Stock Exchange. Now it was fear more than anything else that was making my legs wobble. Between the bank security, NYPD, and video cameras staring down from every corner, this was, with the possible exception of the White House, the most secure patch of real estate in the United States.

Jack held the paper over his face. It wasn't raining hard enough to merit that. I grabbed it and threw it in the garbage.

'But the cameras,' he said.

'You look like a nut. Don't draw attention to yourself.'

I was glad we'd made it up here by lunchtime. I had a list of targets I wanted to hit. We bought a couple of hot dogs and coffees from a vendor on Liberty Street and watched the crowd flow past, jostling us.

The Fed is a fortress rising eighteen stories above street level. Black wrought-iron gates and huge blocks of limestone and sandstone project strength and, above all, impenetrability.

I noticed the surveillance nests high up on the bank's corners.

I handed Jack my cell phone. 'Think tourist,' I said. We circled the building as Jack snapped photos. I had rooted my phone and deleted the shutter noise so we could shoot photos surreptitiously.

Viewed from the air, the building was essentially a long wedge, getting wider as it ran east to west. On the south side, on Liberty Street, there was a main door that led into an ornate lobby. On the north side, on Maiden Lane, there was a crash-proof loading dock and a well-trafficked employee and visitor entrance. Each entrance had at least two cops posted. Every time they looked at me I felt as if I was staring back at them from a wanted poster, with all the details of Sacks's murder printed under my face.

The Fed had been well guarded around the clock since it opened ninety years ago. While I was making my social engineering calls, a former economist there told me an anecdote. The Fed is only a couple of blocks from Ground Zero, and on 9/11, they had to evacuate. Eventually, out of safety concerns, even the Federal Reserve Police were called off. Only then did they realize that there were no locks on the doors, and a smith was dispatched to install some so they could leave the place unmanned for the first time since 1924.

Jack took his own cell phone out and carried it in his hand. He was talking too much, which usually meant he was nervous. Two postal service workers trundled a cart up the sidewalk and guided it into the Fed loading area with no credentials check, just a nod to the cops.

'Bingo,' Jack said.

I shook my head. 'They're known quantities. It's too complicated, and then how do you get in once you're in the dock?'

'The bar around the corner,' Jack said. 'I've been there. The bathroom's three floors down. If we could get into some of the tunnels, get over to the Fed basement somehow—'

I saw a woman approaching. She was Tara Pollard of Murray Hill, the office manager on the trading desk. I'd pieced together photos of the staff of the president's office, the press shop, and the trading desk, all the most likely candidates to have access to the directive before its public announcement.

She must have gone out for lunch today because she was coming my way with a Styrofoam takeout container. I checked her badge. It was helpful that the Fed labeled their employees for me.

'Stay here,' I told Jack.

I walked toward her, eyes down against the rain, reached into my pocket and palmed the USB drive in my left hand. Her purse looked zipped shut, but a side pouch hung halfway open.

I brushed past her and dropped it in. As a pickpocket, it's a lot easier to give than to receive.

'What was that?' Jack asked after I circled back.

'Not now,' I said.

'Where's the suite we need to get to?' he asked. 'The turret? That's where I'd be.'

A tower stood out at the east end of the Fed. As I checked out the crenels, I thought the architects might have taken the fortress idea a little too far. It looked like they could defend the place with bows and arrows.

'The president is on ten. The desk is on nine.'

'So these tunnels,' he went on. 'I found some old maps on the web, construction stuff from when they built it.'

'Shut up,' I said. Jack looked at me angrily until he noticed the cop walking by. I waited for him to pass.

'The vault's eighty feet down, Jack, below the subway. It's on the bedrock. It's three stories of solid steel, weighs two hundred and thirty tons, and is surrounded by steel-reinforced concrete. They lowered it down to the bottom, then built the building around it. The whole infrastructure of New York City is sitting on top of it. Any breach and one button seals it air- and watertight within twenty-five seconds. Maybe tunneling through the bathroom at TGI Fridays isn't the way to go.'

Getting into buildings was my specialty. Jack's strength was sneaking past people's suspicions.

'How are you going to get inside, then?' he asked, looking a little wounded.

'First things first,' I said and took my phone.

We had already learned everything we could about the perimeter from outside, and anyone I needed to check out during the lunch rush had already gone back in. Catty-corner from the Fed there was an overpriced sandwich shop that billed itself as a patisserie.

I walked in, told Jack to order something, and headed for the restroom. I'd checked the place out in advance. It was close enough to the Fed and had free Wi-Fi. Both were crucial. I stood on a toilet and lifted the ceiling tiles.

From my bag I pulled out a small black box with an antenna on the side and placed it above the tiles. For power, I hooked into a junction box for the bathroom ceiling fan. This was essentially a wireless repeater. It would pick up the over-the-air signal from a camera inside the Fed, then send it back out over the Internet. I could watch the feed from anywhere on the web.

Our next stop was a delivery service. I'd already boxed up the baseball and had picked up the display stand from my father that morning. His milling was as good as ever, even though the Ford Steel Works had been shut down for almost thirty years. The base had been hollowed out for a camera and a backup battery, but there was no sign of any modification. The lens was invisible, hidden behind the drilled-out dot in the *i* of 'Series.'

Inside the box was a gift receipt I'd backdated a few weeks and a nice note from a Professor Halloran at the University of Chicago. He had been the lead author on several of the senior vice president's early papers in graduate school and was a fellow baseball geek. That made him a plausible giver for my

Trojan horse baseball, which would soon take up its rightful spot, aimed directly at the senior VP's computer and broadcasting everything he read back to me.

'What about the thank-you note?' Jack asked. 'Or if he calls this professor?'

'Halloran died last week,' I said. I'd been poring over the SVP's résumé and the obituaries for two days, searching for the right candidate. The phone and e-mail address on the invoice led back to my dummy accounts, if he had any other questions.

'Cute,' he said. 'But you still haven't gotten inside. You going to do this all by remote control?'

I wished I could, but at some point I had to put my ass on the line. That time was now.

Chapter Twenty-Three

I handed Jack a paper printout and a wallet full of forged credentials. He looked at the sheet. It was an e-ticket for the Fed tour. We walked toward the Federal Reserve Police guarding the Maiden Lane entrance. They're a formidable group, all required to certify on pistol, rifle, and shotgun twice a year at the Fed's range. Most qualify as experts.

They looked at the tickets first, and then at our fake IDs. The guard looked back and forth between my face, my license, and my face again.

He waved me in.

My eyes darted around the lobby, calculating the possibilities for beating security on the day of the heist. The employees walked into mantraps opened by RFID badges. This place was going to be just as bad as I had feared. Mantraps look like futuristic telephone booths, with two doors that open on opposite sides. A higher-security version of a turnstile, mantraps isolate people so that only one at a time can enter as his credentials are confirmed. Some actually check your weight to prevent two people from going through, or lock you in if your ID doesn't scan.

Jack and I turned to the right. Visitors walked through a metal detector and bag X-ray before going to the traps. It was pretty standard security, typical of courthouses, though these guards were better armed.

Jack went through the security screen first, then I cleared the metal detectors. He stepped into an elevator with the rest of the tour just before the doors closed. The guard pointed me toward the mantrap and another scanned a card to allow me to pass.

'Go with them,' he said. I followed three women to the elevators and glanced down at their badges. Everyone wore credentials on plastic badge-holders clipped to their waists or on lanyards around their necks.

The RFID technology was a relief. Most feds were moving toward smart-card badges encrypted by the NSA, which as a practical matter were impossible to crack or clone. RFID is much easier to hack, but I probably wouldn't even have to go that far. I had some other tricks in mind. I was holding my phone in my hand, and as we entered the elevator, I snapped a couple of shots of the badges up close.

The women exited on three. What the hell, I thought, and pressed ten, the president's floor. It worked. There was no key control for the elevators, another good sign. Still, it was a stupid move. As I rose toward the heart of the Fed, I wouldn't have a plausible story if I were challenged.

The car stopped and the doors opened on ten. There were no guards at the elevator banks. Once past the guns and the guards and the mantraps, it was just an office, full of bankers and economists, people who don't have security in their bones the way they do at the Pentagon or the CIA.

There were doors at either end, also on RFID, and I could see a manned reception area behind them. I stepped out, dropped a thumb drive, and kicked it along the floor. It came to rest near the suite's door. Then I turned and stepped back onto the elevator. The doors closed. I pressed one and began to descend.

I exited into the old public area of the bank, a room of high vaulted ceilings and beautiful wrought-iron cages where once the public could come in to buy and redeem bonds. Now it was a museum of finance where they parked visitors until the tours began. I found Jack just before the program started.

Gathered around a rotating gold bar on display behind twelve inches of glass, we listened to a genial South Asian guide dispel some of the more notorious myths about the Fed. Jack watched the gold bar go around and around.

I was more interested in cataloging the closed-circuit cameras and the visitor badges I spotted on a few people who were filing out past us. People on the tour had no badges, so they were easy to spot if they broke away from the group. Other visitors – contractors, friends, and family – received a red temporary badge. That's what I would need.

We circled back to the elevators, passing through the main lobby on the south side of the building. There were four cops outside, two more at the guard desk. I watched as more people with temporary visitor badges exited the elevator. They had no escorts, no one to make sure they left the building after they were sent down.

That would give me an opening.

The group of tourists was large enough that they split us into two elevators. 'Just press E and hold it,' the guide said.

That was all it took to get to the vault, five floors down. In my mind I'd conjured up something out of *Get Smart*: door after impregnable door, each with technology that was squirrelier than the last. But there was no special key. We just dropped, then stepped out into a claustrophobic basement corridor. I could barely pay attention to the educational video that played on the wall. It sounded as if it was narrated by the same guy who'd done the health videos in my seventh-grade sex ed class.

My focus was squarely on the narrow hallway and, forty feet away, the largest gold reserve in the world. Our guide kept a close eye on us as she told us to put away our phones and warned us not to take any photos, notes, or sketches. We moved toward the vault.

Chapter Twenty-Four

Take a look at the money in your pocket, any bill. Printed across the top you'll see that what you're actually carrying around is a 'Federal Reserve Note.' The Fed is the reason your dollars are worth anything.

The Fed spends a lot of time debunking conspiracy theories, as you might expect from an institution that was founded on a private island by a cabal of New York bankers to control the US economy. That is the literal truth. It gets better. The place was called Jekyll Island.

There hadn't been a US central bank for most of the nineteenth century, and the economy kept going through dangerous boom and bust cycles. Finally, after the panic of 1907, the bankers were fed up. J. P. Morgan was tired of having to single-handedly orchestrate the bailout of the American economy, so he rounded up a bunch of New York money men and politicians. Under cover of night they left the city on a private railroad car from a little-used platform. They secluded themselves on an island off the coast of Georgia, and refrained from referring to each other by name in order to prevent the servants from leaking their purpose as they hammered out what would later become the Federal Reserve System. Some bankers later pretended they were opposed to the plan, so it wouldn't seem like too much of a sweetheart deal as Congress wrangled over it.

As a result, the Fed is by design very friendly to large

New York banks. When the committee in DC decides what interest rates should be, they can't simply dictate them to the banks. They decide on a target interest rate, and then send the directive to the trading desk at the New York Fed to instruct them about how to achieve it. The traders upstairs go into the markets and wheel and deal with the big banks, buying and selling Treasury bills and other government debts, essentially IOUs from Uncle Sam. When the Fed buys up a lot of those IOUs, they flood the economy with money; when they sell them, they take money out of circulation.

They are effectively creating and destroying cash. By shrinking or expanding the supply of money in the global economy, making it more or less scarce, they also make it more or less expensive to borrow: the interest rate. In this way, trading back and forth with the largest banks in the world, they can drive interest rates toward their target.

The amount of actual physical currency in circulation is only a quarter of the total monetary supply. The rest is just numbers on a computer somewhere. When people say the government can print as much money as it wants, they're really talking about the desk doing its daily work of resizing the monetary supply – tacking zeros onto a bunch of electronic accounts – that big banks are allowed to lend out to you and me.

In the Fed basement, I didn't see any guards or any guns, just tour groups cycling through. We walked through a narrow hall toward the gold. And then the reason for what seemed like lax security became clear.

We weren't in a hallway. We were in a ten-foot passage through a cylinder of solid steel. The gold vault has no door, because that passage *is* the door. Picture a giant wheel of cheese laid flat, with a tunnel carved through it from one end to the other.

That's what protects the gold. The cylinder weighs 90 tons.

The frame around it weighs 140. Every night, a guard cranks a heavy wheel and slowly turns the cylinder ninety degrees, then drops it three-eighths of an inch. It then rests against the frame, forming an airtight and watertight seal, an impenetrable bunker sitting on the Manhattan bedrock.

After the walk through that beast, the gold was almost a letdown. The bars were dull, like yellowish lead, stacked in cages. The vault interior could have been an old apartment building's basement storage lockers, except for the huge balance scale in the middle of the room.

What I took to be a friends and family tour actually went inside the cages, where a vault keeper passed them a gold bar from some country's stash – 98 percent of the gold consists of foreign reserves we've kept safe since Europe stashed it here during World War Two – and they all hefted it and oohed and aahed.

Gold is a pain to move. Each bar weighs about twenty-seven pounds and is worth about half to three-quarters of a million dollars – the sizes aren't standard. If one country wanted to loan another a few billion dollars, one of those clerks would just strap metal covers over his shoes, load up a trolley from country A's locker, and walk the bars a few feet over to country B's. I watched Jack's eyes as he schemed like a madman in there. I was afraid he'd pull something, telegraph that we were casing the place, call down the guards. My focus was on the passes the visitors wore: red, cheap printouts with names but no bar codes. The employee hard passes were blue.

After a minute the guide ushered us out. Jack took a last hungry look at the vault, but I could only think about the billions of dollars flowing through the computers upstairs, at the end of an unkeyed elevator, behind a door secured only by RFID, surrounded by friendly folks who don't bother challenging a badgeless visitor.

Some will rob you with a six-gun, some with a fountain pen. But probably your best bet these days is a Bloomberg terminal.

Every morning, on the ninth floor of the New York Fed, the desk gets ready to go out and manipulate the markets according to the instructions laid out in the directive. Its traders are linked by computer with twenty-one of the largest banks in the world. When they're ready to buy and sell, in what are called open market operations, one trader presses a button on his terminal and three chimes – the notes F-E-D – sound on the terminals of his counterparties. Then they're off to the races.

There are usually eight to ten people on that desk, mostly guys in their late twenties and early thirties, and they manage a portfolio of government securities worth nearly $4 trillion that backs our currency. Without it, the bills in your wallet would be as worthless as Monopoly cash. The traders on that floor carry out nearly $5.5 billion in trades per day, set the value of every penny you earn or spend, and steer the global economy.

If you stole their game plan, you could make hundreds of millions of dollars in a few minutes, without picking up a gun or setting foot in a bank. You wouldn't even have to leave the house. You would take your money in the markets, robbing the Federal Reserve in plain sight.

Forget the vault. Forget the bales of currency locked away in the basement. Forget the gold bars. Whoever was behind Lynch was right about one thing. The big money was upstairs. The real score was the directive.

The tour guide herded us onto the elevator back to the main lobby. When the doors opened, I saw a man about Jack's age waiting to board. I knew from my research that he worked on the desk. I dropped another thumb drive as I stepped out, hoping that he might pick it up.

I lingered near the back of the group as we returned to the museum area. Slipping off the tour seemed like a hokey, amateurish plan, though that didn't mean it wouldn't work. I watched the guards. They were sure to notice someone peeling off the tour and doubling back to the elevators. I paused in the lobby, noting every door, every exit, whether they had locks or crash bars, and whether they were alarmed. There were Medeco locks everywhere. Each time I saw one, it tightened up my spine as I remembered my failure with Lynch. I memorized the layout, imagining myself running, soaked in sweat, with a pack of cops behind me.

How would I get out? Where would I go?

The most important part of any robbery isn't getting what you're after, it's getting away after you've got it. Considering that my employers might be setting me up for a fall, on this job the escape plan was even more crucial than usual.

I let the group go ahead, and walked over to the far side of the room to get a view down a corridor. Then I saw motion over my shoulder: a police officer, walking purposefully. I ducked into the museum.

He followed, scanning between the exhibits. I walked a little faster and started mentally cataloging the contents of my backpack. There was nothing obviously criminal in there, though I had seen Jack take a few notes on the access control.

They had eyes everywhere. Had they caught me dropping the drives?

'What's up?' Jack asked as he caught up to me.

'Stay close,' I said. 'May be trouble.'

We did our best to cover ground without seeming panicked, circling around toward the exit to get behind the cop.

I could hear the boots behind us.

'Excuse me,' the officer said.

I started to sweat. Our cover identities weren't backstopped.

That would have cost thousands of dollars more and required a dedicated team. If they ran our licenses, we were done.

I pretended to ignore him and turned through the main lobby toward the exits. One of the police at the guard desks blocked our way.

The pursuing cop stepped in front of us, holding the USB drive in his hand.

I could see Jack getting ready to speak, to string out some bullshit.

'You dropped this,' the cop said.

My eyebrows rose as I wondered what he'd say next: *And I know your game? You're going to jail? I'll be shooting you now?*

All valid options. He held it toward me. It took me a second to realize he was just giving it back. I took it and said, 'Thanks!' in a voice an octave too high. I smiled, turned, and fast-walked toward the open door, the cold rain, and freedom. I didn't stop or look back until we'd reached South Street and the river.

Jack's eyes were wide and he was breathing fast, puffs of white in the cold.

'I knew we were fine,' he said, lying.

I looked out over the tall ships and antique tugs.

'So what do you think?' he asked.

I had hoped the job would be impossible. That would narrow my choices, simplify things. But it wasn't. I had seen a way past the perimeter. Internal access control was beatable, at least until the suite, and I had just carpet-bombed the place with surveillance and malware. That was the only unknown: the security in the target suite around the directive. But if my cameras or malware worked, I would soon have an inside view.

I looked back toward the Fed and the towers of the Financial District. Then I turned to Jack.

'I can do it,' I said.

Chapter Twenty-Five

If the tour wasn't going to work, I needed one of those visitor passes. My first thought was to pose as a financial lobbyist, which opens all doors. But that would introduce too many loose ends. Better something simpler. During the ride home from New York I searched until I found a gym that was set to open near the New York Fed in the next month or two. I tried its corporate parent's office and asked for a packet of materials about workplace wellness programs. They said they would send it.

'Overnight, please,' I said, and gave them my UPS account number.

Next I contacted Human Resources at the New York Fed. I bounced around among a few people until I reached someone in charge of benefits.

I introduced myself as a sales manager at the fitness center. 'I was wondering if we could set up a meeting on Tuesday,' I said. That was Fed Day, the day of the heist.

'Well, we're actually really busy, and we have most of our accounts set for the year.'

I assumed a mood diametrically opposite my own: chipper gym rep. 'Well, I'd just love to tell you all about our corporate wellness benefits. You could be on your way to a happier, healthier—'

'We're only free for lunch.'

'That would be great,' I said.

'Lunch,' he repeated.

'Oh . . .' I realized it was a shakedown. 'I'd be happy to pick up lunch for the team there, if we could discuss setting up a table in the employee cafeteria one day to share some of our exciting membership options.'

'Basil Thai,' he said. 'Tell them it's for Steven at the Fed. They know the order. I'll e-mail you a form to get a pass for security.'

I gave him a dummy e-mail address.

'Can we do it early?' I asked. 'Say eleven forty-five?' It wasn't going to last long, and I needed to be free not long after noon to snag the directive.

'Sure,' he said.

I ordered a pair of fleece vests from the gym so Jack and I could pass as reps, then checked the e-mail Steven had sent. It was what I suspected: for all visitors, they required a name, address, and Social Security number. Maybe they didn't run a full background check on all of them, but I couldn't risk making one up.

I would have a visitor badge waiting for me on Fed Day and a longer leash than I'd had on the tour, but it was going to cost me. I needed to see Cartwright.

I was feeling pretty good about the plan and the casing job after I dropped Jack off. I told him I'd work on our credentials for Tuesday. He had to meet someone, but said he'd catch up with me later to help finish the prep. I pulled out for home. I needed to remind myself: I wasn't actually breaking in. I was only buying time, going through the motions perfectly to keep Lynch happy long enough to play this back at him. Then I noticed someone following me. After five turns, I was certain; I could tell by the radio antenna. It was a cop, making no attempt to hide the tail. Staring at my mirrors, I nearly rear-ended someone.

I turned on the radio to try to distract myself. *Marketplace* was airing a segment about the Fed's committee meeting. For the first time in years, the outcome was an open question. Normally these meetings are scripted affairs, the numbers set in advance. They spend whole sessions arguing over minutiae, because even minutiae – saying 'substantial' developments rather than 'meaningful' developments – can shock the markets. But now there was finally a good-sized voting bloc of dissenters to the easy money policies.

Trading volume was high, and the markets were mixed. The committee meeting was going to be a showdown, and no one knew who would win. That would make early access to the directive even more valuable and security even tighter.

As I approached my neighborhood, I didn't see the cop behind me any longer. It must have just been my nerves. I found a parking spot around the corner from my house and scanned the street again. There was no sign of the unmarked car.

I was halfway up the block when I heard it pull up behind me. It was the same car. The cop rolled along with me at walking pace as he looked back and forth between me and his dash-mounted laptop. I tried to stay calm and think of what a normal, non-murder-implicated, non-lockpick-wielding, non-heist-planning citizen would do, which is a great way to end up acting shady.

Our eyes met. I gave him a nod. He stared back at me. I stopped. He stopped. I turned up my front walk and ditched my pick and tension wrench into a bush beside the mailbox, shielding them from his view with my body. Possession of what are called 'burglarious tools' in the Virginia code is a felony.

A floodlight lit up the front of my house. Enough of this. I turned and walked toward him. The light died. I saw him say something into his radio, then pull away.

So much for my clean getaway. The cops were putting the pressure on. But if I were a suspect in the murder, they wouldn't be playing mind games, they'd have me in custody. I knew who was behind it.

I needed to go deeper on our fake identities to pass the visitor check at the New York Fed. After I grabbed a cup of coffee at home, I went to Ted's. Cartwright was in the back room, sitting at a table stacked high with what looked like life insurance applications.

I explained what I needed. He scratched his cheek with one finger as he thought about it.

'So this is for one-time verification?' he asked.

'Yes.'

'Social search? Are they going to be checking the date of birth to match, all that?'

'Maybe. I'd better be prepared.'

'Then I'll have to find you a grown-up,' he said.

'Sorry?'

'Most of the identity theft stuff these days, you take a kid's Social, sell it to an illegal immigrant. Kids never check their credit. They don't apply for jobs. They don't learn it's been stolen until the parents apply for college loans and find out junior has been working in a poultry processing plant for fifteen years,' he said. 'But for this I need a fresh wallet of someone in the ballpark of your age. I'll have to do some calling around.'

'In other words.'

'Friends and family: three grand.'

'I can swing that,' I said. 'Can you turn it around by next Tuesday?'

He nodded. 'Your baseball work out?'

'It's not online yet.'

'Is that your only way in?'

'I dropped some flash drives, too.'

He made a disapproving hum from the back of his throat. 'They're on to that.'

'You sure?'

'It used to be like a skeleton key. Sprinkle some in the parking lot. If you put wedding photos on there, or kids, or dogs, forget about it. They'd hand it around the whole office, louse up every machine in the place. But every chief security officer read the same article. They're real pricks about it. No one uses autorun anymore. Sometimes they glue the USB ports shut. You want to be careful with the USB drops, you'll have the Secret Service knocking on your front door.'

'Not the FBI?'

He nodded. 'Secret Service does bank and computer fraud. Also counterfeiting, and protecting the president. Makes perfect sense, right?'

'By DC logic.'

'You have the name and workup on your target?'

'Yeah. A woman in the office, a couple of others.'

'Want to back up the USB key drop?'

'What are you thinking?'

'The hot thing now is putting a Trojan on the smartphone and praying they plug it into the USB to charge it. Then you can actually use the phone's network connections and not have to fuck around with the company network and firewall. But that's a lot of ifs. I'd say just spear-phish her.'

I was having some trouble with this conversation, not because of the technical stuff, but because it was coming from Cartwright. He was of the old school, like my dad; I had a hard time imagining him using anything more modern than a smoke-less ashtray. He walked over to the couch and pulled a laptop out of a battered leather attaché. Then he brought it back to the checkers table and pulled up a website. All Derek's pals were there: the webcam girls, the weird Russian fantasy games, the credit card machines.

I looked from the laptop to Cartwright.

'You've got to stay on top of this shit, Mike. You don't even need to put pants on anymore to rob people. So you know phishing, right? Those sketchy e-mails that say "There was a problem with your account, please click here." And then that link hijacks your computer? Spear-phishing is sending a Trojan specifically tailored to the recipient. Tell you what. Send me her e-mail and a plausible origin for the message, and some kind of PDF or JPEG she's sure to open, and I'll set it up for you.'

'Thanks,' I said. 'I can probably write up something right here if you have a second. She doesn't have to run a program or download anything?'

'Nope. She just looks at it and the payload is injected. PDFs are full of vulnerabilities.'

He handed me his laptop, then walked over and poured himself another drink while I drafted the message. I made the attachment seem to be a typical internal Fed newsletter I'd come across in their public archives.

Cartwright looked it over. He must have seen the worry on my face as I thought about my growing bill. I could barely afford a wedding or a bank job, and certainly not both.

'I'll just throw that in,' Cartwright said as he took the computer back. 'I could use the practice, and you've certainly racked up some comps. I'll send it out tonight. And who knows, maybe your USB drives will hit, too. Drink?'

'No. I should probably get going.' I stood, then thought about it. 'You know what? Sure. A beer. Whatever you got.'

Annie was out of town, and I didn't feel like rattling

around the empty house, waiting for Lynch to stick a gun in my face.

He went behind the bar and brought me a longneck Bud.

'It's a damn shame, you know,' he said. 'That you and your dad went clean. I'm fine with all the detail stuff, keeping up the relationships, but nobody could beat your father for the big picture. And you, well . . . I'll just say it's nice having you back.' He raised his drink. 'If only for a little while, of course.'

I clinked his glass with my bottle. 'Of course.'

We caught up for a while, then Cartwright had to take a phone call. I pushed my chair back and was getting ready to leave when Jack stuck his head through the door.

'Good. You're still here,' he said. 'What can I do? Anything on the papers?'

'I took care of it,' I said.

'Sorry I got held up. I had to finish a job. The courier thing.'

'Don't worry about it.'

He poured himself a glass of water from the tap and sat down next to me.

'Nice work today,' he said.

'Thanks. Though you know, when I was thinking about calling you up, catching up with my old partner in crime, blowing off some steam before the wedding, I had in mind something like daytime drinking or a road trip, not robbing the goddamn Fed.'

'Sorry about that. Though you're holding it down like you do it every day.' He looked around the back room. I could hear Cartwright in the office, yelling at someone on his phone. The back still smelled like the old Ted's: cheap cabinets, damp and mildewed.

'Some bachelor party,' Jack said, and raised his glass of water. Tuck had been asking me about putting one together. I didn't seem to have a lot of free time to think about it recently.

'I've been to a lot worse,' I said. 'Your courier job went smoothly, I hope.'

'Yeah. The world's sketchiest Vietnamese dudes out in Seven Corners. I can't keep doing this work,' he said. 'But I think I have a way out. Maybe you can give me your thoughts.' He pulled a folder from his bag.

I rubbed my temple. 'Jesus Christ, Jack. You haven't even finished fucking up my life with the last scam. Maybe now's not a good time.'

'It's not like that.'

I looked over at the papers, slid them closer. They were registration forms.

'You're going back to school?' I asked.

'Yeah. I'm done with the security stuff. There are just too many grays. I was wondering if I could ask you a couple of questions about how it works, with the credits. I guess everyone switched from semesters to quarters.'

'Of course. School's a good move. And you can really appreciate it when you're older.'

'When I think about sitting down for an exam—' Jack shivered. 'But I'm going to do everything I can. I've got to make a change. You ever have trouble, get tempted, the stuff from the old life?'

'Sure,' I said. 'And I miss it. I wish it were different circumstances, of course, but today reminded me of the fun we used to have crossing the line, the old mischief, before everything got heavy.

'But it's like most things when you're young and dumb,' I went on. 'Nearly getting killed makes a great story looking back. But that's not how I want to spend my time. I'm lucky to be where I am, and I don't take it for granted for a second. It's the little stuff: Sleeping through the night. Not fearing the knock at the door. Not having to keep a half-dozen lies straight in your head. Having an amazing girl I don't have to hide stuff from – or didn't use to. Driving past cops without breaking into a sweat. I'd take that over easy money and the thrill of a close call any day. It's all just so much easier, simpler, happier.' I finished my beer, pushed it back on the bar. 'Going straight is the best hustle out there.'

'That's why I'm so pissed with myself,' Jack said. 'I told Dad I'd watch out for you and Mom when he went away. I never kept that promise. And now all this. I just keep fucking it up.'

'You did all right,' I said. I looked over at the scar on his chin. He'd taken his lumps protecting me as a kid. 'We don't have to hash this out right now, Jack. It's not exactly my favorite subject.'

In the old days, it was the kind of thing we'd work out by getting fall-down drunk. We'd either end with our arms draped around each other's necks, shouting how much we loved each other, or rolling on the floor punching each other in the face. Either way was therapeutic.

'This is kind of hard for me,' he said. 'Can I just tell you one thing?'

'Sure.'

'I tried, and I guess I did okay for a while, after he was gone. But it got to be too much. And then when Mom got sick and there was no money, it was just easier for me to be fucked up all the time. It's not an excuse. It's just what happened. I wasn't strong enough. I wish I had been. It was shitty, what I did, bailing on you. You were just a kid. You carried way too much, way too young. And I'm sorry.'

'You want me to forgive you—'

'No. That's not what I'm saying. I've got to earn that, and I haven't. I don't know if I ever will. And the night you got arrested. I'll never forgive myself for letting you get caught.

Never. I want you to know I can't shut my eyes and try to go to bed without all those regrets running through my head, tearing me up. I just had to say it. I don't want you to forgive me, but I need to tell you, I need you to believe me when I say I'm sorry. Truly. With everything I got. That's all.'

He looked down at the bar, then shut his eyes hard. His chin trembled.

'I do,' I said, and put my hand on his back. 'I believe you, Jack.'

Chapter Twenty-Six

After we left Ted's, I stopped by my office to pick up a thousand pages of files on the dark-money case I wouldn't have time to read. But really I just wanted to get to my computer to see if I had any bites on my cameras.

To get to the servers linked to the camera and malware, first I went through a virtual private network, which created an anonymous tunnel over the Internet, and then through an anonymizing system called Tor that bounced my traffic around among a network of servers, hiding its origin.

I didn't understand exactly how it all worked. The impression I'd taken away from Derek was that it was the modern equivalent of the old trick of taping one phone to another, mouthpiece to earpiece, to defeat a trace.

I was paranoid, so I used the Wi-Fi signal from the realtor's office downstairs. They were always parking in my space. The connection was weak and slow, but I appreciated the extra layer. Between all the log-ins I had to go through and the dribble signal, it would probably have been faster to actually find a couple of phone booths and tape the damn handsets together.

After all that, I logged in to the client software for my viruses, a program called DarkComet RAT, which stands for Remote Administration Tool and would let me take over the victim's computer completely. Each time I got the same message: 'Host not found.' I tried each flash drive. I tried Cartwright's malware. I tried my hidden camera in the baseball stand. Nothing.

I needed to prep that deposition and then do a triage on my other cases to keep the rest of my clients from bailing on me. I barely made any headway. Every five minutes, I would log in and refresh all my different backdoors and cameras, clicking over and over like a slots junkie.

When I came up for air, it was getting close to eight thirty. I checked my cameras one last time, hoping to have something to show Lynch. None worked. I gave up. It was time to go home. At least Annie was safely gone, and at least I had a gun there.

As I neared my house, I drove past St Elmo's, a little coffee shop and neighborhood hub where you could run a tab and keep your own mug on the rack. Idling at the stoplight, I thought I saw Annie inside. I parked down the street and came back. Her flight wasn't supposed to arrive until ten.

I checked my phone, saw the missed text messages she had sent. Just seeing her face made me feel better. Her laptop was on a side table beside a cup of coffee, and it looked like she was talking to someone, maybe the accountant from next door.

I walked up to the entrance. As I grabbed the door handle, I saw Annie laugh, all her defenses down, then lean over and touch the arm of the man sitting across from her.

I stepped inside and got a look at his face. She was talking to Lynch, laughing with Lynch.

I walked behind him before Annie's face could give me away. He was sitting on a low chair. I had the knife I'd lifted in New York in my pocket. I'd been carrying it wherever I could.

I flicked the blade open and pressed the tip into his back near his heart, just under the shoulder blade. I balled his collar into my fist, a sure grip, and leaned down next to his ear.

'Not another word,' I whispered.

'Mike, hey, I caught an early flight back—' Annie had started to say as she saw me enter, but her smile disappeared as she watched the anger twist my face and noticed something not quite right about how I was standing over Lynch.

'Wait a minute there, Mike,' Lynch said.

'Get up and get the fuck out of here.'

'Mike, what the hell are you doing?' said Annie.

I tried to conceal the knife, but it wasn't working. A good-sized group turned their attention toward us.

'Good one, Mike,' Lynch said calmly as he patted my hand. He was smiling. In fact, he was the only thing saving me from myself.

I saw a woman in the far corner sitting at a jigsaw puzzle, with a decent view of the knife, as she lifted her cell phone and put her reading glasses on to examine the digits. I could guess which three she had in mind.

'What are you doing here?' I said.

'Eating a cookie,' Lynch replied.

'Mike,' Annie said. 'What the fuck are you doing?'

I looked over. The woman with the puzzle was talking on her phone. The police would be here soon.

'Annie,' I said. 'Run. Get out of here.'

'I'm not going to run anywhere. What's wrong with you?'

'Let's not let this little joke get out of hand, Mike,' Lynch said.

The last thing I needed was to give the police a good reason to take a deeper interest in me. I was a murder suspect carrying two different identities, a wallet in each pocket. Who pulls a knife on a stranger in a coffee shop for telling a good joke?

I pulled the blade back and dropped the knife in my pocket, then let go of Lynch's jacket and stepped away.

'That's just a very old and very bad joke we used to play in the navy, Annie,' Lynch said. 'I wasn't his favorite CO.'

'You know each other?'

Lynch looked at me, waiting.

I swallowed the acid rising in my throat. 'Sorry, Annie. Just messing around.'

'I guess we'll never learn,' Lynch said, and lifted his palms.

Annie shook her head. 'Enough of this. I'll let you keep doing whatever the hell you have going on. I have to run.'

She picked up her laptop and headed for the door. I let her go, glad to be standing between her and Lynch.

'If you come near her again, I'll kill you.'

He looked at me, unimpressed.

'So what do you have?' he asked.

I had nothing. 'This isn't a good place to talk,' I said.

He twisted his head to the side, cracking his neck. Then he swallowed his last bit of cookie, stood, and walked me out to his car.

'The cops cruised my house today,' I said. 'What's the story?'

'Have you been a bad boy?'

'You said you'd keep them off my back.'

'You said you'd get this job done.'

I knew Lynch probably had some law on his payroll. I had a feeling the police drive-by was a warning shot. I rattled off a list of every step I'd taken and filled him in about my new cover to get inside the building on Fed Day.

'What else do you want from me?' I asked.

'There's no A for effort here. And this is not my first time getting jerked off, Mike. How are you going to get the directive?'

'I have a way into the Fed. I can get inside the suite.'

'So what, you went on the fucking tour? A class trip? What do you have inside the suite?'

'Cameras. Trojan horses on the computers.'

'Show me. Or I'll go finish up my date with Annie.'

'I need to show you on a computer,' I said, trying to stall. 'At my office. Maybe—'

He reached into his car, pulled out a ThinkPad, and opened it on the hood.

'All right,' I said. 'But before you connect to the cameras—'

I was about to share some of my newfound expertise in Internet anonymity, but then I stopped myself. The more links between Lynch and this crime, the better.

'—do you have a good signal?' I asked.

'It's fine,' he said. 'It has a mobile card. What do I do?'

I leaned over and started typing.

'Walk me through every step,' he said, and pulled a pad from his pocket.

'It can be a little tricky.'

'Try me,' he said. 'You think I'm going to take this on faith? Let you run this whole thing out of your pocket?'

I had, actually. He took it all down, the log-ins, the software, the addresses of the servers. Not that it mattered. They didn't show a thing.

I started with the least complicated item, and logged in to the web server for the baseball cam. It came up 'Host not found.'

'What does that mean?' he asked.

'Must be a flaky connection.'

'Are you fucking with me, Mike?'

'That's a physical camera I hid in a gift,' I said. 'He may not have opened it yet.'

I tried to access the viruses I had planted with my USB keys. *Connecting . . . connecting . . . connecting.*

I reached my hand into my pocket and felt my knife.

'Host not found.'

Lynch frowned and reached inside his jacket. Great. I had brought a knife to a gunfight.

'It's malware. It can be a little particular,' I said. I tried again, this time Cartwright's spear-phishing virus.

Connecting . . . connecting . . . connecting.

Then a screen popped up with an IP address.

Host connected.

I pumped my fist. I was in, though it wasn't all that impressive to Lynch.

A side menu listed the program functions. It could bounce me all the e-mails sent to that computer, or every password saved on it. I pressed one called 'Cam Capture.'

A video window popped up. But it was all black.

'Get in the fucking car,' he said, grabbing my elbow and digging the gun into my ribs.

What was wrong?

I looked down the street. Another car was waiting, a Charger with his backup. They had me covered.

'There,' I said, and pointed to the corner of the screen. You could barely make it out, the letters were so faint.

'What?'

'The glow. It's an exit sign. The office is closed. The camera's working, but the lights are out.'

'That's on the desk?'

'Yes. And I have more in the executive suite. I have eyes everywhere the directive will be.'

'And you'll be able to see it?'

'I should,' I said. 'They're just coming online now. I can pull passwords. I can see inside the office, see where the restricted information is kept. I can get what you need.'

He let my elbow go. The violence turned off like a switch. It was clinical.

'Nicely done,' he said. 'I'll be back tomorrow, probably closer to five. I want to see screens and passwords and a minute-by-minute for Fed Day.'

He shut the laptop and slid into the driver's seat. 'Tell Annie I said goodbye.'

After he pulled away, I started toward the house to try to smooth things over with Annie, but she was already in her car, driving toward me up the street. She pulled over.

'Where are you going?' I asked.

'Meeting my dad for dinner,' she said. 'What was all that about? You were acting like such an ass.'

'Long story,' I said. The driver behind her leaned on his horn.

'Can we talk when I get back?' she asked.

That didn't sound good. 'Of course.'

She rolled up the window and drove off.

Lynch had seen right through me. I was trying to buy myself time, but he was tightening the leash. I was getting closer and closer to the point of no return, where my only choice would be to pull the job and then face whatever fate he had in mind for me.

But this had come too close to my home, to Annie. He'd crossed a line. I had to find an out. The rule about snitching was simple: Dead kids don't talk. But maybe I could inch up to the line and not cross it. Maybe I could get something for nothing.

I opened my wallet and dug out a business card.

EMILY BLOOM
CHIEF EXECUTIVE OFFICER
BLOOM SECURITY

Her cell number was on the back. I took my phone out and dialed it.

Chapter Twenty-Seven

Twenty-five minutes later, I was looking for Bloom in the foyer of a Georgetown mansion where she'd told me to find her. I'd been to the house before. It belonged to a woman who was a full-time socialite and hostess (such things still exist in DC). She'd married for money, bought a beautiful Richardsonian Romanesque place on Q Street, and started throwing parties, which she liked to call *salons* with the full nasal French pronunciation.

It's not too hard to bring out the VIPs. Despite all the trappings of power on the Hill, most senators and congressmen live like college sophomores during the term, bunking in with other pols in apartments on Capitol Hill, living off takeout and cereal. Some sleep in their offices. Most are just glad for an excuse to get out of a two-bedroom apartment crowded with middle-aged guys in their undershirts.

So here I was in the glittering firmament of DC's social world: a party that ended at 9:30 p.m., where the juiciest discussion was about Congressional Budget Office scoring. I chatted with a derivatives lobbyist I knew as he scanned the room looking for someone better to talk to. He spied a whale of a man in a cream-colored suit, said, 'Ooh, natural gas is here,' then walked away in the middle of my sentence.

I finally spotted Bloom near the bar. I needed to find out who Lynch was working for, and I needed to find a way to go

154

over his head. I knew he had some cops sewn up, so going straight to the authorities was a minefield, but Bloom might be able to help me pick my way through it.

'You haven't run into our friends from the alley again, have you?' I asked her.

'No. You?'

She pulled two glasses of red wine from a waiter's tray and handed me one.

'I may have,' I said.

She gestured for me to follow her. We crossed the sitting room, then headed upstairs. Bloom ducked through the master bedroom into an office lined with beautiful antique books in green and brown leather that had probably been purchased by the shelf-foot by some designer. With all the crimes and threats swirling in my mind, I'd felt like an impostor among these polite Washingtonians, my hands still dirty with blood. But I could relax a little around Bloom, glad to know that there was someone here who sometimes traveled down the same back alleys.

'Have you learned anything else about them?' I asked.

'Not my wheelhouse, but I may know someone you can talk to.'

Our hostess opened the door and saw Bloom leaning against her husband's desk. The woman apologized and excused herself. I imagined Bloom was always doing this sort of thing, strolling into rooms marked Private, commandeering people's offices and then acting so damned natural, so entitled, that the people who caught her were the ones who felt out of place.

'Is your someone law enforcement?' I asked.

'Yes.'

'Can I trust him?'

She didn't respond. She was looking over my shoulder.

Tuck Straus, our mutual friend, had stopped in the doorway.

'Hey, guys,' he said as he walked in and sat down on the arm of a sofa.

'What's up?' I asked.

'What are you-all talking about?'

'Just catching up on some business contacts.'

'Anyone I know?'

'Don't think so,' I said.

Bloom's pocket buzzed. She checked her phone. 'Oh shit. I've got to run.'

As she walked toward the door, she paused and whispered in my ear: 'I can help you out. Meet me outside in five minutes.'

After Bloom left, Tuck sat down and eased back on the couch. 'I didn't know you were friends with Emily.' He had the air of a prosecutor.

There was nothing too odd in our circle about a man and a woman being friends or hanging out one on one, especially when it came to business. Tuck was, however, a little weird on the subject of Emily Bloom. Even though he was practically engaged, he'd always had a thing for her.

'We've met a couple of times,' I said. 'She's great.'

'I know,' Tuck said. 'Everything okay with you and Annie?'

'Sure. We're a little stressed out between work and the wedding. Why? What have you heard?'

'Annie's an amazing girl, Mike.'

'Did she say something?'

'No. I'm just saying don't take that for granted.'

'I never would.'

He gave me a searching look.

'I have to get going,' I said, and started for the door. 'Early morning on the Hill.'

Bloom stood on the corner in the shadows of an old elm, talking into her cell phone. She wrapped the call as I drew closer.

'I told you not to tangle with that crew, Mike. What happened?' She started walking downhill toward the river.

'I was hoping you'd tell me. Are you looking into them?'

'Like I said, I was pretty tangential on that case. But I have a name for you: Paul Lasseter.'

'Metro?'

'A street agent at the FBI. He's heading up the investigation.'

'Trustworthy?'

'Yeah,' she said, as if I'd told a great joke. 'Mormon bishop. Nine kids. Lives out in Loudoun County. Totally on the level.'

'Can you connect me with him?'

'Sure I can,' she said.

'Any chance you can call him now?'

She ignored the question. I guess I wasn't getting it out of her that easily.

'I heard a rumor recently,' she said. 'About you.'

'I'm not a very interesting subject for rumors.'

'It's that you're some kind of break-in artist. Or were. A good one.'

'Where would you have heard that?'

She lowered her shoulders, deflated. 'Where I get most of my gossip. Public records searches.'

'Is that in Accurint? Or are you on the NCIC?' That's the national criminal database.

'Oh no,' she waved away the thought. 'I have a collection that makes the cops' stuff look like a card catalog. My great-grandfather started it before the FBI had one. Michael Walsh Ford. Statutory burglary. Class three felony.'

'That was expunged.'

'Yes, it was,' she said, and smiled. We turned onto M Street, the main commercial drag in Georgetown.

'So can you connect me with Lasseter?' I asked.

Bloom checked her phone. 'I'll call him. He'll take care of you, don't worry.'

I waited, looking from her to her phone.

'But help me out with something first,' she said. 'I'd like to get you into a hotel room.'

'What did you say?' I asked, but she was already darting across M Street.

Chapter Twenty-Eight

I waited for a break in traffic, then caught up with her as she strode into the lobby of the Four Seasons.

'Just one favor,' she said. 'Then I'll set you up with Lasseter.'

She had me on the hook and she knew it. 'Fine,' I said.

She watched the elevators for a moment, frowned, then hurried back outside, nearly crashing into a guy in a suit as she exited the revolving door. I followed her down to the C&O Canal. It's a quiet place at night. Only a stone's throw from the madness of M Street, you can almost pretend you're in the country. We passed another couple out strolling.

As we crossed a footbridge, I noticed someone walking away: a solidly built South Asian guy with an earpiece snaking inside the jacket of his suit. He looked a lot like the man Bloom had bumped into outside the lobby.

Bloom waited for him to round the corner, then approached the back of the hotel overlooking the canal. She gave me a look that I didn't like at all.

'I got a note about my friend, who's staying here. I had hoped to surprise him, so maybe you can help me get in.'

'I'll talk to the front desk.'

'They're really pains in the ass about this kind of thing here.'

'Let's go back to the lobby. Maybe we can ride up in the elevator.'

'He's in the terrace suite. It's all key-controlled. Special access.'

'Can you call him? Surprise him downstairs?'

She was already examining the back of the building.

'So you can pick locks?' she asked.

'No no no.'

'But you can.'

'Well, I could. Some of them, sometimes. But that requires picks and willingness, and I don't have either.'

She looked toward a side door on the rear corner of the building, next to a set of exhaust fans concealed by bushes.

'He's right upstairs. It'll be great.'

'We'll get arrested.'

'I know the head of security for the whole chain. It's fine.'

'Then call him up.'

'No time.'

'There's a camera right there,' I said.

She took her keys out and shined a little laser pointer on the wall next to the camera, then aimed it square into its eye.

I guess she knew that trick. I stepped over and peered at the lock.

'Sorry, Emily. I'm in enough trouble already.'

She clicked her tongue. 'That's a shame. It's getting a little late to call my man at the FBI,' she said, shaking her head. 'What about a credit card?'

'No. There's this thing called a deadlatch – just trust me. Shimming decent locks hasn't worked in a hundred years.'

'How about this?' she reached into her purse. Her light wavered away from the camera.

I steadied her hand. 'Keep your eye on that, huh?'

She came up with a bobby pin.

'In theory I would need two pins, and it still wouldn't work.'

'I only have one.'

'Then surprise your friend with some flowers or send up some champagne.'

'I don't think your heart's in this, Mike. I thought we could help each other.'

We'd now left quid pro quo territory and arrived at straight coercion. I sighed and looked down at the bobby pin.

'You don't have any foil, do you?'

'No.'

I looked around. 'Even better.' There was some on the exhaust unit. I leaned over and pulled off a piece. She wasn't going to quit until I gave her a show, so I would appease her for a minute and then we could move on.

The aluminum tape was slightly thicker than the sort of foil you'd find in a kitchen. I flicked open my knife and cut a section about an inch wide and two inches long, then folded it over lengthwise. I cut six slits in the foil, close together, which left five little fingers sticking out of the top. Each was about the width of a notch on a key.

Using the bobby pin, I slid the aluminum strip into the lock so the fingers lined up with the pins, then pressed them all the way up. I put the tip of my knife in the cylinder, twisted it, and then started shaking the whole thing like a guy holding a live wire.

This wasn't a finesse job. Bloom watched with growing skepticism.

A lot of locksmiths don't bother picking. That gets you in only once. Instead, they do something called impressioning. When you pick a lock, you lift each pin to the correct height. Impressioning works the other way. You lift them all the way up and slowly let them push down to the right height.

When I twisted the knife, the cylinder turned and bound the pins. As I shook it, the stuck pins would push the little fingers cut in the foil down to the correct height, hit the shear line, then push no more. Unlike picking or raking or bumping locks, when done well it leaves no trace for any forensics. It not only gets you in, when it's done with the proper tools – a soft key blank and a file – it leaves you with a working copy of the key.

I didn't expect it to work at all, but as I explained the basics of it, I hoped it would sound good enough to get Bloom to leave me alone.

I jerked this jury-rigged mess around for a minute. There was no magic release, no turning of the cylinder.

'Well, so much—' I started to say, then stopped. I heard keys jingling: a guard. 'We need to go,' I whispered. I relaxed my hand on the pin. The knife twisted. The cylinder turned. The lock was open. I'd never been so unhappy to succeed.

'Nice,' Bloom said.

As the rattle of the guard's keys moved closer, there was no place to go but in. She stepped through, grabbed my arm, and dragged me behind her. I pulled the foil out and shut the door. We were in a stairwell. Bloom climbed to the fourth floor, then listened at the door. She raised her finger for me to wait.

Thirty seconds later she eased the door open, and I caught a rear view of another Asian guy in a sack suit as he passed us in the hallway. He appeared to be carrying in a shoulder holster on his left side and something on his belt.

I wanted to ask why armed men were guarding this surprise party, but Bloom was already moving. We followed him at a distance, passed a housekeeping cart, then waited at the corner until he disappeared from sight. Bloom strolled up to a hotel room door with a card lock on it. She laid her hand on the handle.

'Is your friend inside?' I asked. 'Just knock.'

'Have you ever *been* to a surprise party?'

'Not like this,' I said. I just wanted to get the hell out of the hallway and away from any hidden cameras and private security.

'You need a coat hanger or a strip of metal or something,' I said, and started looking around. Standard procedure for hotel doors was to reach under the bottom with a long wire, grab the handle from the inside, and let yourself in.

'We should get out of here,' I said. I turned back to see Bloom dip a card into the reader, then turn the handle.

She waved me through. We were in a suite that seemed to go on forever, with a wall of French doors opening onto a terrace. The lights were hidden like stars in the ceiling. Dark wood paneling covered every surface. It was the nicest room I'd ever been in. I paused. It even *smelled* expensive, the faintest trace of green tea and ginger.

I didn't know what most alarmed me: that this was no surprise, that Bloom had her own break-in chops, or that this crafty woman had just cornered me in a hotel room after a couple of drinks.

'Who are those guards?'

'Nepalis. Supposedly ex-British Gurkhas,' she said and rolled her eyes. She advanced through the suite, methodically checking rooms. 'Don't worry about them, though. Sheikh and oligarch types like to use them as security teams. It's all window dressing. Though they do have these knives that are like a foot long.' She grimaced. 'Theater. It's the kind of thing Naiman goes for.'

'Can we call your contact now?' I said. I was done. It wouldn't take much to play a lost hotel guest and just walk down to the lobby and get away from here as quickly as possible. 'Because I'm going to get—'

Going. But I didn't have a chance to finish. Bloom put her hand over my mouth, then pulled me toward the bedroom.

I could hear the elevator doors chime down the hall. Bloom

killed the lights, and we waited in silence as the footfalls of at least three people approached. The door to the suite opened.

When the rightful occupant of the room hit the lights, he found Bloom sitting in a wingback chair, facing him, looking totally relaxed.

'You're dead,' Bloom said, beaming.

And here was his security detail: four of them, not particularly large, but steely looking and frightening enough even without the pistols drawn and the jackets pulled back to uncover the knives on their belts: long and gleaming, like heavy machetes with a mean-looking forward bend in the blade.

To my eyes, the oligarch looked like a union plumber who had won the lottery. His hair was thinning and styled into a mullet with short bangs. He had on some sort of shimmery shirt under a four-button black suit. Russian or maybe Central Asian, he had a brutal look about him, and two days' growth on his chin. He was the last person on earth I would have wanted to tangle with, even without the killers behind him.

He walked up to Bloom, and his bodyguards surrounded her chair.

The man in the suit, who I gathered was Naiman, stood for a moment, deep in thought, while his guards grew increasingly jumpy.

'Very good, Bloom,' he said finally, with a light accent. 'You win. Send the papers over.'

Bloom stood and shook his hand. He spent a moment talking to the Gurkhas, calming them down from the looks of it, as a few other members of his entourage entered the suite. A woman in perilously high heels appeared and offered us drinks.

'We have to stay for a bit, accept the hospitality,' Bloom whispered. 'Let him save face. Can you hang for a minute? I'll go call Lasseter. Promise.'

I relented. Naiman was actually a pretty charming guy, and

he started up with some stories about the Soviet army and the invasion of Afghanistan.

Bloom excused herself, and I found her a moment later on the terrace, on the phone. 'Terrific. No. Thank you,' she said. 'Give my best to Bev and the kids.' She hung up.

'The Gurkhas don't seem too happy with you,' I said.

'Well, he can hang on to them for show, but he'll go with Bloom Security for his private detail from now on.'

'You had a bet going with him?'

She nodded.

'Maybe you can let me in on the secret next time we co-conspire.'

'That's no fun,' she said. 'I talked to Lasseter.' She wrote a number on a business card and handed it to me. 'Three p.m. Washington Field Office. You know where that is?'

'I do. That's all there is to it?'

'That's it.'

'And you're sure—'

'Just as sure as I was when you asked the first time. You can trust him, Mike.'

'Thanks. I have a feeling my lockpicking 101 talk was unnecessary.'

'I did need to get past the exterior door. They were watching the elevators, and my lock guy was an hour away,' she said. 'First time I've seen the foil trick.'

'You lifted the card when you bumped into the guard outside?'

'I figured I'd take a stab at Naiman while he was here. And part of me just wanted to kick your tires.'

'Don't look at me that way,' I said.

'What way is that?'

'Whenever someone looks at me that way, it doesn't take too long until they offer me a job.'

She clinked her glass against mine. 'The night is young.'

We took our leave, and I walked her back to her office. As I said goodbye, the atmosphere was charged with that first-date feeling of readying yourself for the kill that – and this is probably just in my case – is ten times more thrilling than any break-in. We head-faked each other twice as I came in with a handshake and she started for the hug, and then again with roles reversed.

Nothing had happened, unless you count a few felonies. And as far as Annie was concerned, I had done nothing wrong, just dinner with a business associate and an exchange of favors. But as I drove home and touched my lips, dry from red wine, why did I come away feeling as guilty as if I had just killed somebody?

Chapter Twenty-Nine

I arrived home late. Annie was asleep upstairs. I knew that going to the law was a dangerous move and that Lynch was watching my house. I went upstairs to my office, logged on to my bank, and double-checked that I was paid up on my life insurance. I pulled a lockbox down from the closet and took out my pistol, a Heckler & Koch I'd picked up from Cartwright during the mess with my old employer. I hadn't touched it since then.

I stripped it and cleaned it, then put an empty magazine in and checked the action. I ejected the magazine, loaded it, and was about to slide it back in when the door handle started to move.

I put the gun in an open drawer as Annie stuck her head in.

'Mike?'

'Could I get a little privacy?' I snapped at her as I blocked the drawer with my body.

'Fine,' she said, and shut the door.

I cursed myself. All this criminal garbage was getting to me, coarsening me. Brilliant move: yell at her because *I* was acting like a sketchy asshole.

I put the magazine in and put the gun back in the box. I locked the office door on my way out. She wasn't in the bedroom. I headed downstairs.

'Hon?' I said.

I looked around the kitchen: my dishes were stacked in the sink, some were on the table beside a pile of mail, wedding business that I hadn't opened yet. One of the downsides of moving up in the underworld is you don't have a lot of time to do your chores.

Annie was sitting at the kitchen table in her robe with a grim look on her face, going through the mail, slitting each envelope with an old Swiss Army knife. CNN played quietly on the TV in the living room.

'We need to talk,' she said. 'What's up with you?'

'At St Elmo's? Stupid joke. I'm sorry, and upstairs, I don't know. Bad day. I just needed a moment to myself. I shouldn't have been such a jerk about it.'

'What aren't you telling me?'

'What do you mean?'

'Are there police watching the house?'

'No – wait. Did you see police watching the house?'

'Driving by a couple of times. Is *someone else* watching us?'

'It's fine.'

'In what world is that fine? You've got the blinds down all the time. Did you go to New York while I was gone?'

She pointed to a receipt from Duane Reade I had left on the table.

'It was last-minute, for business.'

'You didn't mention it?'

'When would I? I hardly see you,' I said. I was getting frustrated, and turning it back on her. It felt satisfying for a half second in a childish way, but I immediately realized it was a mistake.

'There's no easy way to do this,' she said. 'I am just going to ask straight out. Are you sleeping with someone else?'

'What? No! Why would you even ask that?'

'I saw you tonight with a woman at the Four Seasons.'

'That was Emily Bloom. I told you I was going to get help, to go to the police about my brother. She was connecting me.'

She thought for a second. 'Tuck's Bloom? Jesus. I've heard

168

about her. Doesn't she live in town? The hotel is a strange place for an appointment, Mike.'

'Were you spying on me?'

'Don't do that. I was there with my dad, for dinner.'

Jesus. Every break was going bad for me. 'Nothing is going on. She has an FBI contact I'm going to talk to tomorrow about my brother. I walked her to the hotel to meet a friend. I'm trying to make sure this Jack stuff doesn't end up hurting us.'

'Are you? Because it looks like you're having a lot of fun. You always talked about how your brother would roll into town and get you sucked into something. I mean, look at you, Mike. You're snapping at me. You're out every night. You're hiding things.'

'He's my brother, Annie. I can't just let him get hurt, say it's not my problem. It's different this time.'

'Different this time? Do you hear yourself? You sound brainwashed. Are you following him back down that path? Is he setting you up for something? Conning you again?'

'That's not it at all, Annie.' I stepped closer to her.

'Are you sure? Think hard about it, Mike. You're not just screwing around because you're tired of all this, because you miss the old risks, because you're bored with everything, with me? Just tell me the truth.'

On the TV, the news brought up a photo of Sacks. 'Police say they are making progress in the brazen daylight murder of a Washington economist last week.'

I held up my hand, trying to hear. 'Can you be quiet?' I asked.

'Be quiet?' she said. Annie was very level-headed, very patient, but I recognized in the cold timbre of her voice that I had finally succeeded in pissing her off beyond all repairing. It was my tone: I might as well have told her to shut up.

'No,' I said. 'Not like that. I just wanted to hear something on the news. For a case.'

'Are you fucking kidding me? In the middle of this?'

'Sorry. Things are a little tough for me right now. Please don't make me out as some sort of frustrated thug. I get enough of that from your family.'

She threw up her hands. 'You just pulled a knife on a guy at St fucking Elmo's.' She took a deep breath. 'I'm not mad. I wish it were only that, Mike. It'd be a lot easier. But no. I'm thinking very hard about all of this. Listen to me. Really listen. You know me. I don't like theatrics. I'm not going to scream at you, not going to make ultimatums. But this wedding, it's taken on a life of its own. It's getting too big to fail.'

I would have preferred screaming to Annie's slow, deliberate talk, the boardroom voice that suggested shrewdness and calculated strength. She sounded as measured as a hostage negotiator.

'So this is the last exit,' she went on. 'I hope it's like you say. But I'm worried I'm losing you, or that you're freaking out and trying to run away, to get out of this. We can talk about it, Mike. Just don't lie to me.'

'No. That's not it at all.'

'Last chance,' she said.

'Annie. About Jack—'

She slammed her palm down on the table. I saw her grit her teeth in pain. A bead of blood grew on her finger where the Swiss Army knife had cut the skin. I stood to help her.

'I'm fine,' she said, watched it for a moment, then dabbed a red stain on an envelope. 'This isn't about Jack, Mike. It's about us.' She pushed back her chair. 'You know what? I'm exhausted. I don't think I can do this now. We can talk more in the morning.'

We were both burned out on too much work and too little sleep.

'I can explain all this, Annie. It's going to be okay.' I followed her as she walked toward the landing.

'I think I'd like to be alone.'

'Sure. I'm sorry, sweetheart. We'll talk tomorrow.'

'Fine.' She shook her head, then marched up the stairs.

I cleaned up the kitchen, then went upstairs. My pillow was sitting outside the bedroom door. Things would be better in the morning. I could clear this up. I grabbed the pillow, went to my office, and folded myself up on the loveseat.

I woke from a night of fitful sleep around six a.m. Annie was still in bed. I left my office and went to the bathroom. Then I heard a bang from downstairs. I waited, listening, then heard it again. As I came down the stairs, I saw that the front door was open. I was certain that I had locked and bolted every door and window in the house. I'd been particularly good about security recently.

I went to my office and pulled my pistol from the lockbox. I locked the door behind me and headed downstairs. The front and back doors were wide open, swaying with the cold spring gusts and slamming into their frames. I worked the house room to room, following the gun to see if anyone was still inside.

It was clear.

I walked outside. Maybe the neighbors had a problem with a guy in boxers and a robe circling his property with a drawn pistol. Right now I didn't care.

Whoever had broken into the house was gone. I went back in.

'Annie?' I said as I took a second look around the first floor.

No reply. The kitchen was empty. So was the bedroom, the sheets shoved aside where she had slept.

'Hon?' I said, louder now.

No answer.

I stepped back into the hallway. My office door was now unlocked and open.

'Annie?' I said.

Still nothing. I could feel the blood rise in me. Everything

171

seemed brighter, clearer, with the adrenaline. I sidestepped toward the door, pistol at my side, then stepped into the office.

Annie was standing over my desk, holding a lock pick and tension wrench in her hand as she looked over everything I had assembled for the Fed job: schematics of the ninth and tenth floors, office directories, mock-ups of fake ID badges, wallets with credentials bearing my face and other men's names, an open box of ammunition, dozens of locks and break-in tools, and a particularly nasty-looking knife.

She turned and faced me. 'What is all this, Mike?'

I hid the gun by my side, stepped over, and slid it deep onto a shelf, out of her sight.

'What are you doing in here?' I asked.

'Trying to figure out what the hell is going on with you.'

'Did you open the downstairs doors?'

'No.'

'You're sure?'

'Yes.' She put the pick and wrench down. Then she reached for the knife, flipped the blade out, and twisted it under the light.

'This isn't about cold feet at all, is it?'

'No, it's not,' I said.

I looked more closely at the pick Annie had been carrying. It was the one I'd tossed when the cop had followed me to the house.

'It's really not too hard,' she said, looking back at my office door. 'Just scrape it back and forth in there, huh?'

'With the rake pick, sure.'

'You have a right to your own space, but I had to know. You never locked doors before. After everything last night, I woke up this morning and you were gone.'

'What did you expect to find?' I asked. Everything between us seemed calmer now.

'I don't know. Worst case: some infidelity trophy room, matchbooks and receipts, a second e-mail account, a second cell phone.'

I took one of the prepaid cells I used to keep in touch with Lynch from my pocket.

'I have one, but it's not for sneaking around behind your back.'

'Is this what you've been up to?' she asked as she pored over the security diagrams, the photos of the different locks and computers at the Fed. 'Where you've been disappearing?'

I could have played up being offended by the violation of privacy, but I deserved it. I'd been acting shady for days, hiding things from her. I was surprised to feel more relieved than anything else. I needed someone to talk to.

She lifted up a forgery of a Fed document I had been working on. 'This is for a break-in,' she said, and laughed. 'Oh, Jesus. Maybe it would be better if it *were* another woman. What are you doing?'

I leaned over to the computer and started some music playing just in case anyone was listening.

'The men who are after Jack. They're going to kill him unless he does a job for them. They're putting pressure on me to help.'

She lifted up the license in the name of Thomas Sandella and looked at my face staring back.

'So Mike Ford, who may seem like a cool customer but is deep down a total control freak, is just helping out, taking a back seat to his brother who's never done anything right?'

'I'm not going to go through with it, but I had to keep them thinking I would, go through the motions long enough to blow the whistle on them.'

She looked over the diagrams.

'What's the job?' she asked.

'I don't want to implicate you, Annie. If you were in front of a grand jury—'

She leafed through some of the renovation contracts. 'New York Fed?' she said. 'You're kidding.'

'I wish.'

'Is Jack hustling you, Mike?'

'I thought so at first, but these guys will kill him.'

'Kill him? Come on.'

I couldn't fool her, and I didn't want to. I had to come clean.

'That murder on the Mall. I was there. The victim was part of it; he was trying to go to the authorities. They killed him right in front of me. If I don't play along, they might try to hang it on me. The man at the coffee shop is the ringleader. That's why I flipped out on him. They're watching me.'

'You wanted a little excitement. I guess it's working out for you.' She stepped back. 'Why didn't you tell me?'

'To keep you safe, to keep you out of it.'

She raised one eyebrow, and may as well have put me on the rack.

I leaned against the desk. 'Well, let's say your significant other comes to you and tells you some people are making him out as a murderous thug. He swears it's not true, and you give him the benefit of the doubt. That's mighty cool of you. But then, after everything we went through, if I were to come back a second time with a similar story, you would be a hundred-percent justified if you started to wonder, "Hey, what's the deal with this guy? Maybe I can find someone with better luck when it comes to capital crimes."'

'That day,' she said. 'The violence . . . it messed me up for a while, and I never want to see you like that again. But I dealt with it. So be yourself, just don't kill anybody. That ought to give you enough room to maneuver. I figured out a long time ago that I'm not marrying a normal guy. It's what I signed up for. Be straight with me. I don't scare easily.'

'I know. That's part of the reason I didn't tell you. I was worried you would wade in.'

She looked over my notes on the Fed computers. 'Are you trying to hack them?'

'Annie, you don't want to be an accessory.'

'That's only if I help you.' She pointed to the papers. 'The secure terminals would probably be air-gapped, not connected to the public Internet. They have their own networks. And it's all two-factor authentication, at least. You need the crypto card and the PIN.'

'How do you know?'

'From when I was at OMB.'

'Do you have a clearance?' I asked.

'Maybe. I've got my own mysteries, Mike Ford.'

'What level?'

'I'm not supposed to talk about it.' She smiled.

'I'm going to the FBI this afternoon. This ends today.'

'Your date with Bloom went well?'

'No . . . well . . . yes, as far as finding some law enforcement I could talk to. But not as a date. Anyway, I'm going in to the feds. It's all set.'

'Good,' she said, with an air of finality.

'So are we cool?'

'Cooler. You're still in the doghouse. But at least you're being honest with me. I know your tells by now, Mike. You told me you'll put a stop to it, I believe you. Because this sneaking around stuff ends now. Or I'm gone.'

'I'll take care of it.'

'You'll be careful?'

'Always.'

She wasn't buying that one.

'I didn't mean to bring this home,' I said. 'I know everything's crazy now, but I'm taking care of it. You're heading out of town?'

'Yes. My dad's house and then the spa retreat thing with the bridesmaids.'

'Good. Maybe I should come with you. With all that's going on, it'd give me peace of mind.'

'You want to come to my ladies' spa day?'

'I could just hang outside, keep an eye out. I've got the FBI thing at three. When are you leaving?'

'After breakfast.'

'Maybe I can send someone.'

'Like a guard?'

'Yeah. To keep an eye on things. Make sure nothing bad happens.'

'I'll be fine. I can take care of myself, and my dad's a little obsessed with the security, so don't worry. And don't let this get to you. You haven't been sleeping. You're paranoid. It's probably not as bad as you think.'

'It's not great. Though you seem pretty relaxed.'

'I've been through a lot, and I don't know – there's something about the whole thing, about what you told me about Jack, that just doesn't add up. Is there a chance it's all a scam? It wouldn't be the first time.'

'That doesn't make any sense, though. It's gone too far.'

'I'm only thinking out loud,' she said. 'I know you're trying to get your family back together. I know what that means to you, but don't let it blind you to anything. Family's not all they make it out to be. Trust me.'

'Will you tell your dad's security guys to keep their heads up?'

'Sure.'

'Okay.' I took back my pick and tension wrench. 'Get out of town. Take it easy. You're doing an amazing job with everything. I don't deserve a girl like you.'

'That may be true. We'll see how it goes.'

Chapter Thirty

After Annie left, I went to my office and reviewed everything I knew about Lynch to prepare for my meeting with Lasseter at the FBI. As I walked past the hall mirror on the way to the bathroom, I saw a trace of the red wine stain still on my lips. That probably wouldn't help my credibility, so I went upstairs for a long shower. I wrapped a towel around my waist, then sat down on the bench at the foot of our bed. I felt something poking into my leg. I leaned to the side and felt the blankets where Annie had cast them off.

It was cold, small, about an inch long. I lifted it in front of me and tilted it in the light: a jacketed hollow-point bullet in .45 caliber. It wasn't mine, and it sure wasn't Annie's.

I went back over the morning. I wasn't imagining things. It had been sitting there, like a warning to back off. Someone had broken into my house, into my bedroom, where my fiancée and I slept, and laid a bullet at our feet.

I tried calling Annie, but she must already have been up in the mountains.

The next stop was my brother's town house. I couldn't stop thinking about what Annie had said about Jack. I had to get my story straight before I talked to the FBI, but more than that, I was pissed off and suspicious, and it seemed only fair to take it out on him.

I knocked on his door, hard. He answered it with half his body hidden. He let me in, then laid his gun down on a side table.

'What's up, man?' he said. 'Any word on those cameras? You want some coffee?'

'I'll take a cup,' I said.

He took a mug down and filled it. I sat at the kitchen table. Jack took the chair opposite and laid his cell phone down in front of him.

'I need you to tell me everything again, from the top,' I said.

'What's going on?' he asked.

'I'm risking my life for you, so just answer the goddamn questions. Now tell me, how did you start working for Lynch?'

'A referral.'

'Who?'

'A guy I knew from Florida.'

'What's the name?'

'I always knew him as Flores. Jeff Flores.'

'And his number?'

'I can get it for you.'

'Go ahead.'

'Now? It's up in my office. In my old cell phone. I have to find the charger.'

'We'll get it before I leave. I need every time you met with Lynch. The tick-tock on the Sacks approach. Every address. You know his real name?'

'Hold on. Why are you asking me all this?'

I stood up. My chair skidded back.

'Because someone left a fucking bullet in my bedroom this morning. Because Annie's going to leave me if this doesn't stop today. Because you've ruined my life. How's that? I deserve some answers, and I'm going to get them.'

'Was it Lynch?'

'Just answer the questions, Jack.'

'I'm sorry you were dragged into this, but you can't keep me in the dark, Mike. Did they threaten Annie?'

I laid the bullet on the table.

He stood and moved closer to me. 'You've got to trust me, Mike.'

'Trust you? There's no one I know better, and no one I trust less.'

'We do this job and nothing bad will happen. You have to believe me. I swear. We do it, everyone will be fine.'

'How are you so sure?'

'I'm sure.'

'These guys sent you to the hospital.'

'Squabbling is only going to hurt us, Mike. We need to focus on doing the job and getting out of this.'

'Wait. How are you so sure?'

'Because I know these guys. Because—'

'You're absolutely positive?'

'Yes.' He was trying to reassure me, but he'd just given away his own game.

'You asshole,' I said, my voice cold, my body numb, in shock from what I was beginning to understand. 'I was right all along. You were in on it. That first night.'

I'd always known that Jack had the potential to be one of the great confidence men. In the old days, I often thought that he could do something beautiful, ingenious, something like art, if he would only finally get his head clean. This was it: the long con, the calculated, expert play I'd always known he was capable of. It had been as good as I dreamed. There was only one problem: I was the mark.

He held his finger across his lips and looked down at the phone, suddenly afraid.

They were listening.

I walked over to Jack and put my hand on his shoulder. It might have been a consoling gesture, but then I turned and, holding his shirt, brought my arm across his neck as I stepped behind him. I dragged him off the chair, back on his heels toward the bathroom.

I turned the shower on as high as the water would go and shoved Jack in, tripping him backward over the tub. I turned up the radio on the counter and blasted music as the room filled with steam.

No one could hear us. No bug would survive that water.

'You set me up,' I said. 'You were working for them from the beginning.'

'No, Mike,' he said. 'I told you I was honest. It was the truth, but then they came after me. I had no choice.'

I grabbed his soaking shirt and shook him hard.

'Stop lying!' I shouted.

'Fuck you.' He punched me hard in the cheek. I didn't let go.

'My whole life. My job. Annie. It's all falling apart because of you.'

'Some part of you wanted in. You can't con an honest man.'

'You're blaming *me*?'

'That's the problem. It *is* all about you. There are a million guys better suited to pull this off, so why are they so set on you? They set me up just to get to you, Mike. You dragged *me* into this.'

His gall was unbelievable, his willingness to not only pervert the truth, but flip it completely.

'Don't you dare,' I said. 'Is that why? Are you behind this whole fucking thing? Is everyone working for you? I'll kill you.' I shook him harder, banged his head against the edge of the tub. He shut his eyes and wrinkled his face as he started crying.

'I'm sorry, Mike. I'm just a piece of shit. I tried. I really did, but they caught me out. I can't change, Mike. But you have to know that none of this was supposed to happen. No one was supposed to get hurt. And no one will. We just need to do the job, and we'll be free and clear. Let's go back and figure something out. We can fix this.'

Oh Christ. I preferred Jack punching me in the eye to this sputtering self-pity.

'I'm done with you.'

'They'll kill me, Mike. You know that. You've seen them.'

'I'm not buying it anymore, Jack.'

'We need to go out there and walk this back. If they find out that you know this is a setup, it's my life.'

'No, Jack.'

'If you leave, they'll know. They heard what you said. They've been watching me. I wanted to tell you, Mike, but they would have killed me.'

'You need some new material.' I turned and walked out.

As I drove away from Jack's house, I was so keyed up with rage I barely noticed that I was doing sixty on a residential street. I eased the brake down and took a deep breath. I didn't know what was going on, whether Jack was really just a pathetic piece of bait or whether he had somehow been orchestrating all this, trapping me from the beginning.

My phone rang. It was him. I should have ignored him, but I'd thought of a couple more items I wanted to throw in his face. I answered as I palmed the wheel to the right through a red light.

'Don't even call, Jack. You're dead to me.'

'Michael?' the voice asked. It was Lynch.

'What?'

'I thought I would let you know that Jack isn't dead yet,

but he will be in, I don't know, ten to fifteen minutes. I'm no doctor. So you should probably hurry back. Stop fighting this, Mike. It only gets people hurt.'

The line went dead. I pulled a U-turn. My tires skidded through the gravel on the shoulder, and I raced back to Jack's house.

The front door was open. As I entered, I could see his feet through the kitchen door. He lay facedown on the tiles. I moved closer. A puddle of blood surrounded him, slowly pooling around his chef's knife.

Lynch had cut deep into his scalp. I folded paper towels into a compress, clamped it down on his matted hair, and called 911. He was breathing, drifting in and out of consciousness. The cup of coffee I'd left untouched was still cooling on the table.

It took about ten minutes for the EMTs to show up. They seemed remarkably calm as they lifted Jack down the stairs and into the ambulance, at least until they read his blood pressure. One said something about a thready pulse and blood pressure of 65 over palp. They started pouring a clear IV into his arm with a thick needle. He opened his eyes for a moment, looked at me, then passed out again. I called my father as we drove.

At the hospital a surgeon was waiting with two assistants. They took him straight into the trauma bay. I watched through the open door as they transferred him to a table. 'Cut his pants, prep a femoral line, and bring me a Cordis and a cutdown kit,' the surgeon said. 'We need to get some volume into him fast.' He lifted a scalpel, then looked back, saw me staring, and barked at an aide to shut the door.

Someone marched me to the waiting room. I passed the time with the other unfortunates, watching the clock advance toward my appointment with the FBI.

Chapter Thirty-One

The procedure took an hour. They led me to a recovery room, where a woman from billing hovered near the door like a vulture.

'We have some forms for you to sign if you have a moment,' she said as I walked in.

I stepped past her.

Jack was still unconscious, his cheeks white as wax.

I sat in a hard chair beside him and waited, watching *Access Hollywood* and counting down the minutes until I would miss my meeting with Lasseter, my only way out of this nightmare.

'You've got to be kidding me,' I said as the doctor stepped in. It was the physician assistant from last time. 'Is he going to be all right?'

'Sure. It was just the blood loss. Weird cut, though. The head just oozes and oozes forever. What was he doing?'

'Making a curry.'

'Huh. Weren't you in here before?'

'You're probably thinking of someone else.'

'I don't think so. You guys should be more careful.'

'I agree.'

Jack finally came to, swallowing and wincing in pain as he traced the various plastic tubes going into his body.

'I'm sorry, Mike,' he said, and cleared his throat.

'You should be.' I threw my coat on. I had only waited to

see him wake up, to make sure that he would survive. 'Dad's on his way. I'm going to settle this, one way or another.'

'What are you going to do?'

I walked away. The woman from billing followed me down the hallway, saying something about ID and the responsible party.

'He's awake,' I said. 'Go talk to him. I'm done paying for his mistakes.'

Seeing Jack lying in a pool of blood convinced me of one thing. This was personal. I had been the target from the beginning. I tried to think through it methodically, but the names came too fast. There was the dark money, whoever was behind it. There was Mark, who I always suspected of being on the hustle somehow, maybe fighting the corporations while shorting their stock. There were all the secrets I had learned, all the corrupt politicians who had fallen as I cleaned up the mess after taking down my old employer. Every case was another suspect.

I grabbed another cup of coffee in the cafeteria on my way out, then took a walk through the parking lot to clear my head. I still had time to make it to my meet-up with the FBI.

I saw Cartwright rolling through the hospital parking lot in his old Cadillac Eldorado. My father sat on the passenger side. I met them as they parked.

'How is he?' my father asked.

'Fine. They cut him. He lost a lot of blood, but he'll be out tonight or tomorrow.'

'And you?'

'I've had better days,' I said.

'We're going in.'

'I just said goodbye to him. He's awake.'

My father nodded. Cartwright told my father he would meet him inside, then hung back with me. When my dad was out of sight, he gestured me toward the car. We sat in the front seats. From a false panel under the dash, he pulled out a packet.

'Here's the full kit.' There were licenses, credit cards, and Social Security cards.

'The Socials are clean?' I asked.

'Yes. Recent deaths, haven't been reported to the SSA. Their master file is a mess anyway.'

'The security badges for the Fed?'

'I'm still working on them. They'll be fine. You did a good job with the pictures.'

I bundled up the papers. 'Thanks. Can I ask you something?'

'Probably not. I've only lived this long by being uncurious.' I stared at him for a second. He sighed and checked the mirrors. 'Fine.'

'If someone is shafting you. And you can get the law to get them out of the way. And they deserve it, one hundred percent. That would be okay, right? If none of your own people would be involved? No betrayals. Just knocking out an enemy?'

'This is getting pretty heavy.'

I looked back at the hospital. 'Yes.'

'There's no line between black and white, Mike. But you only realize that once you get up close to where it should be. You understand what happens if my name gets brought into it.'

'I never would.'

He nodded. 'Good. Everyone with any profile works out some accommodation with the feds. It's another piece on the board. But leave it for the grown-ups if you can. It's dangerous ground. I appreciate you checking in with me first.'

'Sure thing.'

'You should know, once they get their nails into you, they never let you go. They're worse than the wise guys. They'll lever you with it, and they make plenty of mistakes. Forget all the G-man stuff, it's still government work.'

'What are you saying?'

'Be very careful.'

I laughed bitterly. I didn't need to be reminded of that.

'What's up?' Cartwright asked.

'I was thinking of the last man who tried to dime on these guys.'

'How'd that work out?'

'Shot in the heart on the National Mall.'

He raised a finger. 'I've got something you might be interested in.' He stepped out of the car. I followed him around to the trunk. From a compartment on the side he pulled a duffel bag and started rooting around in it. I saw something that was either a flare or a hand grenade.

'You carry that around?'

He ignored the question, then pulled out a vest. 'Here you go.' He knocked on the chest with his knuckles. 'Chicken plates. This is what the cops use. Level two. Good for everyday wear, will stop most handguns.'

'I was hoping to avoid getting shot altogether.'

'Belt and suspenders. Can't hurt.'

I lifted it up. It seemed awfully thin. 'Put that on my tab, too.' He stuffed everything into a plastic shopping bag.

'I hate to seem insensitive, Mike. But based on what you just told me . . .'

It took me a second: dead men don't get credit. I reached for my wallet.

I pulled up outside an Ethiopian coffee shop with free Wi-Fi and took my laptop out of its case. I had a broadband card, but I didn't trust it for this hacker stuff. I double-checked the Trojans Cartwright had sent by mail first. They had taken root. Then I tried my flash drives. One pinged back. It gave me a great view of the bulletin board in a cubicle, mostly obscured by a very French-looking economist's enormous head. As he scratched the side of his nose and pondered some unseen spreadsheet, I surveyed the room behind him. There were no passwords I could make out on the bulletin board, just a few business cards and xkcd cartoons.

I put my thumb over my own webcam. I knew it was silly, but it's hard to believe when you're staring someone in the face that they aren't staring back.

I felt a certain pride in myself and Derek and our little flash drives. Next I tried my baseball. I watched the little string of periods crawl across my screen and then the pixelated image pop up in a window in my client software.

It worked. Anyone walking by would have seen me, a guy sitting alone in a parked car, hunched over a laptop, shouting 'Yes!' and raising his fist in the air.

I had eyes in the office that would receive the directive. Jesus, all I would have to do was sit in pajamas at home and shoulder-surf the guy, and I'd be done with all this. At the very least, it would keep Lynch from putting a coin slot in the top of my skull.

That camera sent back still photos, taken every few seconds to conserve power. I checked out the first batch. The office looked familiar, same paneled walls, same desk.

Except this time, the desk was clear except for a phone. I pulled up one of the original photos I'd found of the senior vice president's office. The baseball with the camera in its stand was on the correct shelf, exactly where I had hoped. The computer should have been there, in plain view of the camera.

I could make out wires on the far right of the image, and a flat surface on some kind of metal mount. It didn't make any sense until the guy showed up a few frames later. He ate carrots out of a Tupperware dish, then stood facing to the right, half blocking the camera as he typed.

He'd moved his computer.

I grabbed the steering wheel and shook it hard in anger. The guy was working at a goddamn standup desk, as if he had a bad back or something – which I guess made sense given that he'd just worked through the biggest economic implosion in eighty years, but still, his ergonomics jones was going to cost me my life.

That was my main gambit. Unless I pulled a miracle with my other cameras, I was done. I went back to my one good webcam shot, of the exit sign that I had shown Lynch last night. At least this time the lights were on.

The camera showed the inside of a suite. To one side I could see a glass-walled conference room with a few cubicles around it. The only good view was of a printer, a fax machine, and a few reams of paper. Taped to the wall was a sad 8½-by-11-inch sheet that read 'Execute Policy Like a Champion Today' in inch-high letters.

I had nothing. Lynch had access to these cameras. He must have known by now. He probably knew by this morning. That's why he had left a bullet in my bedroom.

There was no easy way to do this job, and Lynch would be gunning for me now. My only out was the FBI. I reached into the back seat, took the bulletproof vest out of the bag, slipped it over my head, and strapped it on tight.

Chapter Thirty-Two

The Washington Field Office of the FBI was in Judiciary Square, next door to the US Attorney's Office from which I had unwittingly lured Sacks to his death.

I drove a route along the Metro Red Line on my way down, doubling back over bridges and turning randomly until I was certain I'd cleaned any tails.

The pressure was getting to me. A white floater crowded my vision, building with a pain behind my eye, and in every black sedan I swore I saw Lynch smiling back at me.

I parked four blocks away from the field office and cursed myself for driving my car again instead of taking Jack's. Up the block, I saw a patrol car with cameras mounted on the hood and trunk moving slowly down the street. The District is the home of the automated license-plate reader, cars that rove the city recording every vehicle. It takes some of the fun out of cat-and-mouse on the two-hour zone limit, but today it might tie me to Sacks's death.

I'd brought my pistol from home. I stashed it under the passenger seat before I stepped out. The field office looked like a giant gray crypt with a green tinge to the stone.

I paused as I came around the National Building Museum, a massive pile of red brick that looked like a turn-of-the-century warehouse. I thought I recognized a car across the street, a Dodge Charger, but this is cop-land, and there were dozens of that model.

I slowed down as I walked through the museum parking lot, across the street from the FBI office. It was another paranoid Lynch sighting. Just in case, I ducked behind a truck. As I peered around the corner, there was no mistaking him. He cupped a cigarette against the wind, lit it, and took a drag.

At least now I wouldn't feel like a crazy person for wearing body armor. This whole setup was turning into a sickening rerun of Sacks's death outside the courthouse. I waited for Lynch to get on the far side of the truck so I could run back the way I'd come, but when I looked that way, I saw Lynch's partner, the guy with glasses, coming toward me.

I moved through the lot. They were on the northern sidewalk. I hid behind a van and waited. My appointment was in three minutes. I couldn't run without them seeing me. I glanced over. They were talking on the street. I counted down the seconds.

I saw an older woman walking between the cars in my direction, so I straightened up and started pretending to check my phone, trying not to look like a hunted man.

The van behind me beeped twice and its lights flashed. She had just clicked her key fob. I shot her a half smile, checked the gap, and dashed behind another car. The next time I looked over, Lynch and his man were walking south. They would see me in a few seconds. I inched around the car, keeping it between us, and once they had gone around the corner of a building, ran back toward my car.

I called Lasseter, my FBI contact, once I was three blocks away, standing under a huge Chinese archway covered in dragons and pagoda roofs.

'It's Michael Ford,' I said.

'Are you here?' he asked.

'I'm nearby. There are men watching the entrance.'

'Of course there are.'

'No. The people you're investigating. They must be watching for witnesses.'

'This is the heart of US law enforcement. If you think—'

'Jonathan Sacks,' I said. All it took was that reminder of what had happened to their last source.

'Where are you?'

'Chinatown,' I said. 'Can we meet away from the office?'

'I'll send a car. He'll bring you into the garage. No one will be able to see.'

'Calvary Baptist. The red-brick church,' I said. 'Eighth and H Street. I'll be standing on the steps.'

I paced on the corner until a black Chevy Tahoe with tinted windows pulled up. The driver leaned out the window. 'Michael Ford?'

'Do you have some ID?' I asked.

He showed me his credentials. I stepped inside. It went against every instinct to get into the back seat of a cop car. He drove around the corner, behind the field office, then pulled into the underground garage. Lasseter was waiting as I exited the elevators. There was a permanent vertical crease above his brows.

'Mr Ford,' he said, measuring the extra bulk in my chest and back. 'Is your attorney here?'

'I'm a lawyer.'

'Suit yourself,' he said. 'Let's go.'

We walked down the office corridor. It was all white walls and beige partitions. Challenge coins decorated the cubicles. A few agents had nameplates in English and Arabic script. Older guys with muscle gone to fat filled the place, alongside a few younger men and women in fighting shape. It was cell-phone-holster heaven.

He led me through a bullpen office and then down a long corridor to an open door with a sign beside it that read 'Interview 3.'

I stopped. It was clearly set up for interrogation.

'You have a conference room or anything?' I asked.

'No.'

I had no choice. I went into the box. Three hard plastic chairs stood around a cheap-looking desk. It was less grim than the rooms I had seen at a lot of cop stations, but the U-bolt screwed into the desktop didn't look all that reassuring.

He slammed the metal door closed with a clang. I was starting to feel more and more as if walking into the arms of the law was a major misstep.

Lasseter sat opposite me and put a coffee mug down on the table. There was a chair to my right that was usually used later in interrogations, when they started crowding in, getting into the suspect's face.

I was wearing the vest under a zip-up sweatshirt. Thanks to the near miss with Lynch, the shirt underneath was soaked with sweat.

'So, do we do this like a proffer agreement?' I asked.

When you have what defense attorneys like to call 'exposure' – i.e., you're guilty – you can make a proffer. You arrange one magic meeting called a Queen for a Day to go spill to the district attorney about what you know and what sort of deal you want. They can't use any of it against you later in court, unless you contradict what you said during the proffer.

'Queen for a Day?' he said. 'That would be the, uh, prosecutor's area. This is more under the confidential informant rules. My supervisory agent wanted to sit in anyway. He's really handling this case. You can ask him about that. So, what do you have?'

I didn't know where to start. At Jack's the first night? Covered in blood on the National Mall? At Bergdorf Goodman?

'You want anything to drink?' he asked.

'I'm fine.' I looked in his mug and saw that it was full of water.

I took a deep breath. 'I have some information about a crime that I believe is going to be committed. And some crimes that have already taken place. Unfortunately, I've become involved—'

There was a knock on the door.

'Sorry,' he said. 'One second.'

He opened the door, and one of my ghosts walked in. For a second I wasn't concerned, because my mind had been screwing with me all day.

But when the ghost spoke I knew this was all for real.

'Thank you so much for your help,' Lasseter's supervisor said. 'We want to do everything we can to nail these guys who are after you.'

My tongue just scratched across the roof of my mouth, dry as a file.

It was Lynch, or, as I gleaned from the hard pass on his belt, Supervisory Special Agent Daniel Waters.

Chapter Thirty-Three

'Michael Ford, is it?' Lynch said as he reached across the table to shake my hand. My own seemed to rise on an invisible string to take his and move up and down with it.

'What's the scoop?' he asked.

'I . . . well . . .'

Lynch was excellent in the role. He tilted his head, looked at Lasseter then back at me.

'You know what, Paul,' Lynch said. 'Why don't you go help Sue with those photos. It might be a little more relaxed for Mr Ford without two lugs crowded in here.'

Lasseter nodded and left.

Lynch locked the door behind him. He double-checked the camera to make sure it was off, then came around and thumped me on the chest.

'A vest, Mike? You worried about something?'

'My house? My brother?' I said. 'You crossed a line.'

'And what are you going to do about it? Now that crying to the teacher is out, I don't see a lot of options for you.'

He sat down next to me, reached into a briefcase, and pulled out a laptop. 'Down to business. I've been watching your peep show.'

He typed a few things, drummed his fingers on the table as he waited, then turned it to face me. 'What do you see?'

'The desk at the New York Fed.'

'I see squat,' he said. 'Unless they send the directive by acting it out with a game of fucking charades in the middle of the office. I've given you enough leash. No more stalling. Just tell me, how are you going to get it?'

'How do you even manage to hold down a job like this?' I asked. 'You've been up my ass for four days.'

'I'm retiring.' He waved his hand back toward the office. 'This place used to be Candyland, then Mueller came in. Now the Eagle Scouts are running the show. I'm done. They probably think I'm out playing golf, counting down my days until the pension kicks in. I'm moonlighting, have a nice second career all set. Once you see how your hundredth rich asshole gets away with murder, you start to realize you're playing for the wrong team. *Your* future, however, is not so sunny. There's only a day left until you have to head to New York to stage for Fed Day. So I want to hear some answers, or else I'll start cutting the people you actually like.'

'This isn't about the Fed,' I said. I remembered Jack's accusation at his house: that somehow I was the target from the beginning. 'Why do you have such a hard-on for me in particular? For wrecking my life?'

'I don't know, Ziggy. Maybe you fucked with the wrong guy. I just do what I'm told. This is business. It's about the Fed. You hurt your brother and you're going to get yourself hurt, because you're wasting your efforts on everything but the one thing that matters: get me the directive. So tell me, come Tuesday, how you will get the job done? That's all.'

'I have badges,' I said.

'They work?'

'Not the electronics, but that's fine. I have an appointment. I have the access control and interior security down. I can get into the suite.'

'And then what? Ask extra nice? This is the grail of market-moving data, restricted at the highest level.'

'I can get into the suite, and then I can get it from the office manager. She must be the one who's cleared for it. I'll just get in there, and . . .'

'Wing it?' he laughed. 'So what's it going to be?' He rested his hand on his hip. I could see his 1911 pistol holstered on his right side, beside an expandable baton, and his two phones clipped to the front of his belt. 'Annie or your father?'

'Don't even say their names.'

'Their names? That's the least bad thing I'm going to do. But I'll let you pick. You've got to learn to take this seriously, and clearly your brother isn't the most valuable piece of leverage. So choose.'

'No.'

'I'll do both if you don't pick. So you're doing the one a mercy. You're a real hero.'

'Don't do this.'

'I didn't picture you for the begging type.'

'Please!' I said.

He sneered. 'Come on, Mike.'

I threw myself on my knees at his feet. As much as it nauseated me to kowtow to this guy, I needed the cover. On my way down, I slipped his flip phone out of its holster. As he pushed me back, I palmed it. Someone was giving him orders, and they were coming through that phone. With it, I could find out who was behind Lynch.

'Have some self-respect,' he said. I sat back down and slipped his phone into my pocket. 'My sympathies aren't what they used to be. So which one?'

'Me,' I said. 'I'll take whatever punishment is due.'

'On top of what you already owe?' He shook his head. 'Doesn't work. I can't kill you; you're getting those numbers

196

on Tuesday. I can come close, though. It's admirable, I guess, though I think you're going to regret it. People always imagine they're so tough. In a few minutes, you'll be begging for me to go after the others.'

He put his laptop on a metal shelf on the wall next to the desk.

'You're going to work me over in the middle of an FBI office?' I asked.

'There's great soundproofing.' He looked around on the shelf. 'They've let the lawyers dial everything back since the 9/11 stuff calmed down.' He pulled a thick stack of papers off the shelf.

'Interrogation policies and practices,' he said. 'They make us take an exam on this every six months, like schoolkids.' He handed it over to me. When I reached for it – lawyer's instinct, I guess – he came up fast from underneath it with a pair of handcuffs and slapped one around my wrist. Then he hit me hard in the stomach with the baton and pulled me across the desk by the cuffs. The metal dug hard into the bones of my forearm. He ratcheted the open bracelet shut through the bolt on the desktop.

He spun the desk around so I was spread across it on my stomach, feet in the air. He hit me again, at the base of my skull, dazing me. Then he cuffed my ankle to something. I couldn't get up, couldn't turn over. I was laid out on top of the desk like a roast.

He lifted up the interrogation manual. 'This is all about how I have to Mirandize you, and hold your hand if you get scared, and get your lawyer coffee just how he likes it.'

He shoved my bulletproof vest up, laid the manual on my lower back, then stepped back. He let the baton extend to its full length, and brought it down hard on the papers.

'Besides being a good way to hide some cuffs, I find it's a

great way to bang up someone's organs without leaving too much bruising.'

I grunted. It hurt like hell, but I'm pretty good with pain. What really worried me was a feeling of profound unwellness in my insides, like he was pulping something important.

He wheeled back and brought the baton down again like he was splitting wood.

I groaned. Something was definitely not right in there. I stared at the wall, at Lynch's laptop on the metal shelf, anything to take my mind off the injury.

But some things are impossible to ignore. I felt cold water splash onto my pants, and then pressure on a very sensitive area. I looked back. I couldn't see, but I quickly figured out that he was using Lasseter's mug like a garlic press, slowly crushing my nuts against the table.

'Wait a minute!' I said, and looked straight ahead at the shelf.

He levered it down. 'Thinking of a family, Mike? Because it's easy to do some permanent damage here.'

I howled. It hurt my ears as it echoed in the box.

'Wait!'

'Not happening.' He pressed down again, with both hands this time, nearly lifting himself off the floor.

I screamed. 'No! The video. Go back.'

'What? I can't hear you.'

'That's 'cause you're fucking killing me! The camera! Look!'

He walked over to the laptop. 'What?'

'Go back.'

'How do I do that?'

'The little thing at the bottom.'

'If you're just trying to get out of this, Mike . . .'

'Press the goddamn button.'

He rewound the video. I was panting and sweating from

the pain blooming through my groin. My face was pressed against the cold desk. On the screen, a woman walked up to a fax machine, inserted a card into a port on the side, then typed in something.

'So she's sending a fax? You think that's going to save your balls?'

'It's a crypto card,' I said. 'That's a secure fax.'

'A fax?'

'Yes. It's NSA-encrypted, STE standard. Have you ever dealt with a bank? They fax everything. The desk was using a chalk-board for securities quotes until the late nineties. The directive has to go in writing, signed. They fax it. What time did that happen?'

'Two thirty,' he said.

'They must have been the staff economist's reports, to get ready for Fed Day. They're Class I Restricted. That's it. Can you see the numbers she typed, the PIN?'

'The keyboard's a little small.'

'Look at the pattern.'

He squinted at the screen.

'I'm getting a six, maybe a five.'

'Let me up, I can figure it out.'

He hesitated.

'That's the way in. I can get it. Just let me up.'

He freed my ankle carefully, ready to club my brains out with the baton. I came around the table and watched it, again and again. There were eight digits. I had determined six, and I was close on the other two.

I called Lynch over. 'Look close,' I said. 'Is that a three or a six?'

I knew it was a three. While he peered at the screen, I pulled his phone from my pocket and looked through it. No messages. No numbers. He must have purged the history every time.

'You should have pointed that out before I got started.' He collapsed the baton. I slipped his phone back in my pocket before he could see it.

'I just saw it.'

The one thing scarier than Lynch's skill with violence was how easily he dropped it, like a surgeon putting down a knife.

'So what?' he asked.

'We can make the malware we already have installed in the suite act up, then come in posing as IT, check out the fax, and get the directive.'

'How do you get the crypto card?'

'I can snag it. See?' I pointed to the screen. 'She put it back in her purse, hanging in the cubicle. That's easy to pick up.'

He weighed that option for a moment. I found his doubt about my pickpocketing skills pretty rich, given I had his phone in my pocket. Still, feds take those crypto cards seriously. If you lose one, you call a number anytime day or night and agents are at your house in fifteen minutes.

'That might work,' Lynch said. He pointed to the chair next to the desk.

'I think I'd rather stand,' I said.

'Oh, right.'

'What else do you have to do?' he asked.

'Just work on that PIN, play with the video, and nail it down. My guy is printing up a couple of badges so we'll be able to move around once we're past the perimeter. We need rehearsals, more contingency planning on escape routes.'

'You understand what happens if you step out of line again?'

'I do.'

He leaned across the table to undo the cuff on my hand. While he was working the key, his phone started to buzz in my pocket. Any second now he'd hear it and realize it was stolen.

200

I winced and crumpled over, pretending the injuries he'd just caused were acting up. That bumped our bodies together, my hip against his waist, long enough to cover my movement as I slid the phone back into the holster. That's the key to picking pockets: covering the criminal touch with some larger accidental press. I stayed bent over, free hand on my groin, while Lynch put away the cuffs.

He checked the phone, looked down at it, then at me.

'Speak of the devil,' he said. 'You can take a minute to get yourself together. Lasseter will be around. Lesson learned?'

I was walking bowlegged as a cowboy, eyes shut against the pain. 'I won't be forgetting anytime soon.'

'Good. Stay close to home. Don't do anything weird. We're heading up to New York on Sunday to stage.'

Lynch carried his flip phone in his hand, checking his messages as he walked toward the stairwell.

As I headed toward the elevators, I watched him walk through a heavy fire door that led to the stairs on the other side of the office. I slowed my pace to see which direction he went, then took the elevator down a floor and moved through the offices below, back toward the stairs to follow him.

In the box, Lynch had switched in a second from gelding me to letting me walk. It wasn't a sudden attack of conscience. I was disposable, and I knew it.

My father had been right. They weren't just going to let me pull this job. They must have known I would try to turn it back on them. As soon as I handed over that directive, I was done. They would either let me take the fall or just kill me outright. I had to know who was on the other end of that phone. I couldn't walk into a trap.

Everyone on the floor below had badges in plain sight. The only exceptions were the men and women in raid jackets – blue

FBI windbreakers. I was wearing a bulletproof vest and walking like John Wayne. It wasn't too much of a stretch to look the part. I grabbed a jacket off the back of a chair and held it draped over my arm, obscuring most of my waist, where most of the workers wore their badges.

I wasn't exactly impersonating a federal law enforcement officer, but as I thought through what I would do when challenged, that distinction started to sound pretty weak.

No one stopped me. I was just your average suspected murderer strolling through the relevant FBI field office a few hundred yards from the crime scene. It was a fifty-yard walk to the stairwell, but with all that law around, it felt like one of those nightmares where your goal keeps moving farther and farther away as you move toward it.

I entered the stairwell and started down, careful not to overtake Lynch. At the second basement I heard a door close just ahead of me. I peered out and saw him walking through the mostly empty lower level of the parking garage, the phone in his hand as he turned a corner. His car was parked at the far end. There were only a few vans nearby.

I eased the door shut behind me and hugged the concrete walls, hiding behind columns, trying to get close enough to eavesdrop on him.

He stopped beside a chugging piece of machinery inside a steel cage. I crept to the other side. I watched him dial, and traced the path his fingers made. Certain things – patterns on keypads, log-ins, and codes – stick in my mind. I'd spent a lot of time practicing it once, when I was younger, and the habit has never left me. I had the number, or most of it. I entered it into my phone.

He began to speak, but I couldn't hear him over the machinery. I squeezed closer and could just make out his voice:

'—I don't understand why we don't just deal with him right now. Think about what he knows. Well, sure . . . but— If you say you have it covered, I'll hold off. I can't really talk about this here. Where? Sure. I have to check out that shipment anyway. I'll take care of one more thing here, then I can meet you. About an hour. Sounds good.'

He turned back. I dropped and crammed myself in between the machinery and the wall. My face was four inches from a hot pipe that stank of diesel. I couldn't hear a thing with all the noise.

I waited what I thought was a minute but was probably only ten seconds as I felt my heart jumping against the vest. Then I heard a door close. I eased back up, expecting Lynch to pop out from behind the next column, his coffee mug at the ready. But when I stood up, I had the basement to myself.

He was going to meet his boss. Maybe it was my paranoia in overdrive, but it sounded like my fate might be on the agenda. He hadn't given me nearly enough to know where he was going. I could have tried to follow him, but my Jeep was a giveaway.

I walked over to his Chrysler. The vans gave me some cover from the security cameras. In a complex this big, the cameras on the second basement, however scary, would most likely be glanced at periodically, if that, and reviewed only if there were an incident. Though given how my day was going, I wouldn't have been at all surprised if I still managed to catch the moment exactly wrong.

Getting inside a car isn't very hard, but actually stealing one is another matter. Engine immobilizers took all the fun out of auto theft in the 1990s. When I was growing up, there was a magic moment for joyriding, around the time the Club came out. There were still plenty of mid-to-late-1980s cars on the road that you could hot-wire. You needed a lot of leverage to break the steering wheel lock, though, and you looked awfully suspicious walking around a parking lot with a breaking bar.

But then, God bless them, drivers began strapping metal bars to their wheels for you: the Club. You'd wire the ignition, crack the lock with the Club, and all you needed was a hacksaw blade up your shirtsleeve to cut through the steering wheel and take the bar off. The whole city was your showroom. Once chip keys became standard the party ended. No more hot-wiring. Your options were carjacking or the bus.

I needed to get in and leave no trace. Slim jims haven't worked reliably in years, so locksmiths use the wedge tech-nique. There were yellow bumpers on the column behind me. I pulled the hard plastic cap off one and drove it in at the top of the driver's side door, then jammed the plastic in deeper, opening up a small space between the door and frame. I unscrewed a threaded rod from the pipe conduit running along the walls and gave it a slight bend. I angled it in past the wedge. My hand started shaking as I got the rod halfway in. If I left scratches all over his doorframe, I would tip Lynch off. I stopped, steadied my wrist, and guided it toward the door-lock button.

It skittered off the top twice. And then I managed solid contact. The button levered down. The door locks clunked open.

Lynch kept his car clean. I was hoping for a GPS unit that might tell me his usual meeting places, but there was nothing to find except a *Best of Frank Sinatra* CD and the musty trace of ten thousand cigarettes lingering in the upholstery.

I sat there for a moment. This was my only chance. Lynch would be back any second.

I took my cell phone out, turned off every ringer, silenced it completely. I checked it four times, and slid it under his rear seats.

Then I locked his doors, sealed my phone in, and stepped away.

I heard someone coming up behind me. I started walking calmly toward the exit.

A round, middle-aged man with a nicotine-stained mustache approached me from across the garage. He was wearing a military-style black uniform, but these days everybody from mall guards on up was playing SWAT Team, so that didn't mean much.

As I neared him, I realized he wasn't FBI. He was Federal Protective Service, the government's version of rent-a-cops. Still, he had a radio, and that meant he could rain hell down on me with a few words.

I brought my shoulders back square, my chest out, recalled every tic of posture I had learned in the navy, and strode right at the guy. I gave him a respectful nod.

He looked at me, then dropped his head slightly in return.

I walked back toward the garage stairwell, climbed two flights up, then exited into Judiciary Square. I enjoyed a second of freedom before I recalled that I was still deep in enemy territory, near the site of Sacks's execution, surrounded by police, marshals, prosecutors, and judges. I got away as fast as I could, by walking north and taking the long way around back to my Jeep.

Chapter Thirty-Four

I sat in the driver's seat, pulled out my laptop, and went to my phone carrier's website. I searched until I found the 'Where's my cell phone?' feature and then I pinged my phone. There it was on the map, sleeping peacefully in Lynch's car under the field office.

From there I drove to a neighborhood called Shaw, where my car had less chance of being recognized from the day of Sacks's death. I parked outside a Laundromat and waited. Ten minutes later Lynch was on the move, heading west.

I followed, staying about five minutes behind him so that my Jeep wouldn't give me away. District traffic is dangerous enough without the need to check a laptop every twenty seconds. We drove northwest through the towns on the Maryland side of the Potomac, and soon – far sooner than you would think when coming from mid-city DC – we were driving past ten-million-dollar houses and horse farms.

We headed for the historic estates high above the river, over-looking Great Falls. These towns – Great Falls, McLean, Potomac, Bethesda – are home to lobbyists and government contractors and are now some of the wealthiest zip codes in the country. I pressed *67 on my prepaid – which blocks your number from showing up on caller ID – then tried the phone number I'd seen Lynch dial. There was no answer.

The land grew more rural. I passed forests and equestrian

schools. Then the dot stopped. I refreshed my computer again. It didn't move. Lynch had arrived at his destination. On a winding country road, I pulled up to within three-quarters of a mile of him.

Through the woods from time to time I caught glimmers of the river running far below. At the end of the road, I could make out a massive stone building that looked like a former luxury hotel or resort, a hundred years old at least. The wings lay partly in ruins, backing into overgrown woods. Boards covered the high arched windows. You could just make out the green copper ornaments along the roof: Poseidons and mermaids swimming along, choked by the kudzu that covered half the building. It looked as if no one but vandals, bums, and graffiti artists had set foot in the place since the Hoover administration.

As I drove along the rusting fence, I saw that there had been some recent improvements at the main building: a gleaming steel door and an electronic gate. Clearly a new tenant had arrived, and he was hiding something, or someone, very valuable. Two cars and two vans were parked in the long circular driveway.

There was nothing good about this setup, but I had to find out who was behind it all, which part of my past had come back for me. I almost believed that it was Jack who was giving Lynch orders, running this game. But was my brother twisted enough to put a four-inch slice in his scalp in order to hook his mark?

Who knows? Maybe it was the florist we fired a couple of months back.

I drove along the edge of the property in my Jeep, bucking along a trail in the woods until I was out of sight, then parked. I pulled the pistol from where I'd hidden it under the seat and slid it into my belt.

Graffiti and empty bottles of MD 20/20 testified to the recent clientele of the resort, but even in the back of the building, the new security regime was clear. The two wings of the hotel were just husks, but the domed central portion had been secured with steel plates over the windows and new locks.

I made my way past overgrown gardens, empty pools, and defaced Roman statues, then crawled along a low parapet until I was close enough to dash to Lynch's car. It was nearly dark, and there was no sign of anyone inside. I found a scrap of old molding and tried using it to wedge his door. The wood crumbled, nothing but dry rot and termite holes. I looked around for another wedge, then thought to try the door handle.

It was unlocked. We were in the middle of nowhere.

I sat inside and started rooting around in the back seat. My phone wasn't there. I dug my hands deep between the cushions, took a chunk of skin off my knuckles on a bolt head, then finally felt the cold plastic.

I eased the door shut, then ran back to the parapet.

Around the side of the building, I found a steel door in an inside corner that offered decent cover while I worked. An American-brand padlock held it shut. It was a good lock, but still shouldn't have taken too long. I was jumpy as hell, however, and kept false-setting the pins.

Finally the cylinder turned. I stepped inside, following the thin beam of my keychain flashlight. The corridor was eerie. My steps echoed, and I could only just make out the contours of the wooden paneling and porcelain fixtures.

I heard a low rumble ahead and followed it. I took one wrong turn, and my foot punched through rotten flooring and debris. As I fell I speared my kneecap on something jagged.

I pulled myself out, then circled around. Once again the noise grew louder. A long section of wall was missing along the hallway, and I crossed through it.

In the gloom I found a thick metal door, open a foot or so.

As I stepped through, I realized I was in a strong room. There were old safes in the corner, too heavy for anyone to bother pulling out. The whole place was trimmed in Gilded Age decadence – carved columns and friezes and crashed-down chandeliers.

I was closer to the pulsing sound now. It seemed to be coming from behind a door with an old-fashioned keyhole, the kind you could actually peep through. That meant a lever lock. Under other circumstances this might have been an interesting puzzle, but not with Lynch and his squad waiting nearby.

I had the wrong sort of picks, which meant a nightmare of awkward angles and too much pressure. It left my fingers red and raw. I finally managed to set the levers and drew the bolt.

When I eased the door open, the noise boomed out loud, and light flooded through the crack, blinding me for a few seconds.

I was close, suddenly too close, and I could hear voices. The thick walls of the strong room had led me to believe I was much farther away.

As my eyes adjusted, the scene grew increasingly surreal. I was in the rear of an old casino cage, where money was counted and swapped for chips. It was an ornate tangle of wrought iron, wood, and brass that took up one side of the gaming floor. Looking up, I saw the vaulted ceilings over the main gambling area and the dome high above me. A quarter of the ceiling had caved in, and I could see, past the wood molding and cracked frescoes, the sky turning plum with dusk. There were a few craps tables decaying on the floor. Grass grew all around them in the casino pits, with wildflowers blooming here and there. That dome must have been open for decades.

I could hear people close by. I was shielded from their view by a counter and a safe, but through the brass bars I could see, at the far end of the floor, two glaring halogen floodlights aimed my way. There were men moving near them – maybe ten – but I couldn't make out faces with the blinding lights behind them. Dozens of crates were stacked on the floor, towering over the heads of the men. I could see guards off to both sides, carrying assault rifles.

The throb of the generator partly drowned out the voices, but I thought I recognized Lynch speaking. I craned my neck farther out to try to see who he was talking to, but could discern only silhouettes. I moved a little closer, and I could make out what he was saying.

'I don't understand why you don't just put some fear into the fiancée. Or why you think you have him under control when he's clearly out to get us—'

The other speaker cut him off. 'Fine,' he said. 'Fine. It's your show.'

This was the man behind it all. I crawled out farther, desperate to see the face of whoever was bent on ruining me. We had narrowed down our search for the men behind the dark money. We were close. If I could only hear the voice, I would know.

Lynch moved a few feet. The other man remained only a shadow framed by the lights. If he would just turn, move a few feet, I could see.

I inched out. The floorboard under my elbow creaked. I transferred my weight back. Wood cracked under my foot.

'What's that?' someone said.

'There!'

I lunged back.

Beams of light flashed through the darkness, shot toward me. Men came running.

Chapter Thirty-Five

I leapt through the door, slammed it shut behind me, turned the bolt back, and jammed a pick inside until it broke. There was a light far ahead, and I hauled ass toward it. The ruined corridor walls flashed by, a long wing of ballrooms built from stone with beautiful wood-frame ceilings. I hurdled a pile of debris. The ceilings were gone, the second floor half collapsed. I ran into the ruins. The stone walls stood high above my head.

I'd put some distance between me and the guards when I heard a loud bang far back, then voices. Gunshots cracked. Bullets skipped off the walls, tore the air, and sent up puffs of dirt and marble around my feet.

I ran through a stone archway held up by jack stands, then stopped. I doubled back, wrenched the supports down, then dove away, waiting for what remained of the upper floor to fall and give me cover. The stone creaked, chunks of masonry crumbled down, then nothing. Bullets sang past me. I sprinted away.

I reached the end of the corridor. The walls rose unbroken to fifteen feet. Steel plates covered the windows: a dead end. The only way out was back the way I had come, the vault where I had kicked out the stands.

I ran toward the shots, darting side to side. I heard cracks and settling from the stone archway ahead. Great. *Now* the vault had decided to cooperate. Chunks fell. I sped up straight for the

211

passage, and rounded the corner in a flat-out sprint, arms pumping as the ceiling collapsed and the bullets slit the air.

It all came down. I dove, then felt the stones striking my legs, my back. Maybe I hadn't gone far enough. A cloud of dust swallowed me, coated my mouth like talc. I struggled to my knees, throwing myself forward, waiting to be crushed.

A heavy stone hit me in the small of the back. I stumbled. I was going to get buried alive in this creepy pile. Some kids playing manhunt would find my bloated blue body months from now. I kept going, half crawling. The dust stung my eyes. The falling rubble eased. I ran, crashed into a wall, groped my way forward blindly.

The air cleared. The walls tapered down into piles of stone. I felt dirt beneath my feet as I ran, jumped a low pile of stone, and started across the grounds toward the fence.

Someone with a rifle must have arrived at the party, because the bullets were moving closer, indicating the practiced hand of a marksman taking his time to correct for distance and the cold wind coming off the water.

Over my shoulder I could see muzzle flares in a high window.

I ran, and saw ahead of me a last chain-link fence and then the wooded descent to the river. I jumped up, grabbed the links, and started climbing.

A bullet sparked off the fence by my head. I threw myself over the top. The twists of chain link tore at my ribs as I went over. I lost control and landed hard on the other side, driving my knee into my chin and dazing myself for a second.

A hill dropped off to my left as I kept on.

Before I heard the crack of the gunshot, I felt it hit me, like a twenty-pound sledge crashing into my lower back. I tumbled forward, whipping my head against the ground at the last second. I managed to get my feet below me, but by then the descent was too steep. I was sliding through dirt and leaves. My gun fell from my waistband, tumbled away. I took a roll and landed on my back.

I groaned. The world went red, shot through with stars and sparking lights. I fell end over end down a ledge, and came to on my stomach in a gully.

I wasn't far from the river. There was no sign of my gun. I limped through the trees toward where I'd left my car. As I came around a bend in the water, I saw my Jeep. Thank God. I might make it out of this. I started to run, but the pain in my back flared, crippling me. As I drew closer, I saw figures ahead, flashlights scanning. They'd found my car.

The lights panned through the woods. I ducked behind a tree and waited for them to pass.

I turned and started back down the river, tearing through brush, pain arcing up my back with every step. There was nothing for miles but the men trying to kill me. As I mucked through cold standing water, I saw headlights coming down a trail. I threw myself down in the mud and waited. Minutes passed. Spiders crawled from the leaves near my ear. Something that felt like claws skittered over my legs. I held on.

The car stopped. Flashlights crossed the field, lit up the wet earth around my head. I buried my face, tried to breathe out of the corner of my mouth.

I don't know how long I lay like that, feeling the insects crawl down my collar, the mud seep into my ear.

The lights moved on, flashed back once more. The car engine growled. They left.

Three-quarters of a mile down the river I came across an old bait shed, closed for the season. In the creek behind it there was a skiff, abandoned and half full of brown water. I clambered in and pushed out toward the river. I let the current take me away as I collapsed on my back, staring at the stars in that cold soaking mess.

I felt the blood flow from my lower back, felt the warmth mingle with the filthy water. I knew that I had been shot. I had to hope they would peg me for dead, and pray they weren't right in the end.

It was a wide, calm section of the river. The boat ran into a snag of trees. I pushed it off with my foot. Then an eddy caught me and took me to shore on the far, Virginia side.

I made my way through the freezing water by the bank. I seemed to be in some kind of county park. As I trudged up the hill, I felt the heat from my blood as it spread down my buttocks, my leg.

I reached back and felt the vest with my fingers, traced the hole in the plate. The bullet had gone through.

The trail led to a rural road. I fished out my cell phone. Water was beaded on the screen, but it still worked. I tried Annie. No answer. I was about to call my dad, but that was a last resort. If he didn't make it home in time for his parole curfew call, he could be sent back.

I could have knocked on someone's front door, but they would have been justified in answering it with a shotgun. I looked every bit the escaped murderer.

I started to feel faint, and tripped over my feet a couple of times. This was getting bad fast. I had to take a break. I stepped into the cover of the roadside trees and sat down with my back against a log.

I needed an ambulance. I was about to call for one when I remembered that they report all gunshot wounds. I couldn't bump into the cops with this. I lay on my back, breathing slowly and deliberately. I'd never felt so tired, or so cold. My eyes closed and I slumped over.

The pain and the damp and the chill seemed not to matter anymore. Unconsciousness came over me like a veil. I let the darkness in.

Chapter Thirty-Six

Bells rang. I don't know if they would have done the job of waking me on their own, but as I lay half conscious on the ground, a fat, cold drop of rain landed in my ear. I came to with my teeth chattering. The bells were the shrill digital ring of my cell phone. I lifted myself onto the log, hunched forward.

I had to keep moving.

I answered the phone as I tried to stand.

'Hello,' I said.

'Mike?'

'Who is this?'

'It's Emily. Emily Bloom. I wanted to check in on how the meeting went. Are you okay? Is this a bad time to talk?'

'A bit of trouble,' I croaked. 'You aren't up around, I don't know, I guess I'm near Herndon?'

The pain made it hard to breathe. Every word came out as a groan.

'You sound awful. Are you okay?'

'No.'

'Are you hurt?'

'Yeah.'

'I'll be there in ten minutes.'

I didn't want to drag her into this, but I preferred not to die of politeness. 'Thank you,' I said.

'Just give me an address.'

215

I looked myself up on my phone's GPS and read it out to her.

While I waited, I called my dad.

'Hey,' I said, doing my best to sound like one of the living.

'What's up, Mike? Jack okay?'

'I haven't checked. I was wondering about that doc that you and Cartwright know. The veterinarian.'

'Macosko?'

'Can you give him a call, see if I can stop by there tonight?'

'What happened?'

'I'm fine. I just need something stitched up.'

'What? Go to the damn ER. You've got insurance.'

'I can't.'

'Why can't you?'

'I got, just a little bit, I got shot.'

'You can't get a little shot, Mike. What the hell is going on?'

'I'll tell you all about it later. I can't talk now. But in the meantime, can you get Macosko, see if I can come in? Please?'

'I'll come get you,' he said. He was at least a half hour away.

'I have a friend coming. I'll give you a call if there's any trouble.'

For a second I could only hear breathing, then my father relented. 'I'll call him.'

I tried to stay conscious, but I started to go dark again, despite the rain. I woke, blinded by headlights.

It was Bloom. She wanted to know what had happened, how I'd gone from the field office to bleeding out on the side of a county road, but I didn't have the strength to get into it all now. She dumped out a large Neiman Marcus shopping bag from the back seat, tore the sides, and laid it on the passenger seat.

'You mind if I just rest?' I asked. 'I don't want to seem ungrateful, but it's been a tough day.'

'Sure. Hospital?'

'No,' I said. I checked my messages and gave her an address off Lee Highway.

A half mile off the main drag we pulled up to a storefront with a lighted sign that read 'NoVa Veterinary Clinic.'

The vet was a friend of Cartwright's. I think the doc owed him, for gambling or some other sins. He served as the go-to for injuries you'd prefer not to explain to the police. I'd first heard about him because of the trouble my father and I were in a while back with my old boss.

The bleeding was slow but steady. The pain had died down some, or I'd just grown used to it. I started to hope that maybe the bullet hadn't gone through, that the mess in my back was just a result of the force of impact. When I had tried to pull the vest off, the pain made me pass out again, so I was still wearing it.

Macosko met us in the lobby, carrying a mug, wearing sweatpants and a flannel shirt.

'Shot?' he asked me as he pulled the tea bag out and tossed it in the trash.

'I think it hit the vest.'

'Mmm hmm,' he said. He walked past the receptionist's desk. I followed. A few dogs snapped their teeth against the doors of their cages along the wall. He sat me on a metal table. The place looked nicer than the last hospital for people I'd been in.

Macosko undid the Velcro on the vest and lifted off the front. I ground my teeth together.

'That okay?'

'Uh huh.'

217

He tugged the back of the vest gently away from my spine, testing it.

I let out a few choice obscenities.

'I see,' he said.

'What?'

'Behind-armor blunt trauma. What shot you?'

'A rifle, I think.'

He prepped a hypodermic and slid it into a vein in the hollow of my elbow.

'You're going to want that,' he said as he dropped the plunger. A pleasant, woozy feeling drifted through me.

He lifted some gauze with a pair of forceps and told Bloom to grab the shoulders of the bulletproof vest. All the Velcro was hanging free.

'Pull it when I say,' he said. 'Ready?'

She grabbed it.

'Go.'

She yanked it away. I felt as if someone had jammed a flaming Roman candle through the flesh of my back. I groaned low in my throat and gripped the edge of the table. Something clinked against the tiles behind me. I looked over to see a deformed rifle slug skitter across the linoleum and under a cabinet.

I felt warmth spill down my back as Macosko jammed the gauze in the hole left by the bullet. That burned worse than the original tug. I was too tired to grunt anymore, so I just clenched my teeth, and redoubled my grip on the table's edge.

'Did it go through?' I asked.

'Yes and no.' He looked through his reading glasses at the wound. 'A case like this, it enters, but not too deep, and brings the vest material with it. It's sort of like a magician stuffing a handkerchief into his fist. You're lucky I see a lot of GSWs. Most docs would assume it went right through, open you up

218

and spend a couple hours doing a laparotomy and poking around in your abdomen looking for it.'

He slapped the table, indicating I should lie on my stomach. I complied, slowly. He set to work stitching up my back.

'This isn't nearly as bad as it looks.'

He almost sounded disappointed. Bloom came back with the slug and took a second to examine it. 'Looks like a five five six. You're lucky you're alive. These tumble.'

The stitches took another ten minutes. I sat up, and Macosko gave me some pills. I looked at the bottle.

'These are for dogs,' I said.

'It's all the same stuff,' he said. 'Will help with any mange, too.'

'Are you the wife?' he asked Bloom.

'No.'

'Well, that's none of my business.' He started loading his autoclave. 'But this one—' he pointed to me '—has a pony's worth of oxycodone in him. Keep a close eye for the next eight to twelve hours. He should be fine, but Lord knows I've been wrong before.'

Bloom walked me outside. With the bullet out and the drugs in, I felt like a new man.

'So I take it the meeting didn't go as planned?' Bloom asked as we stepped into her truck.

'No,' I said. 'I just need to get home and lie down.'

'Annie there?'

'No.'

'Anybody?'

'No.'

'Then you're coming with me. Doctor's orders.'

Chapter Thirty-Seven

I woke and nuzzled my cheek against cool sheets and a mattress more comfortable than anything I'd ever slept on. It sure wasn't mine.

On the dresser, I saw family snapshots: skiing in the Alps, riding horses in what looked like Montana, a Stanford graduation. All featured Emily Bloom.

I let out a long, quiet 'Oh no.'

Last night was a haze. What had I done? When I rolled over I barked in pain, but found, fortunately, that I was alone. I lay there and took in the bedroom, all perfectly arranged. I couldn't imagine a real person lived there; I felt as if I'd conked out in a Restoration Hardware. Last night grew clearer in my mind. I slowly pieced together the events, the shot, and why I was sleeping in a strange woman's bed.

Bloom opened the door.

'Morning,' she said. 'You want some coffee? Vicodin?'

'Both. God bless you. Sorry I put you out. I should have slept on the couch or something. Did I pass out?'

'You earned the bed. Don't worry about it.'

I sat up and swung my legs to the ground. I was wearing a T-shirt and a pair of Bloom's sweatpants.

'Should you be moving around?'

'I feel pretty good, considering. A lot of it was just having the damn thing in there, not knowing how bad it all was.'

She'd slept in the living room and checked in on me every few hours. A bag of bagels and coffee from Dean & DeLuca sat on the kitchen counter.

'All right,' she said. 'What happened?'

'The good news is that I got very close to finding out who is after me and my brother. The person at the top.'

'Who is it?'

'That's the bad news. I don't know. I keep going over it in my head. There are a few cases I have going now that could be related, a few guys I tangled with in the past.'

'Are you being cagey? You can trust me, Mike.'

'I genuinely don't know. It must be this anticorruption work. If I can get to my files, I can narrow it down, maybe get some audio.'

'You were close enough to get shot. I guess that's something. You want to talk it through?'

'Everyone who learns about this case seems to end up in the hospital, or the morgue, or the vet's office, so I'll save you the details.'

'Are you still going to the feds?'

'That's how last night started. They have sources everywhere.'

'Lasseter?'

'Above Lasseter. But don't say or do anything. They kill informants. I've seen them do it. Promise me.'

'Of course. So what's next?'

'Can you take me home?'

We pulled up to my street in Bloom's truck. My clothes from yesterday, caked in river muck and blood, sat in a trash bag between my feet.

Even through the narcotics, my back was screaming. As we approached my house, I saw familiar cars: a 1950s Bentley, a

Lexus convertible. They belonged to Annie's grandmother and her aunt.

A white windowless van – to my mind, the preferred ride of kidnappers – was parked in my driveway. If Lynch and his higher-up knew that it was me at the casino, they would come after me with everything.

My hand went to my knife, and then I saw a waiter in a white shirt and black pants, ferrying an empty tray from my backyard to the van.

He emerged with a bunch of hors d'oeuvres with toothpicks sticking out of them. We parked in front of the house. Bloom stepped out of the car at the same time I did.

'You might be a little shaky,' she said.

'I'm okay,' I said. Despite the pain, I was able to get around pretty well.

When I turned back to the house I saw Annie on the front porch. I thought she wasn't getting back until tonight, but I may have had that wrong.

If I had known she would be home, I probably wouldn't have rolled up to the house after being out all night with the woman I swore I wasn't sleeping with. And I definitely wouldn't have worn the clothes I got from Bloom: a threadbare girls' Catholic school T-shirt and red sweatpants.

Annie regarded me with barely contained rage. Given the evidence against me, I was getting off easy. I climbed the steps to the porch. After last night, I was just glad to be alive to hug her. It was like squeezing an oak. She pushed me away.

'Are you serious?' she asked.

We had a good-sized audience of aunts and cousins and friends in the picture window now, pretending to eat canapés while watching the action on the porch.

'I can explain.'

'You're unbelievable.'

'I tried to go to the FBI, but—'

Annie's father stepped onto the porch. I threw up my hands. This was bad enough without Clark in the front row watching as my life imploded.

'Maybe we could talk about this later,' I said to Annie. 'I've had a truly awful night.'

'Looks like a decent night to me,' she said, looking from my clothes to Bloom, who was standing beside her car. Annie glanced at her father, then moved closer to me. 'We are absolutely going to talk about this later. There's going to be a goddamned *symposium* on this. Make yourself presentable.'

Was today her shower? Then what was the spa thing? I may have had other things on my mind besides Annie's social calendar, but there seemed to be an endless chain of pre-wedding events, of female relatives and friends throwing around gadgets and champagne and tissue paper. It was hard to keep them all straight.

At least having a house full of guests bought me a brief reprieve from the trouble I was in with Annie. I looked back at her.

'What are you grinning about?' Annie asked. I hadn't realized. I was just so happy to see her, for us both to be safe. But I really should stop smiling like someone who'd just had the night of his life. 'Are you high?'

Just dog pills. And I had a prescription.

I didn't answer her. All my attention turned to a car coming around the corner. It was a Dodge Charger. I peered at the window. Lynch's man in glasses was driving, with three other men in the car.

The Charger double-parked in front of our house, blocking the driveway.

'Get inside, Annie!' I said.

'You're giving me orders now?'

I put my hand on her back and steered her toward the front door. Then two hundred and fifty pounds of future-father-in-law stepped in front of me to protect his daughter.

'I don't have time to explain, Annie. Just get inside. These men—'

'Stop it, Mike. I know what's going on.' She reached into her pocket and pulled out an envelope crammed with thousands of dollars in twenties.

'The police came by today in front of my whole family. They were here to bring you in for questioning about that murder on the Mall. Have you completely lost your mind? You're a lawyer. You can't run around robbing or conning people or whatever the hell you and your brother are really up to. I thought that was sort of a given. I can't even believe what I'm saying here. It's like a bad dream.'

'Annie. You're not safe. Just go inside.'

'I can't believe I fell for your bullshit yesterday. You lost your main client and didn't tell me? Who are these people you're hanging out with? Did your brother get you involved in some kind of . . . a gang? Are you in a fucking gang?'

She clearly didn't care anymore who heard her.

'I'm trying to protect you.' I took her arm. Clark put his hand on my chest.

'Just stop,' Annie said. 'Stop lying. And her.' She looked over at Bloom. 'You're obviously sleeping with her, so don't insult me by pretending otherwise. It's two weeks until our wedding. What the fuck, Mike?'

'I swear nothing happened. I—'

'I thought you wanted all this,' she lifted her hand toward the house, the tidy garden. I saw her grandmother inside, watching us and enjoying my comeuppance. I couldn't argue with Annie now. I didn't have time. Soon Lynch and his men would come for blood. I just had to get her to safety and hope I survived. Then I could find some way to explain it all, to ask forgiveness for the unforgivable.

'But you can't stand it,' she went on. 'You can't stand me. You think this is about your brother? It's not. You're using him as an excuse to get your hands dirty and steal away from me every chance you get. You told me you could change, Mike. But I don't know anymore. You act like it's the right thing, a means to some honorable end. But it's your whole family. It's in your blood. You're one of them. You're a lost cause.'

She threw the money down at my feet.

'It's better I find out now, before I make the biggest mistake of my life.' She gave me a look I knew well. It was the look she'd been hiding from me ever since she'd seen me kill a man. It was a mix of pity, suspicion, and fear.

She held her forehead and sighed. 'I can't believe what I'm saying, but this is over.'

'Annie. Please, just give me a chance to talk to you, but not now. Now I need to get you someplace safe.'

I reached out for her. She backed away. Her father blocked my path.

'I think she's finally seen you for who you are, Michael. Now I suggest you go.'

'Me?' I turned on him. 'I'm the fucking criminal?'

I'd told myself I wouldn't do this. It would only blow back in my face, only make me look petty. But I was too broken down to hold back. The sight of that smug prick basking in my downfall was too much, the hypocrisy of it all just too much.

'I may be trash,' I said as I stepped toward him. 'But at least I'm not some self-loathing hypocrite con man whose whole life is a lie.'

He shook his head.

'Has it ever seemed odd, Annie,' I asked, 'that he gets fifteen percent returns for twenty years in a row, no matter what happens in the markets? That a London real estate guy pulls together a billion-dollar fund in a few years while everyone is hiding their money under their mattresses?'

Annie looked down. She was entering the embarrassed-for-me stage.

'Your father is the real crook. Ask him about his first deals in London. Ask him about blockbusting. Ask him about the fires in Barnsbury.'

She looked at her dad. And for a moment I saw the doubt flicker on her face, saw that at one time or other she had wondered about him, too. She turned back to me. I had her.

'This is just pathetic, Mike,' she said.

I turned to the side. I knew I shouldn't have said anything.

My prepaid phone rang. It was Lynch. I had to answer, to at least negotiate Annie's safety, no matter what it cost me.

'One second,' I said.

'You're taking a call in the middle of our life falling apart?'

'It's an emergency. I swear.'

I stalked across the lawn. 'You or any of your men come near my home, and I'll fucking kill you,' I said into the phone, seething.

'Oops,' he said; I watched as his car pulled around the corner and stopped. He stepped out and started walking toward my house.

Bloom had stood silent beside her truck the whole time, examining the edging around my sidewalk and doing her best to spare me any further embarrassment. Maybe she was hanging around because it was clear I was going to need a lift soon.

I looked from her to Lynch, then back.

I lifted my phone and then dialed the number I'd seen Lynch call back at the FBI. My cell rang in my hand. But it wasn't the only one. Another ring echoed it. It was coming out of Bloom's pocket. She silenced it.

'No.' I said. 'You?'

I walked closer.

'You? What the hell did I do to *you?*'

Bloom stepped over and put her arm around me.

'Just business,' she said.

I flicked open the knife. 'Get these men away from my house.'

'Lovely,' she said. 'But I don't think sticking me in plain view is going to help your nice-guy case with Annie. You see that truck?'

I looked past the grass beside my house. There was a black Chevy Suburban on the side street. The rear window was open.

Annie stood on the porch, clearly shocked that I had decided to huddle with my mistress in front of our extended family at a time like this.

'Let me tell you how this plays out,' Bloom said. 'You tell Annie that you're coming with us. We'll call it a bachelor party. Then you get in the car, and we go do this job. No one gets hurt. Understand?'

'Don't you dare threaten her.'

'I haven't, actually. I don't think that's necessary. But if you need convincing, here are a few things you should know. Lynch has a guy at your father's house right now. I just talked to him. He's watching your dad read a paperback on his deck. There's also a man in that Suburban. Both have suppressed HK416 rifles and two-way radios, and both are waiting on a single word from Lynch. He, as you may have noticed, is getting increasingly erratic, so it's best not to give him an excuse. He might try to wing her, but there's no such thing as a safe shot. He could just as easily end up paralyzing her from the waist down or worse, you know?'

'You wouldn't.'

'Of course he would. You've seen him do it. Do you want him to put the red dot on her to prove his point?'

I looked back at Annie, at our appalled families. I knew that if I went with Bloom, it would be the end of the best thing that had ever happened to me. The price was Annie. She would never speak to me again, but at least I could buy her safety. And that was more important than anything else.

'Tell Annie what I just told you,' Bloom said. 'And then get in the car. One wrong word and the triggers get pulled.'

I looked at Lynch, his push-to-talk phone held up to his mouth, ready to give the order. I took a step toward the porch.

'I have to go,' I said to Annie. 'I can't explain. Go to your father's.'

'What are you talking about?'

'I'm sorry, Annie.'

'Don't,' she said. I could see her fists clench, the muscles in her jaw tighten.

I walked toward Bloom, then looked back at Annie one last time. It was like standing too close to the edge of a cliff. My body refused to move. I had to will it, step by step. Bloom climbed into the driver's seat, leaned over, and opened the passenger door.

'If you leave now, Mike,' Annie said, 'this is the end.'

I'd been feeling sick since the morning before, when I realized that Jack had been playing me from the beginning. Now, as this trap closed around me, shame and regret filled me, crawled down my spine like the worst hangover I'd ever had.

'I love you,' I said, standing beside the open car door.

Bloom pulled me in by my belt. 'Come on, Romeo.'

She put her arm around my shoulder and smiled across the passenger seat at Annie. She gave her a little wave as she kissed me. Then we pulled away.

Chapter Thirty-Eight

'That's Annie, huh?' Bloom said, and wrinkled her nose. 'Is she always like that? Seems like a drag.'

'Pull your men back,' I said.

She raised Lynch on the radio and confirmed the order. In the rearview, I saw the cars line up behind us as we pulled out of my neighborhood.

'Keep your enemies close,' I said, shaking my head.

'Something like that.'

'Who's paying you?'

'This is my show, Mike. Give me a little credit.'

'That's bullshit.'

'Believe what you want.'

'So you're the police *and* the thieves?' I said, and thought it through for a moment. 'I guess it makes your investigations a lot easier. Bloom Security, always somehow able to penetrate the underground, to navigate the most corrupt nations on earth. And if you have any criminal competition, you just snitch them out, burnish your credentials with law enforcement at the same time.'

'I wish it were that easy. But you know how these things go. There are no bright lines on the ground. Sometimes we're bad guys pretending to be good guys, sometimes we're good guys pretending to be bad guys. Sometimes we do the necessary evils the good guys can't. Half the time I don't know what the fuck is going on. I just cash the check.'

'Don't even try to sell this as some elaborate undercover job. You're a criminal.'

'If you work in this field your whole life, you find that straight/criminal distinction less and less meaningful. I imagine you can relate. Let's just say I'm a pragmatist. An opportunity seeker. A good American entrepreneur.'

'You forgot murderer.'

'No. As far as the Sacks business goes, I'm a general contractor with some quality assurance issues in one of my subs.'

'Was your billion-dollar inheritance not enough? You needed more?'

'It's not about money, Mike. After the first ten million or so, it's all the same hamburger. You just start to worry about how not to fuck up your kids with all the cash around.'

'Bloom senior clearly did a bang-up job.'

'My family's been doing this sort of thing a long time. You have to get your hands dirty. We were losing our soul, turning into a handmaiden for a bunch of law firms and hedge funds.'

'A rich girl steals for thrills. What could be more obnoxious? You just like slumming?'

'I do, actually, and so do you. But the point was to buy back the company. I needed to revisit some revenue streams we'd turned away from. And sure, I get bored sometimes. What am I supposed to get excited about? Dining room tables? A new place in Mustique? Trying really, really hard to earn a pat on the head from the board, a bunch of old men who divvied up my family's legacy and sold it off to the highest bidders? It's just my nature. And it's important work. You can't have the white market without the black. There needs to be a go-between. That's where we come in.'

'You seem so on the ball, and yet this is so fucking crazy.'

'So I've heard,' she said. 'It's the times. The government's outsourced everything. Intelligence. Interrogations. It's one of the downsides to privatizing security. You end up with a lot of grays.'

'You end up with paid enemies who do better the worse things get.' I watched the cars following us in the rearview. 'All very interesting. You should write something up for the Outlook section after you dump my body.'

We were driving out near where the Beltway intersects 395, an agglomeration of recently built apartment complexes and office parks tangled between highway overpasses and cloverleafs.

'I like you, Mike. This isn't a kidnapping.' We pulled into an underground garage. 'It's a corporate apartment, a pretty nice one. Think of it as an off-site meeting, some team building. We're just going to do the job you agreed to do.'

The rest of the convoy trailed in and parked beside us. Lynch searched me thoroughly, taking extra care to poke me hard in my fresh stitches. We trooped over to the elevators.

It was a brand-new apartment tower. We took the elevator up to twelve and entered a beautiful open-floor-plan apartment that looked like a realtor's model. The only thing I had going for me was that there was an espresso machine built into the cabinetry next to the fridge.

'Welcome,' Bloom said. 'And since I believe you were just tossed out of your house, you can crash here until we head up to New York for the job.'

'The job? You're unbelievable. You just shot me—'

'It didn't even go in that far.'

'—you threatened my fiancée—'

'Ex-fiancée.'

'—and you nearly killed my brother.'

231

'Only because you tried to be sneaky with us, Mike. So those are all good reasons to cooperate this time. See how easy it can be.'

She walked over to a bowl on the granite counter, lifted an apple, and bit a chunk out of it.

'And who knows where this will lead?' she continued. 'You're a competent guy. I'm very impressed so far. You do dirty. You do clean. You're fun to have around. So come work with us. You already have been, so what's the big deal? We're crooks, Mike. You can't change your nature. Stop being tortured and have fun with it. I wish somebody had told me that fifteen years ago. It would have saved me a lot of time and pain.'

She offered me a bite.

'Very subtle,' I said.

'You're angry. I get it. And this isn't the Soviet Union. It's your choice.'

'What's the choice? What if I say no?'

She waved that notion away. 'Let's keep it positive. That's the key to success. One day I asked myself, why should cops and robbers be going round and round in a zero-sum game? So much entrepreneurial spirit wasted. Let's make it win-win. Grow the pie. And right here, Mike,' she said, pointing back and forth between us, 'I see a lot of synergies. Let's focus on those.'

That was the nicest way anyone has ever threatened to kill me. It was almost possible to forget that this was coercion at the point of a gun.

'I'm sorry about how this all worked out,' she went on. 'I was hoping to bring you in without the unpleasantness. You should rest up. We're heading to New York tonight or tomorrow morning. Then it's Fed Day. So what do you say? This is in your blood, same as mine. So stop lying to yourself and just go with it. Are you in?'

'You don't know a goddamned thing about me.'

'Don't I? I know about what happened to your father, Mike. You know the thieves have more honor than the law. So why bother with their bullshit distinctions? Don't try to pretend you'd be happy with fantasy football and rote sex twice a month. You need this, haven't you realized? You try to live between the lines, you'll die of boredom.'

Bloom was speaking out loud the thoughts that kept me up at night, staring at the ceiling of my American dream house, the thoughts that haunted me when I nodded over china patterns or picked out the gold ring I'd wear until I died.

The moves I had tried against Lynch and Bloom had left me with my life in shambles and a hole in my back. I had one out left. The only option was to play along. I could take them all down, but I would have to take myself down with them, and I would have to pull the heist first.

'I'm in,' I said.

'Excellent.'

'I'll need help.'

'Jack will go in with you. He'll be ready. It's only fair he has some skin in the game.'

'There are some supplies. ID cards, a few other things. I need to get them from my guys before we head up to New York.'

'Tell me their names,' she said.

'A guy named Cartwright, and my father. I don't think they'll be ready until tonight.'

'Your father?'

'Nobody's better with paper.'

'We'll get them.'

'They can be a little jumpy. I can go—'

'Not a chance.'

'Then at least call first. I'll give you the numbers.'

'Sure. You need anything else. Breakfast?'

'I'm not hungry,' I said. 'But there is one thing. You know the crypto cards the feds use? I think they're called Fortezzas.'

'Sure.'

'Can you get me one of those? It doesn't have to work. It just has to look okay.'

'That's no problem,' she said, and started for the door.

Bloom had set me up in the alley, back when she popped up to save me from Lynch. It was all so I would trust her, the Good Samaritan con, so she would be able to intercept me when I tried to go to the law. She had set me up at the Four Seasons. She must have known Annie would see us. And this morning, she had gone out of her way to break up my relationship with Annie beyond fixing. I'd like to think I'm just catnip for the ladies, but there was something more going on. Why salt the earth? So I would have no legit life to go back to?

'Tell me one thing,' I said. 'Why me? You must have half a dozen crews who could pull off something like this. Why bring in an amateur? Why am I so goddamned special?'

'Don't sell yourself short, Mike,' she said. 'You're the right man for the job. I told you. This is just business.'

She and her men left, then shut and locked the door.

Chapter Thirty-Nine

I leaned out over the twelve-story drop, my hands gripping the rail behind me. It had seemed like a much better plan this afternoon. I stood on the edge of the terrace, outside the railing, like a kid too scared to plunge into the water after his friends. I turned, grabbed the vertical bars, and started to lower myself. Dangling from the bottom of the railing, my feet were still six inches from the railing below.

At least it was better than sitting trapped inside that apartment, feeling numb, unable to think about anything but the fact that Annie was gone for good.

The man in glasses was guarding my room, posted just outside the door. I had tried to stall by saying I needed gear and maps from my house for the heist. But they must have broken into my place the night before. Everything from my office was at the apartment complex, in file boxes in a room down the hall.

They seemed to control the whole floor. I had heard a tenant below me, watching basketball all afternoon. After dinner, once his apartment went quiet and I could see there were no lights on, I slipped out onto the terrace. It was recessed into the side of the building.

I didn't want to escape, but I needed a few items before we headed up to New York, and now seemed to be my only chance.

I let go with my right hand and gripped the edge of the

cement floor of my terrace. My right toe could just touch below. I brought my left hand down. I had my toes on the railing of the downstairs apartment terrace, but I was angled back, leaning out over the drop. A cold gust pulled me back.

The stretching tore at my stitches. My hands were slick with sweat, and the cement edge was slipping past my second knuckles. I let go with my left hand and began to teeter back toward the cement sidewalk a hundred and fifty feet below. I dragged my left hand on the underside of my terrace, uselessly, as I began to fall, and then against the brick wall on the side of the terrace below.

That gave me a small amount of the momentum I needed. I grasped again, found some purchase in the mortar, and pulled myself forward as I jumped onto the floor of the terrace under my own.

Sliding glass doors are easy. You install them by lifting them up and in, so you can get past them by lifting them up and out. If that doesn't work, you gently apply a brick. But here on the eleventh floor, this guy hadn't even bothered to lock his.

I went in. It was a classic DC workaholic setup. The furniture was rented. I could see the tall movers' boxes full of hanging suits, and one bowl and one glass drying near the sink.

There was a desk in the corner, piled with papers. I scanned the apartment. The occupant was gone, for now. I picked up the phone and called my dad.

'Hey, Dad,' I said. 'It's Mike.'

'You okay? What the hell happened over at the house?'

'A little banged-up, but okay overall,' I said. 'Can't talk much now. Can I ask you for something?'

'Please. I'd hate to be the only Ford who hasn't been sent to the hospital this week. You should have asked for help, Mike.'

'I'm not getting you sent back. I've got it under control.'

'Clearly.'

'I have to be quick. Some people may call you. They'll ask for some gear for the break-in. It's okay. Can you get the ID badges from Cartwright and give it to them? Bring it to me yourself if they let you?'

'Sure.'

'And could you sneak a couple other things in there, just in case? I'm worried they're going to try to pull something on me after the job.'

'Tell me where you are, and we'll get you out.'

'They have an army, Dad. And they'll come after everyone. I have a plan. There's no time. You just have to trust me. I want to go through with the job. It's the only way out.'

We bickered for a while until he finally gave in. 'Fine,' he said. 'What do you need?'

'Picks. I broke mine. When you're getting the package together, you don't have to hide them. I'll say they're for the Fed. And I need a razor blade and a handcuff key, hidden in the same package with the picks. Nonmetal, if you can manage. You think you can keep them from finding it? They'll probably search it.'

'I spent sixteen years inside, Mike. They won't find a thing. You're really going to do this?'

'I have no choice. They'll kill Annie. They'll get you. They can put a murder on me.'

'But you know too much now. They're not just going to let you walk. It doesn't make sense. Why would they send in someone who hates them, who is dying to get back at them, to get something they need?'

'They must have me covered. I'm going to take the fall, or they'll kill me after.'

'What are you thinking?' he said.

'I'm going to pull the switch, beat them at their own game. They might be expecting it. I just have to hope my tricks are better than theirs.'

'Does Jack know?'

'I haven't told him.'

'Will you?'

'He was conning me this whole time.'

'He's not an evil guy,' my father said, pained. 'But sometimes he might as well be.'

'Maybe he's their insurance. He'll watch me on the inside and sell me out if I try anything.'

'You think he'd go that far?'

'They nearly killed him,' I said. 'That definitely wasn't part of his con. So now he's either scared to death and will do anything they want. Or he's scared and angry, and will do anything to get back at them.'

'I can't tell you what to do, Mike. You're a good guy, and that'll get you killed in this world.'

'I just wanted to believe I could get us all back together, bring Jack along, help him get himself sorted out. I wanted to believe he could change.'

'You can't save him, Mike. He has to save himself. And you are your own man. If he stumbles, that doesn't mean you will.'

'Thanks. I sneaked out to a phone. I've got to run, but I love you. Hopefully I'll see you tonight.'

'You too.'

Chapter Forty

In the empty apartment I sat down at the computer, a ThinkPad. The log-in screen asked for my fingerprint. I held the power button down and rebooted it into the recovery mode. From there, using the Command prompt, you can modify files on the main operating system.

If you press Shift five times on a Windows machine, a utility called Sticky Keys will run. It's a feature for people with disabilities that helps them hold down keys like Control. It's also a security hole.

From recovery, I replaced the Sticky Keys program on the main system with cmd.exe. When I restarted the guy's computer and faced that log-in screen, I just pressed Shift five times. Instead of Sticky Keys, it gave me a command line on his main operating system. From there, it was a single command to reset the password.

Once I was in, I went online, logged into my Dropbox folder, and pulled up two forgeries I'd been working on since I'd first discussed the switch with my dad. I had modeled them on past Fed directives. They matched the format and language of the official documents, right down to the letterhead and the 'Class I FOMC – Restricted Controlled (FR)' printed across the top.

I needed those fakes to make the switch. One directive told the desk to hit the brakes, let the interest rates rise, and shut down the special programs that were pumping up the economy. The other said to keep the throttle wide open.

I downloaded an open-source photo-editing program and started playing with the filters until I found one that made the pages look like bad photocopies. Once I had the grainy-fax look down, I went to Google Image search, found some scans of faxes, and started clipping numbers from the time stamps. I pasted them onto the top of my forgeries so they appeared to have come in at 12:05 p.m. on Tuesday, when the directive would be sent to New York.

I printed out both versions of the directive. Now, no matter what the committee did, I could slip Lynch and Bloom a forgery that said the opposite. They would bet exactly wrong, and I would blow up their position.

Of course, that meant I would have to pull this heist and steal the real directive first.

I printed out another copy of each version, just in case. As the last page spooled out of the printer, I heard the elevator doors down the hallway.

I trashed everything I'd put on the computer and shut it down. I could hear the apartment's rightful occupant working the lock as I pulled my printouts. I ran out onto the terrace just as the front door opened. I only managed to shut the sliding door partway.

I hid to the side, but I was visible from about half of the apartment. I heard the TV come on, *SportsCenter,* and ventured a look inside. With the lights on, all he could probably see was his own reflection, but still I felt exposed. I eased the door shut centimeter by centimeter, waiting for a squeak to give me away, for the man to find me out here.

I probably shouldn't have worried. I glanced inside. The guy was on the couch, eating a burrito out of his hand while reading from a thick sheaf of legal documents. I saw him bite the foil, grimace, tear it away, and continue. Half my friends from law school were like this: holed up in some extended-stay or corporate apartment across the street from the court or the doc review warehouse, clocking twenty-two hundred, twenty-five hundred hours a year, working every waking minute, sleeping four hours a night. The guy probably wouldn't have noticed if I'd sat down next to him and helped myself to his chips and guac.

I may have been in mortal danger, but at least I wasn't an associate anymore.

I folded the papers over once and put them in my back pocket. Steadying myself against the wall, I planted a foot on the railing and stepped on top of it. I hooked the fingers of my left hand into the brickwork and pivoted on top of the railing. I leaned back into the void, left hand on the brick, then pressed my right against the terrace ceiling.

My foot started to shake like the needle of a sewing machine.

I started to lose my balance. I pulled forward with my right hand and brought my left hand up to grab the terrace floor above me. My full weight dragged my right fingers back toward the fall as I pressed up with my toes and clamped my left hand onto the cement above.

I eased my right hand upward to a better grip, then walked my feet up the bricks of the wall and hooked my foot between the railing and the floor of my own terrace. I was in agony from the wound on my back. I hoisted my hips up to the edge. From there I walked my hands up the railing, planted my feet on the terrace's edge, and pushed myself over.

As I sat down and caught my breath, I could hear knocking on the front door of my apartment.

The guard stepped in and looked around nervously. I rapped on the glass. He walked over, slid open the door, and stuck out his head.

'The chief talked to your guys. The stuff's not going to be ready until tomorrow morning.'

'Okay.'

'It's freezing out here,' he said.

'Cabin fever. Can you bring me a copy of a book called *Locks, Safes, and Security* from down the hall?'

'Yeah. You coming in?'

'In a minute.'

He looked at me like I was nuts, and slid the door shut.

I sat back against the brick, touched my bandage, and hissed. I must have opened up a few stitches. I had what I needed to blow up Lynch and Bloom, but I'd missed my chance to call Annie.

My father dropped off the package the next morning. The man in glasses brought them to the door. The ID badges looked fine. They would definitely pass a quick visual inspection.

'There were these, too.' He held up a black leather case: the picks.

I put my hand out.

'You only touch them under adult supervision.'

'Fine. Grab me a couple of locks for practice, then: the Schlage Everest and the ASSA V-10.'

He came back with the lock cylinders ten minutes later and handed them over with the picks.

'I counted those, so don't try to pull anything.'

I sat at the table and opened the pouch. There were fifteen picks and tension wrenches inside. I double-checked the pouch. No sign of any blade or handcuff key.

Had they found them?

As I looked more closely at the picks, I noticed a tiny symbol stamped in the steel that I hadn't seen since I was a kid. It was a cannon crossed with a hammer, the maker's mark for Ford

Steel. The metalworks had been in my family for generations, until it was cheated away from my father. Fighting back against the man who ruined him was what started him doing cons. The date was 1976. These must have been some of the last pieces ever made at Ford Steel. I could always tell my father's work. They were beautiful, hand ground and polished.

I felt the hard plastic handles. They seemed odd, cheap and out of place.

As spectator sports go, lockpicking is slightly less exciting than ice fishing. After I'd worked the cylinders for about twenty minutes, the guy in glasses started playing a video game on his phone.

That gave me time to look more closely at the handles on some of those picks. I put my fingernail into a seam on the plastic at the end of a double-ball pick and pressed in. The plastic slid back. It was a cap. I eased it off and tilted the pick down. A thin blade slid out of a perfectly formed hollow in the plastic. I felt the razor. It wasn't metal, probably ceramic. I let it fall to the floor, then slipped it under the edge of the rug with my foot.

I started examining the other picks and found a barely visible seam on the handle of a wafer-lock pick. I slid the plastic cylinder all the way off the metal part of the pick. It was a short barrel, about an inch long, and once I had it off I noticed a square plastic tab, about three by four millimeters at the end that I could push out from the cylinder. It was a handcuff key. The other end of the cylinder had two notches, enough to get something in there to twist it, a fingernail or a pin or a blade. Handcuff keys are more or less standard in the United States. If my dad had the tolerances right, this would open any of the majors: Smith & Wesson, Peerless, ASP, Winchester, Chicago.

The old man had learned a lot during his time away.

I pulled the handcuff key part off, slid the remainder of the handle down, and capped it. It looked like the rest of the picks. I dropped the key on the rug and slid it underneath, alongside the blade.

With my contraband hidden, I turned back to my locks, mostly to keep myself distracted from the fact that I was going to rob the Federal Reserve Bank of New York and then, most likely, be executed.

I managed to pick the sidebar on the ASSA. The Everest was still giving me trouble. That was fine. My get-out-of-jail-free tools under the rug were the only thing that mattered.

After two hours, the guard called lunchtime and collected my picks and locks. He brought in some deli sandwiches. Once I was alone, I tied my shoelaces near the rug edge, putting my body between my hands and the places where Bloom was most likely to have stashed a camera. I palmed the blade and key, and went into the bathroom. Bloom's people had brought me a few changes of clothes. I picked out some of the threads on the shirt I was wearing, then slipped the blade into the front button placket and the key cylinder inside the cuff.

I looked over my forged copies of the directive again: two versions, two copies each. I was ready for New York.

Chapter Forty-One

Bloom put us up – though I guess 'imprisoned' is the right word – in another corporate suite in Manhattan. It was *American Psycho* deluxe, with glass, chrome, and black leather furniture and a monolith of a TV commanding the whole room.

The phones didn't work. The doors were locked from the outside, and even if I managed to get through them, there were guys with guns at both ends of the hall in case I needed a tuck-in.

Not that I wanted out. I had nothing left except revenge. I was going to claw into the heart of Bloom's operation and detonate. I couldn't wait for the heist to begin.

Bloomberg News was on. The main story tonight, as it had been for the past week, was the Federal Open Market Committee meeting in Washington and whether the dissenting Fed presidents would manage to shut down the easy-money efforts.

Someone knocked on the door. I opened it. It was Jack, flanked by the guy in glasses and the Irish guy from that first night at my brother's town house.

I stepped toward him. The guards moved closer, on the balls of their feet, ready to jump in if I attacked him.

I smiled and put my arms around him. I needed help. I needed my brother.

'Your head looks good,' I said. I could barely see the stitches under his hair. 'How does it feel?'

'It's manageable, unless something touches it. Still a little shaky, all in all. How's the back?'

'Hurts like a bastard. We make quite a team.'

'Sorry about that.'

This whole operation had targeted me from the beginning, had pulled Jack in as a means to an end. He was collateral damage. I could let in a trace of sympathy for him. In fact, making nice with Jack was a crucial part of my plan.

'Should we get into it?' I asked.

'Sure.'

I walked Jack over to the kitchen table, where I'd laid out floor plans for the Fed entrances and the desk. I looked over the stills from my cameras, double-checking the daily routines. The office manager hung her purse with the crypto card in it on the same hook every day. Without that card, the whole plan would fail. We had to rehearse, and I had to give Lynch some basic lessons on my malware. We would need those viruses to act up in order to get into the suite at the Fed.

There was enough to keep us busy that Jack and I could leave most things unsaid. We filled the hours drilling the heist. It was a relief, because if I talked to him about what had happened, or even thought about it too much, I was afraid I would kill him or forgive him. I didn't know which was worse.

Every time the guard stepped out of earshot, Jack would lean in. 'They're not going to let us get away with this, Mike,' he'd whisper. 'They're setting us up. We need a plan. We need some way to get back at them, to get away.'

'Don't worry about it. Just stick to this.' I pointed at the map where I had traced how we would get to the trading desk and our escape routes if something went wrong. 'It will all work out.'

He wasn't satisfied. The next chance he had, he came back to it. 'They are just going to get rid of us after.'

'I have it under control, Jack. Don't pull anything. You'll only get yourself killed. Or me.'

'But how?' he asked. The panic was clear in his eyes as we drew closer to the heist. We would hit the bank in twelve hours.

'I've got it figured—' I said. The door opened. Lynch walked in.

Jack and I straightened up.

'What are we talking about, boys?' Lynch knew something was up.

'Escape routes,' I said. He looked us up and down, shouted for the man in glasses to get out of the bathroom and keep a closer eye on us, then left.

We didn't have another chance to talk before they split us up that night. I knew Jack was up to something. I knew he would try to drag my real plan out of me. I was counting on it.

Chapter Forty-Two

Heist Day

I hadn't slept at all that night, just stared out my window at the gray glow that passes for dark in Manhattan. I stepped out of bed, showered, dressed, and watched the East River cap white with the gusting wind.

Why were they after me? The question wouldn't leave me alone.

You fucked with the wrong guy, Lynch had said. And as I double-checked for the hundredth time the forged directives, the tiny cylinder and blade stitched into my clothes, I finally realized who was behind all this.

Lynch knocked on the door. We were ready. I knew I was walking into a trap, but with what I now understood, and after all that time waiting alone with the fear, I'd never felt so relieved in my life.

We rolled out for Maiden Lane in a black van. The signs on the side said it belonged to a courier service. Lynch drove. Lynch always drove. Irish took the passenger seat. The guy in glasses was on the back bench, watching us. First we stopped at the Thai restaurant. I'd called in the order that morning.

Glasses stepped out of the van door and ran in to pick up the food. Jack and I were alone in the back.

The radio was on: '. . . and the markets are mixed on unprecedented volume as Wall Street waits to hear the results of the Fed meeting in Washington . . .'

We had push-to-talk radios that we could use to connect with Lynch's team and send two-way messages to the lookouts. There was no way to call an outside line.

Our cover story for the first phase, getting past the perimeter, was that we were sales reps for the gym, going in to meet with Human Resources. I had a binder of promotional materials with my picks hidden in the spine.

For hitting the desk, Jack had a laptop in a backpack. I hid the dummy crypto card and a rare-earth magnet where the DVD drive on the computer had once been in order to get them past the metal detectors.

As we approached the Fed, Jack looked at me. He always projected a galling confidence, the certainty that no matter how far he went, or what he did wrong, he'd make it through unscathed. But in that moment, after all these years, it had disappeared.

I'm ashamed at how satisfying it felt for me to watch it go, to see him realize that this time there would be no easy out. All that was left in him was simple fear.

'They're going to fuck us over,' he whispered.

'Yes, they are. I'm not sure if we'll take the fall or they'll just kill us.'

He kept swallowing over and over, his mouth dry. 'I'm just going to run, or give myself up to the cops. I—'

'Don't. They'll go after Annie, after Dad. We need to handle this.'

'But I can't. I botched everything, Mike. We're done—'

'It's not over. I told you, I have a plan.'

'What?' Jack demanded.

'You guys are pretty fucking chatty back there,' Lynch

shouted through the metal partition that separated the cab from the cargo area.

'Just going over the last details,' I said.

Lynch's man came back with the food and set it down on the seat beside me. I heard Lynch say something to Irish.

I reached into the takeout bags and checked the order.

'Okay. Search them,' Lynch ordered.

'Stand up,' Glasses said as he slid the door shut behind him.

'What?' I asked.

'Just making sure you're all squared away,' Lynch said from the front seat. 'I'd hate to have any surprises.'

Glasses started searching Jack. They knew I'd pull something. If they found my fake directives, this was all over. I eased the papers out of the binder where I'd hidden them, and waited as Glasses patted down Jack, poring over every bit of gear he was carrying for the heist. He had to crouch down to search, and as he came around the seat, I slipped the papers to my brother.

Jack looked confused for a second but took them, and slipped them between the seat cushion and his leg as he sat back down.

Glasses checked me next, feeling around my waist and in my groin and my armpits. His fingers went past my cuffs, but he didn't seem to feel the tiny cylinder inside. As he ran his hands down my front, he passed right over the ceramic razor, but it was small enough, like a two-inch section of fretsaw blade, that only I felt it. It pricked my skin.

'They clean?' Lynch asked.

His sidekick looked me over again. I could swear he was staring at that razor, though it was pretty hard to be sure where his gaze was aimed. 'Yeah,' he said.

Lynch started the car.

'We need coffees, too,' I said through the partition.

'You just had some.'

'For the job. I can get anywhere in that building with two cups of coffee.'

'Fine,' Lynch said. There were four Starbucks within a one-block radius. Irish ran down the street and came back with two paper cups in a carrying tray.

We pulled up around the corner from the Fed. The police would be on top of anybody double-parking a van on that block, so we were going to stop only long enough to jump out.

The van door banged open.

'Don't fuck this up,' Lynch said.

Jack and I grabbed our gear and stepped out.

'I'm going to run, Mike,' Jack said as we started down Maiden Lane.

We were fifty feet from the entrance, fifty feet from the van. The police were already watching us.

'Don't.'

'Tell me why I shouldn't.'

'They'll kill you.'

'Eventually, but not here, not in broad daylight.'

I had to tell him or else he would ruin everything. If this job went south, it would take more than me and Annie with it. They would go after my father. They would hang me with the murder on the Mall. Pulling it off and feeding them the false info was the only way I could bring them down, the only way I could win Annie back.

And so I had to choose: After everything, could I trust Jack? Had the fear for his life finally put some honesty into him? I remembered him bleeding out in his kitchen, lying on the floor unconscious, nearly dead.

He was my only brother. People can change. I let him in.

'Those papers I gave you,' I said. 'I can blow up Lynch and Bloom and whoever's running them. I'm going to pull a switch. Whatever the directive says, I have a forgery that says the opposite. When we get out of this, we'll give Lynch the wrong info. They're going to get their faces ripped off by the markets. We'll take them down at their own game.'

He felt for the forgeries I had slipped him.

'You still have them?'

'Yes.'

Lynch was watching us from the van.

'Those are the only things holding off our death sentence, so hang on tight.'

'You trust me with them?'

'You're the most deceitful bastard I've ever met, but you're still my brother. We've got to do this together. We have to trust each other, Jack, or we're dead.'

'Thank you, Mike. God. I'm sorry for everything. I'm sorry.'

'Save it.' I turned toward the Fed. If I was wrong about Jack, he would bury me. But there was one thing about Jack that I could be absolutely sure of. And that was going to save my life.

Jack's radio buzzed. He lifted it and tapped out a message as we walked toward the Fed doors.

'What's up?' I asked.

'Nothing. Everything looks good. Let's go.'

Chapter Forty-Three

Federal Reserve Police guarded the front doors, but there was something off. There were twice as many as usual, and a lot of them carried assault rifles and wore SWAT gear. Maybe the crackdown at the Board of Governors after Sacks's death had been extended to New York. Maybe they were just on high alert because it was such a historic Fed Day. Or maybe they had run our Social Security numbers and they had come back sour.

I walked up to the two cops at the Maiden Lane entrance.

'Hi,' I said. 'We have an appointment with Steven Merrill in Human Resources.'

They looked at the bags of food, then at each other. I guess Steven shook down his fair share of people for lunch.

I transferred the take-out order to one hand, took out my wallet, and handed over the fake license. Jack held the coffees in their cardboard tray and showed his.

The guard radioed in. 'Wellpoint Fitness?' he asked.

I just pointed to the logo on my vest. With our lack of sleep, injuries, and red eyes, nothing about Jack and me suggested health.

'You should come check us out,' I said. 'I can send you a guest pass.'

He listened to his radio earpiece.

'Maybe not today.' He stepped to the side. 'Reception will give you a badge.'

We walked through the door. A guard at a desk gave us clip-on visitor badges, then directed us toward the X-ray machine. Employees streamed past toward the mantraps.

We waited behind a pair of Italian tourists in puffy coats.

'Next,' the guard said, and waved me forward. I stepped through the magnetometer: not a chirp. The conveyor on the X-ray machine backed up as he examined our bags.

I stared at him nervously, like he was a judge presiding over me. He gave me an odd look back.

Our bags emerged. The Federal Reserve cop at the end of the X-ray waved his card in front of the mantrap.

We were in. He told us to wait for our man from HR near the elevator doors. I kept my elbows wide in my best gym-rat posture as the elevator numbers ticked down. A doughy man with a beard stepped out of the door.

'Oh, you brought lunch,' Merrill said as he introduced himself. 'I was just joking around. But thank you.' He hadn't been joking, but I guess he was covered if they came down on him for accepting gifts. We followed him to a second-floor suite where a half-dozen heads rose like prairie dogs from the cubicles. I placed the food out on a side table near the conference room, pulled out a take-out menu from one of the bags, and put it in my back pocket.

Merrill sat down with us in his cube and dug into a plastic takeout tray of pad prik khing. He was clearly just hearing us out for a free lunch, but still I was impressed by Jack's gusto as he marketed our nonexistent gym. I was actually worried Merrill would want to sign up on the spot; I didn't have the papers for that.

As Merrill looked around for more to eat and Jack said something about Zumba, I checked my watch. Five till noon. The committee was sealing its decision as we spoke. The directive would be here soon. Time to go.

'Well,' I said, 'we can leave you some of these materials. Then call back about maybe setting up one day in the cafeteria or break room?'

'We'll see,' Merrill said. 'They can be a little weird about vendors.' Stomach full, he was now cooling us out. He must have thought he was quite the operator.

I stood. 'Great. We'll talk soon.' We shook hands and left.

We took the elevators up to six, then ducked into the bathrooms that were just around the corner. We grabbed two stalls and switched out our visitor badges for the hard passes that Cartwright had mocked up from my photos. The bathroom is the one spot you're guaranteed freedom from security cameras.

Jack pulled the dummy crypto card out of his laptop and handed it to me under the partition. I slipped it in my pocket, then exited the stall and grabbed the two cups of coffee from the counter by the sink. I shoved the carrying tray and the gym vests we had been wearing deep into the trash.

We walked out. Jack carried a notebook computer in one hand and the backpack in the other, looking every bit an overworked IT guy.

On the way back to the elevators I glanced out the windows at Maiden Lane: more SWATs had arrived. They were blocking off the street at both ends. What the hell was going on?

We took the elevator up to nine, where the trading desk was located. I hadn't had a chance to check out the security on this floor when we had first cased the Fed. At the end of the elevator banks was a small reception area with a manned desk. It seemed like the least they could do, considering the keys to a four-trillion-dollar portfolio lay behind those doors.

I was carrying a coffee in each hand, and Jack was looking down at his laptop. We walked slowly down the hall as we hashed out the finer points of some urgent-sounding tech nonsense. It was a stalling tactic to let a young woman go ahead of us.

'Fine,' I said. 'We'll start with your BackTrack Live, and when that doesn't work, we'll go with Knoppix.'

We followed her, keeping up the patter. The technique is known as tailgating, and it's a lot easier than picking locks. You need a good excuse for having the doors held. That's why two coffees will work as surely as a skeleton key to open any door. People are fundamentally nice, or at least afraid of confrontation and getting dressed down if they're wrong. She held the door for a moment and glanced back at me and Jack, who also had his hands full.

You need to look the part. She did a quick visual check that we were wearing hard passes, and that was it. This was a relatively security-conscious place, so at least she looked. The most severe facilities try to drill a 'challenge mentality' into their workers. You don't just check the badge; you slam the door in the person's face and make them swipe in. But like most stringent measures, that is such an off-putting hassle that people just ignore it. As long as you project an attitude of total confidence that you belong where you are, you'll be fine. One glimmer of doubt and it all falls apart.

She watched us enter behind her. I smiled. She gave me a nod. We were in. Even though our badges had no working chips, they had just ushered us into the heart of the Fed. That saved us the technical hassles of trying to actually clone an RFID or hack the administrator's database to add our cards.

I tapped out a message to Lynch: 'Act up.'

That was the last step before we took the desk. I paused, and took a deep breath. At least we were past the door.

It opened again behind us, and an older black man with close-cropped hair stepped out. I recognized him from the desk out front.

'Excuse me,' he said.

'Yes,' I said.

'You gentlemen work on this floor?'

'We're with information security,' I said.

He tilted his head, examined our passes. You always want to backstop any fake identity: Xerox repair, FedEx, and so on. The bigger the organization the better, so it's hard to track you down. You give any challenger a phone number and have someone answer and vouch for you. But we needed to be Fed employees for this, and if this guy checked us out internally, we were done.

'Who called for you?' he asked.

I looked down at my phone. 'Workstation 923. It's—'

Jack looked at his laptop.

'Tara Pollard.'

He held his chin, looked us over again. 'One second,' he said, and took out his cell phone. He was going to call down.

I checked my watch. The timing was razor tight. I had sent that note to Lynch to trigger our malware, make Pollard's computer act so strangely that our target would have to notice it, which would give us an excuse to be in the suite. If we were too early, we'd be caught out, responding to a problem that didn't exist. Too late, and she would have already called down to IT, and when they arrived they would know we were frauds.

'Stay right there,' he said, and began to dial. Jack shot me a panicked look.

Chapter Forty-Four

I was so absorbed by our impending doom that I hadn't seen the alarmed woman coming up behind us.

'Are you with IT?' she asked.

'Yes. We noticed some unusual network traffic. Are you in 923?'

'Thank God. It's over here.'

She walked us past the man from the front desk. He closed his phone, gave us a last suspicious look, and walked toward the front door.

The pulsing heart of American capitalism was actually a bit of a letdown. It didn't look too different from a local bank branch. A conference room with a chest-high glass partition of wood and glass filled most of the space. Seven traders sat at computers along the wall, quietly steering the fate of the economy with a few mouse clicks in between sips from their water bottles. Cubicles filled most of the floor. High arched windows flooded the room with sunlight. An older man walked over to the traders and conferred with them for a moment.

I guess I expected a chaotic trading pit with people shouting orders, signaling trades, and raining down paper tickets. But this was everything the Fed tried to be: slow and deliberate, a deep keel on the economy. It would have been interesting to see how calm things were at 2:15, when the decision went public and the markets went berserk, but I would be long gone by then.

All was not well in workspace 923. Lynch had outdone himself with the malware. As we neared her cubicle, I could see a dozen pop-ups: 'Click here!' 'You won a free iPad!' 'Your computer has been compromised!' 'Virus alert!' The printer nearby was spitting papers onto an overflowing stack in the tray.

'I don't know what's going on,' she said.

'Hmm . . .' Jack said. We stepped into her cubicle.

It was noon. The decision would be here any second, if it hadn't arrived already, queued up in the fax waiting for her to log in with the crypto card.

'You haven't plugged any strange USB drives in here, have you?' Jack asked her. 'Or clicked on any PDFs from someone you don't know?'

'No.' We knew she'd taken the bait, because we had fed it to her. He looked at her with that special derision the computer-savvy reserve for their lessers.

'Well,' she said. 'There was one that looked like a newsletter, but it wasn't from communications.'

While they looked over the laptop, I walked over to her purse and did a quick dip looking for the card.

It wasn't there.

I waited until Jack distracted her with a detailed question, then pulled the purse open and scoured it. I'd seen RVs with less stuff inside. I shifted it one way, then the other.

No crypto card. Through the window in the main door of the suite, I saw the guard from the front desk. He wouldn't stop peering at me. Without that card we'd have to wait for the directive to come in, and then what? Peek over someone's shoulder? Tackle them and take it?

Jack looked at me, desperate: *get on with it*. I looked back toward the main door.

Maybe she had already taken out the card. I checked her mouse pad: left-handed. Then I looked at her left pants pocket, where there was a contour in the fabric. It could have been a wallet.

'I'll check the DNS name change,' I said and pointed at her chair. 'You mind?'

She stood up. I sat down. In the confines of the cubicle, there was nothing out of the ordinary about my hip brushing past hers. I could feel the card in her pocket. On top of all my crimes, I would now probably be arrested for trying to get into the pants of this efficient young woman.

Pickpocketing is all about attention. If you're looking at someone's eyes, they start to get very nervous when you're within a few feet. Look away, though, at the focus of his or her attention, and you can get within inches without setting off any alarms.

I stared at the screen and ran a few things from the Command prompt. It looked very technical, but I wasn't doing anything. Then I pushed back the chair, put my hand on the desk, dropped to one knee, and checked out the Ethernet ports.

When you're in someone's pocket, they're going to feel it, so you cover the touch. In this case I pushed the chair against her as I dipped two fingers into her pocket.

I had the card. Under the desk, I switched it with the dummy card I'd been carrying. On the way back up, I nudged the chair again and dropped the dummy into her pocket. When she did get around to checking the fax, she would get a card fault condition. By the time she sorted out why her card wasn't working, we would already have stolen the directive and be halfway back to DC. Or in handcuffs. Or dead.

I stood up. 'I'll check the other ports and the printer.' On my way over, I messaged Lynch: 'Stop printer.'

The guard from the front desk was now talking to someone on the phone, his attention fixed on me.

With the card palmed, I walked over to the fax. It was in an out-of-the-way cube. The only good thing I had going in my favor was that there were no security cameras aimed directly at the fax. In the highest-security areas, where restricted information is processed, you can't have a camera staring at the state secrets. It would give the bad guys a way to spy.

When we were rehearsing, I had told Jack there might be a mechanical lock to deal with before we could get to the fax. I knew there wasn't, but I had to guarantee that I would handle this part of the job myself.

I put the card in the slot on the side of the fax.

Please enter PIN.

I punched in the eight numbers.

PIN not recognized.

That was one attempt. Three wrong guesses would lock me out. I had divined the PIN from the pattern of Pollard's hand on the video. The last digit had been the least clear. I re-entered the first seven digits, then moved down one in the column for the last number.

PIN not recognized.

After all this work and all this pain, I was about to learn my fate standing in the middle of a badly lit cubicle, staring at the inky black-and-gray display of a fax machine like an intern. Whatever happened to Butch and Sundance?

I punched the PIN in again, and for the last digit moved from a six to a nine.

Secure access granted. 1 Fax in Queue . . .

I busied myself at the Ethernet ports, trying to look like my heart wasn't shuddering inside my chest at 180 beats per minute.

The fax let out a high electronic screech.

Printing . . .

To my mind it was an air raid siren, but apart from a look from one of the traders, no one seemed to notice.

Then Pollard glanced in my direction. I saw her reach down and touch her pocket.

The fax ran on a regular phone line and could receive both normal and encrypted transmissions. It would only print the encrypted material when the card was in and the PIN had been entered. She couldn't be sure I was receiving restricted information. And her card, she must have thought, was still safely in her pocket.

Jack said something to her. We had practiced a half-dozen terrifying-sounding computer security breaches to tell her about that would keep her occupied. Pollard blanched and looked down at the computer. He asked her to keep watch on a progress bar while he did something on his laptop. If the progress stopped, that meant there might be a serious data breach on Fed Day.

Heaven forbid. I watched the fax.

The cover sheet inched out. I saw the words form: 'Class I FOMC – Restricted Controlled (FR).' With every line return, every screech of the printer, I was sure the guard would come back, the real IT department would show up, the SWAT team downstairs would flood the suite with rifles drawn.

The cover page fell into the tray. Pollard stood up. She was examining the dummy crypto card, and me.

The text of the directive began to print. I saw it spool out, the boilerplate introduction that was always used. Through the main door, I could see the guard talking with a cop.

'The Federal Open Market Committee seeks monetary and financial conditions that will foster price stability and promote sustainable growth . . .'

We'd been made. I watched the paper crawl, an eighth of an inch at a time.

'To further its long-run objectives, the Committee in the immediate future seeks conditions in reserve markets consistent with . . .'

The main door opened. The guard stepped inside.

I waited, watching the fax.

And finally, I could see the numbers. I had the directive. The decision was in: they were going to keep the throttle open, keep pumping up the economy. That's all it was: a single paragraph in a dry government memo, a single number – the funds rate – but it was enough to shake the markets to their core, to pivot the global economy. There were billions funneling through those computers over my shoulder, and whoever held this number at this moment stood to make hundreds of millions trading ahead of the announcement. Yet after all I had been through, it seemed like such a small thing for all the trouble it had caused.

I pulled the directive out and read the next few lines. Then I dropped it into the locked bin for the paper shredder.

'What are you doing with that fax?' Pollard asked me across the room.

I ignored her. I needed one more second. I pulled another sheet from my back pocket, where it had been folded inside the take-out menu, and dropped that in for shredding as well.

I glanced back. The guard stepped out. I heard men moving fast down the hallways. Quiet time was over. Any second, the cops were going to burst through that door.

I pulled a blank piece of paper from the fax tray, scrawled a line on it, then folded it in half.

'Ports look good,' I said across the room to Jack. That was our code to get out.

I started walking toward the second exit, past the empty office of the executive vice president who ran the trading desk. He was in DC; the desk manager always attends the committee meeting. That's why I had planted my camera in his deputy's office. I dropped the paper to the ground, then slid it under his door.

Chapter Forty-Five

'I'm going to get another CD,' Jack said to Pollard. 'Could you keep your eye on that hourglass?'

The Federal Reserve Police were at the front door.

We fast-walked, then all-out sprinted, for the secondary exit, and made it to the stairwell.

'Stop!' someone shouted behind us.

I wrenched a piece of electrical conduit off the wall and wedged it across the landing between the door and the stair. I heard the cops banging on the other side.

We ran down one level. There were cameras everywhere. From the request-for-proposals and bids on renovations, I knew they had an access panel every three floors.

The Reserve Police watching the monitors were world class. The cameras were bulletproof. The security contracts to fill the place with all-seeing eyes had cost tens of millions of dollars. And the wires connecting it all? They were sitting in a sheet-metal box, protected by a two-dollar wafer lock.

We hid in a doorway. Jack pulled a keychain laser pointer from his bag and aimed it at the camera. That would blind it, but central control was sure to notice the flaring.

'I can maybe crawl up and smash it,' Jack said.

'Give me your bag.'

He handed it over. I reached in, pulled the tab out of the

end of the binder, and dumped my picks into my palm. I used a C rake and had the panel open on the third pull.

'They'll be here any second,' he said.

There were an awful lot of wires.

'I think the camera's red,' I said. That detail hadn't been in the RFPs.

'I thought it was green.'

'You sure?'

'No.'

A black dome of smoked glass housed the camera, which meant it was a pan-tilt-zoom type. An empty shell would have been just as effective a deterrent, because you never know when they're watching. Most cameras with conspicuous blinking red lights *are* fakes, just as intimidating to bad guys and cheaper than the real thing.

With the green light of Jack's laser shining through the smoked glass, however, I could see the hardware inside slowly panning back and forth as it monitored the flight of stairs.

I pulled the twist nut off a connection in the green wires and slowly separated the copper strands. A fire alarm suddenly shrieked and strobed above our heads. I jammed them back together.

'Okay, red.' I pulled the red wires. The stairwell plunged into blackness. I groped in the dark until I'd managed to get them back together, then twisted the nut back on.

'Blue?'

'Blue,' Jack said with a nod.

I pulled blue, and watched Jack's laser shine through the housing. The camera stopped.

'Which exit?' he asked.

'Maiden Lane.'

It was on the north side, on a floor higher than Liberty Street.

We sprinted down the stairs until the muscles in my legs were on fire, then stopped at the door that led to the rear lobby where we had first entered. There were normally four police officers at the mantraps, but now it was a wall of black uniforms. Clearly the alarm had been called. We didn't have a chance. Why was there so much extra security today? Had Bloom and Lynch called them in?

We descended another level, to the larger, south lobby, the bank's old public entrance. I peeked through the window. It was even worse.

'What the hell are we going to do?' Jack asked. 'The tunnels?'

I thought through my planning, the escape work. 'It's all sealed. Heading closer to the vault will only make it worse. We have to get to the loading dock. It's the only way.'

'They had four cops there,' he said.

I heard footsteps above us on the stairs, the squawk of a radio, more police. 'It's our last chance. Let's go.'

We went back up a level, toward the cops. I killed the cameras through the access panel, and we exited the stairwell and took a quick right into a corridor. It went straight for a hundred feet, and then turned left. Heading that way should have led us around to the loading dock.

I could hear the door open and close once more behind us, the police closing in as we made the left-hand turn. We entered a long, wide hallway that ran toward the dock. There was only one other door, ahead on our right, set back a few feet in an alcove.

I started down the hallway, and we had made it about twenty feet when I saw the barrel of an assault rifle poke out at the far end of the hall, between us and our exit, about two hundred feet away. Two more guns appeared.

It was the SWAT teams, coming our way. Jack and I stopped dead and threw ourselves into the alcove. I reached up and tried the knob behind us: locked, no time to pick it. We were stuck. Any minute, either the cops or the SWAT guys would pass us and we'd be cowering in plain sight. It was over.

The dive had wrenched the stitches in my back. I could hear the beeps and chatter on the radios of the cops following us, coming closer, about to turn the corner we had just made.

'Whoa!' a shout echoed down the hallway from the direction of the SWAT team. 'You can't be in this hallway.'

They had seen us. I took another look at the lock. It was probably better to give ourselves up than surprise a bunch of heavily armed crack shots in riot gear. I looked at Jack. He shook his head.

'Federal Reserve Police!' came the voice of one of the cops who'd been following us. They must have already come around the corner and were standing close by.

The SWATs yelled back, 'This hallway has to be clear for special operations. We have a gold handoff. Didn't you hear the comms?'

They hadn't seen us. They were hailing the police behind us.

'We have a potential breach,' the cops shouted back. 'Did you see anyone run down this hallway?'

Whoever was speaking for the gold team laughed. 'We've got eighty-five million dollars of bullion over here. Anyone running this way would be long gone. You'll need to clear the hallway.'

'Okay, okay.' I could hear the Reserve Police retreat. A door closed behind us, the way we had come. The police would leave us alone for a moment, but it was only because some jumpy commandos were coming our way.

A gold shipment was rolling through. That explained the extra security and the street closings.

I saw Jack glowering at me, as if I could have predicted this disaster. I was already on my feet, examining the lock. It was the electronic card-and-code that Cartwright had shown me how to bypass. We might make it out of this.

But then my stomach turned. Above it was a brand-new Medeco M3, the sort you might install if you found out your $1,300 electronic lock was useless.

We'd have been better off charging the assault rifles at the end of the hallway. The M3 is the lock of choice for government and intelligence agencies. It's on the White House and the Pentagon. It was the direct descendent of the Medeco that had defeated me during Lynch's tryout, three generations more advanced. It usually leads a locksmith to say 'To hell with it,' put his picks down, and drill out the shear line. A break-in artist would just smash a window or call it a day.

I didn't have those options.

I could feel the floor rumble as the gold rolled toward us, slowly but surely. There was no way I had time to pick this beast.

I stabbed the LED on the card-and-code with a pick, shorted the board, and turned the handle. Then I slid a pick across the card-and-code's bolt to keep it open so I wouldn't have to deal with it anymore. That took about four seconds.

The gold rumbled closer. I could hear *clank clank, clank clank, clank clank* over and over again, like footsteps but louder, metal on concrete.

The M3 is something of a fetish object among lockpickers because of its difficulty. On top of the mushroom, spool, and serrated pins, there were new ARX designs: harder to rotate, with false gates to throw off pickers. I had to move them all to the shear line and then set the rotation on each one to allow the sidebar to retract.

Even if I managed those two miracles, I wouldn't be done. Finally, there's the slider: a third piece of brass that stops the key from turning unless it's pushed forward to the correct position. The normal feedback that tells you when a pin has set is a thousand times harder to feel with all those extra pieces securing the cylinder. There were two trillion possible combinations of pin heights, angles, and slider positions, and only one will open the goddamn thing.

I had to find the right one, and here's why real-life lock-picking is hard: I had to do it through the tiny, oddly shaped keyway in the front of the lock while fear tightened my gut into a hard black ball. Imagine trying to change all the spark plugs on your car engine. With the hood open one inch. And a drunk guy driving.

That was my task. I figured I had a minute or two until the SWATs arrived, maybe enough for a lock with only security pins if I was lucky. There would be no gimmicks or easy bypasses, just the slow, painstaking work, millimeter by millimeter, of metal on metal and the feel in my fingers. I put a light torque on the plug with my tension wrench and started setting the pin heights.

I felt the ground shake as they wheeled the gold closer. I knew it was impossible. But I couldn't give up.

It took a minute to set the pins to the shear line. Step one seemed complete, but there was no way to know for sure.

Clank clank. I could hear the footsteps of the SWAT team, hear the rattle of their gear coming closer.

I took out a thin wire with a right-angle bend at the end to start playing with the rotations, feeling for the faintest possible give while trying not to screw up the up-and-down set on each pin.

I cleared from my mind the images of Jack and me, lying here in our own pooling blood, two up-and-coming fitness sales professionals who had met a bad end. I cleared from my mind the vision of Annie in the courtroom gallery as I was found guilty of a long list of crimes culminating in Sacks's murder. I cleared from my mind the image of Lynch standing behind me again, shutting his eyes in anticipation of the gore as he pressed the gun to my skull.

And I cleared the sidebar.

Clank clank. God it was loud.

'They're right here,' Jack whispered in my ear.

I could hear the SWAT team's breath, feel the vibrations from the gold shaking in my fingers, threatening the balance I'd managed inside the brass labyrinth of the Medeco.

I should have been elated by the sidebar's release, but something was wrong. I could still feel it binding. A pin had dropped, or had tricked me the first time around. One by one, keeping just the right tension on the wrench to hold everything in place, I tried them all again. It was number four in a false set.

'Okay,' I heard a voice say. 'Let's do a quick count.'

He started tallying the bars. He sounded as if he was right next to me.

Jack crouched. Sweat matted his hair, and I could see the ugly cut Lynch had given him. He went through the picks and took a W rake in his hand. The W looks like a saw blade at the end. He held it like an ice pick. Terrific. We could give some poor clerk a puncture wound while the guards filled our bodies with NATO rounds. I didn't mind ruining my own life, but on top of it I was going to get an innocent man hurt because I was too incompetent to play out my own crook fantasy.

The clerk kept counting.

I eased pin four up a click and then another, feeling my way past the serration to find the real shear line. The cylinder gave the subtlest motion. The pin resisted my pressure, stronger now, surer. I had it. But the rotation was now off. I held everything steady, picked up my right-angle wire, and felt along the bottom of the pins.

'All here,' the clerk said. They started toward us.

The fluorescent lights threw their shadows across me and Jack.

Jack rose onto the balls of his feet.

I pushed the slider forward, slowly, until it clicked. The cylinder spun. I eased the door open.

I forgot the pick I had left across the bolt of the card-and-code. It fell. I reached for it as it rotated slowly through the air toward the hard floor.

They would hear it. They would know.

Jack was already there. He snatched it inches from the ground.

I grabbed his shirt and hauled him through the doorway behind me. I threw the door closed. At the last second before it slammed, I stopped it, held the bolt back, and eased it gently into the frame.

All I could hear in the dark was our breath. I knew the direction we had gone put us closer to the far end of the loading dock. My eyes adjusted. I could make out the contours of the room in the glow of a few LED lights. There were benches along both walls and a huge balance scale in the middle of the room.

I heard a key in the doorway behind us.

We were in the count room. No wonder it had a Medeco on the door. They were coming in to double-check the gold.

'Hide,' I said. Jack and I threw ourselves onto shelves under the tables. I lay on a lumpy pile of plastic packages. An odd smell, like an old penny jar, drifted up.

The door opened. Light flooded the room.

Chapter Forty-Six

'I'll just grab them,' I heard the clerk say. He clomped into the room. The door shut behind him. All I could see was his black comfort shoes with metal caps strapped over the toes. The vault keepers wore them so that gold bars wouldn't shatter their bones if dropped.

Clank clank.

The shoes moved toward me, reminding me absurdly of a knight. Jack and I were staring at each other, looking and feeling totally exposed. In the light, I could see what Jack and I were lying on: bundles of currency.

The Fed distributes $550 billion a year in cash. Money goes into straps of a hundred bills, then bundles of ten straps, then bricks of four bundles shrink-wrapped together. Finally there are cash packs made of four bricks – 16,000 notes – bound together in thick plastic, as big as a microwave.

I was reclining on a hard bed of tens of millions of dollars. Next to my head lay transparent plastic bags with tamperproof openings that were full of used currency stained red and black: blood.

The clerk started singing a pop country song as he shuffled his legs a foot and a half from my face.

The Federal Reserve banks handle contaminated currency. While reading everything I could about the place, I'd seen the video about it on their website, with the same droning narrator

and 1980s actors from the vault video. They all seemed remarkably calm, given the subject matter: *So you have a blood-soaked
hoard of cash . . .*

The Fed will swap it out for clean money and then destroy it.

I saw the vault keeper's hand come down with a clipboard.
He was looking for something. I heard the rustle of papers.

That gave me some time to examine our options. This was
a strong room. I figured it was for temporarily holding cash
from the loading dock that was in transit to the vault. We had
come through a door on one side, and there was another door
on the opposite end of the room, marked with an exit sign and
secured by another Medeco. But now, at least, we were inside,
and it's a hell of a lot easier to get out of a strong room than
it is to get in.

From what I knew of the layout, that door would lead us
to the loading dock, where armored cars parked for transfers.
With all the money in here, there were sure to be some heavily
armed guards watching it from the outside, even with another
Medeco on the exit door. If we somehow survived this SWAT
team, we still couldn't just waltz out.

But that door was our only shot.

The clerk hit the chorus, lost the words, tried a few different
arrangements, then settled on humming. 'Here you go,' he said
to no one. He opened the door and stepped back into the hall.

'Just a few things to sign,' he said. 'Then we can weigh.'

The door closed behind him. We only had a few seconds
until they would come back.

'The backpack!' I said to Jack.

He tossed it over as I stood and went for the exit to the
loading dock. I drew back the bolt, then pulled the rare-earth
magnet and slapped it to the frame over my head. I didn't
want a screaming alarm announcing our exit, and the magnet
would keep the sensor from tripping.

I opened the door six inches, glimpsed through, then stepped out. Jack picked up the backpack and followed.

I could hear the door on the other side of the strong room open as ours closed.

We stood in the rear corner of the garage, at the end of a short hallway. The garage and loading docks were all inside the building perimeter. Two vehicle entrances led to Maiden Lane.

An exhaust duct thrummed above our heads. SWAT team members covered both exits. An armored truck idled loudly in the bay. There was no way past them, but we couldn't go back.

I listened to the air rush by in the ducts above our heads.

'The money, Jack.'

'What?'

I turned to face him. He played dumb.

'You've been giving me that look since I was three,' I said. 'I'm not buying it. Whatever you took, I need it.'

'I don't know what you're talking about.'

'You're a thief. You were just lying on about thirty million dollars. Don't bullshit me. They have the serials. They bagged it already. It's worthless.' I didn't know if any of that was true, but this last part I was sure about: 'If you don't hand it over, we're dead.'

One of the guards stepped into our line of sight. We pressed ourselves against the wall, but if he looked our way he would see us. Jack pulled out a plastic bag full of hundred-straps. It was half a million dollars, give or take, some stained with blood.

I put my hand out. 'I trusted you, now you trust me.' He looked at the money once more, then handed it over.

I pulled the tape off the ductwork over our heads and bent out the thin galvanized steel. I could feel the air rushing in. I tore open the bag, peeled the strap off a bundle, and dumped it in, then another, then another.

Jack's eyes filled with horror.

'What the—'

Maybe he thought I'd finally cracked, or turned into some sort of potlatch radical. But soon he heard the shouts near the entrance. His eyes opened wide, and he started tearing the bundles apart and throwing them in after mine.

We were two blocks from Wall Street, the capital of American greed. I was counting on one thing to save us: that the bankers hustling down the sidewalks, with their cuff links and contrasting collars, weren't above chasing a little dirty money.

Cash streamed through the ducts and flew out the vents above the garage. A dye pack exploded and boomed further down the duct.

Jack started to move. I held him back.

After a few seconds, you could hear the beginning of the free-for-all. 'Stay back!' a cop yelled.

'Holy shit!' someone on the street shouted. 'Those are hundred-dollar bills!'

The police and SWAT teams fanned toward the entrances. We crept along the wall. The street scene absorbed all their attention.

I didn't know why they should be upset. Washington had just voted to keep propping up the economy. Jack and I were doing our small part to expand the monetary supply, same as the traders upstairs, though I think our approach was a lot more fun.

We could see Maiden Lane. The notes whirled and flipped through the air like autumn leaves. The crowds chased them down, stuffed them into their clothes. The police tried to hold them back, and here and there I could see that the cops weren't above snagging a hundred or two for themselves. They needed to keep the mob at bay, to keep people from rushing in, so two guys in white button-downs trying to get out weren't their top concern.

We hit the sidewalk and turned away from the main action.

The cold wind spun the bills into cyclones, lifted them high between the office towers, plastered them against the stone facades. I stepped through a brown puddle. Ben Franklin looked up at me through the murk.

It was beautiful. Secretaries, shawarma guys, bike messengers, bankers, tourists, movers, cabbies, all snatched hundreds from the air, bundled them to their chests, laughed and fought in the middle of the street.

Only two seemed not to care. Jack and I wove through the crowd, walking fast toward quieter streets, toward freedom.

Chapter Forty-Seven

Our meet-up with Lynch was near Pier 11 on the East River. As soon as we cleared the cops around the Fed, I grabbed Jack's arm.

'Give me the forged directives,' I said. We had to make the switch, then get as far away as fast as we could. We didn't have much time until 2:15. Before Lynch and Bloom realized they had been conned, I had to warn Annie and my father and get them to safety.

'I don't know, Mike.'

'Come on! We'll make the switch and take them down.'

He stepped back. 'I'm sorry, Mike.'

I turned, too late to get away, and saw Lynch and the man in glasses close in on me from both sides. Each grabbed an elbow and barred my arms behind my back.

'You fucking Judas,' I said to Jack.

His whole act before the heist, all that fear, must have been a ploy so I would tell him what I had planned to turn the tables on Lynch and Bloom. They knew I was going to pull something to make it blow back on them. Jack was their insurance, and once I revealed myself to him, they thought they had me covered. Only then would they let me do the job. That must have been the message Jack sent just before we went into the Fed.

'It was between setting you up and losing my life,' Jack said. 'What would you do?'

I knew. I had made the same choice before the heist, when I handed Jack those papers, but he didn't know it yet.

Lynch searched my pockets and found the directive.

As they marched me down Pearl Street, I tore into Jack some more, until Lynch clamped his hand over my mouth. I could taste and smell the tobacco on his skin. A van pulled up. They shoved us in the back.

As we drove down FDR Drive, I watched a ferry pull up to Pier 11. We U-turned, headed north, then exited toward the heliport over the East River. In the front seat, Lynch's man rested the directive on his leg, snapped a photo with a smartphone, and sent it off.

The van stopped. They pulled me out, and we walked toward a building of gray and white stone that occupied a pier. Behind it lay a helipad. The air churned and the blades deafened us as we crossed the landing area and climbed into a small chopper. It rose and spun. The city shrank below us.

As soon as the directive went to Bloom's and Lynch's boss, he would pull the trigger on tens, maybe hundreds of millions, of dollars' worth of highly leveraged trades, building a sure-thing position while the world waited to hear from the Board of Governors. After the decision went public, in less than two hours, he would collect his winnings and cash out.

'Where are we going?' I asked Lynch.

'You are a true pain in the ass, Mr Ford. We need to keep you buttoned up until two fifteen.'

I had tried to avoid helicopters in the navy, part of my living-past-thirty strategy, but had taken a few rides. I was used to jump seats, cold metal, and five-point restraints. This chopper was kitted out like a limo, with a bar and leather upholstery and copies of the *Financial Times* neatly stowed beside every seat.

We flew over the Hudson and the stone palisades on the Jersey side. It was less than ten minutes to Teterboro. We stepped out. A hundred feet across the tarmac, a private jet was waiting. As we climbed aboard, the pilots greeted us. A stunning stewardess gave me a smile. Once we were in the main cabin, Lynch handcuffed my wrist to an armrest.

I checked them out: Smith & Wessons. Good.

If you're planning on being kidnapped, I highly recommend a private flight. No bag check, no X-ray, no security line, shoes on and all the liquids you want, a huge seat, and a couch and bar in the back. It was a nice splurge on my way to my own execution.

We were in the air for just over an hour before we touched down at a small airport. Rolling hills stretched away on all sides.

As we taxied, I recognized the truck sitting on the tarmac. It was Bloom's Land Cruiser.

She was waiting for us on the airfield as Lynch dragged me out of the plane.

'Oh, Michael,' she said. 'We tried to warn you about being too curious. This is really a shame.'

Lynch slid a baton between my cuffed wrists and twisted it. The metal cut into my skin as he tightened the chains, growing visibly excited about the prospect of doing me harm.

'It would have been so easy if you had stayed in the dark. But now . . .' She shook her head.

Lynch squeezed harder.

'Load him up,' she told him. 'I'll take the other one.'

Jack walked to Bloom's truck and stepped in. His hands were free. Lynch shoved me into the passenger seat of a black van. I winced as the thin blade hidden in my shirt placket dug into my chest just below an old scar.

Lynch took the cuff off one wrist, and I could feel a painful burn in my pinky and ring fingers as the feeling came back. I felt only a second's relief before he slid the bracelet through the door handle, ratcheted it shut on my wrist, and double-locked both cuffs.

He took the driver's seat. Holding the wheel with his right hand, with his left he aimed his 1911 Colt pistol at my torso. I could feel blood trickle out from the cut just under my sternum. I leaned forward, trying to hide it and keep Lynch from finding that hidden razor.

'Seems like an awful lot of trouble just to find a good spot to kill me.'

'I agree. But she works in mysterious ways.'

I picked at the stitches on my shirt cuffs, feeling for the key. My hand had never healed quite right from my last time in cuffs, when I'd broken my thumb. Finally I felt that hard cylinder of plastic beginning to emerge from the cotton.

We twisted through wooded terrain, rising and falling with the hills. From the road signs I could tell we were somewhere in Virginia.

The trees cleared, and the road went downhill. There was a long curve as we approached a two-lane bridge over a shallow river valley at the edge of a town. The span was an old-fashioned arch of stone with sidewalks on both sides and metalwork lanterns hanging from poles.

I eased the cylinder out of my cuff. The bloodstain on the front of my shirt was the size of a quarter and growing. I had two things going for me. One was that Lynch always drove, some kind of control thing. And two, he was good about wearing his seat belt. Maybe he'd been in an accident once. I looked at the wedding ring on his gun hand. Maybe he had kids.

The curve before the bridge would require his full attention. I would have no better chance. I clicked open the tab at the end of the cylinder with my fingernail. I twisted it around in my fingers and put it in the keyhole on the cuffs, then waited until he looked at the road.

It was a sweeping left turn. When Lynch looked back, I'd

already taken the cuffs off one wrist and dropped the bracelet through the door handle.

He brought the gun up as he saw my hands moving. I knocked his gun arm forward with my left hand while I reclined my seat back with the lever on my right, laying it flat. The gunshot in that small space was deafening. It blew my window out in a shower of glass that cascaded over the hillside leading to the river below.

The shot was closer to his ears and had rattled him more than it did me. Leaning back, I grabbed Lynch's gun hand with my right and twisted the wrist a hundred and eighty degrees. With my left I grabbed his seat belt, pulled it up and back over his seat near his right shoulder, and choked him hard.

His face began to turn red, then purple as we rolled onto the bridge. I was hoping he'd bring the van to a stop rather than just punching it and killing us both. He let go of the wheel with his right hand for a second, reached down, and released his belt.

I still had his gun hand tied up. As the seat belt loosened and he reached back for the wheel, I sat up and threw my left arm around his neck. I settled it into a choke, dragging him across the center console with his throat in the V of my elbow.

His face was turned to the ceiling. Neither of us could see the road.

'Brake!' I shouted. He couldn't say anything through the choke, and given how far he'd come out of his seat I didn't even know if he could reach the pedals. His main goal seemed to be angling the gun, which was about six inches from my face, so he could kill me. I gripped his wrist and tried to aim the muzzle away from my head.

The van must have had decent alignment, because it seemed like a long time before we veered into oncoming traffic and clipped another car.

Metal shrieked. The van skidded and bucked hard to the

right, throwing us over my reclined seat toward the back seats. I let go of his gun hand for a second and reached back to brace myself.

I only succeeded in shoving the handle of the passenger-side sliding door. It flew back, wide open.

The collision knocked us away from the median. We jumped the curb and ran along the sidewalk, edging closer and closer to the railing and the long drop to the river.

I had the choke in deep. Lynch was lying half on top of me. We both faced the ceiling, far back on the tilted passenger seat, no one in control. He had no good angle to get me with the pistol now.

Lynch reached back with his right hand and drove his thumb into my eye. I twisted my head away, but suddenly neither the pain nor the gun seemed to matter.

I was slipping off the seat, toward the open door. Only my hips, pinned by Lynch's weight, kept me inside the vehicle. The last wheel jumped the sidewalk. The van shuddered, knocking me farther out. My head was hanging upside down, past the doorsill. The bridge's white stone parapet strobed past, coming closer and closer to crushing my head against the steel frame of the van.

I waited until the last second, dug my left arm into the choke, and groaned as I levered my torso up with every bit of strength I had. I pulled up just before the body of the van ground against the railing, raining sparks on the cement sidewalk.

We slowed, then stopped – as did most of the blood to Lynch's brain, from the look of him. He was like a rag doll. I relaxed the choke hold, then took a deep breath. I was draped over the seat with my head resting on the sill a couple of inches from the railing. It wasn't ideal, but at least I wasn't dead.

On my third breath, Lynch's body tensed. 'Christ,' I muttered. He started to turn over, his gun hand now free.

He aimed the pistol at my face. I grabbed his wrist and the gun with both hands and jerked it down beside my ear as I pressed both legs hard into his waist and sent him over the bridge railing.

I looked over. We were near the end of the span, and it was only a short fall to the brush on the hill below.

I glanced up and down the sidewalk. The driver of the other car had gotten out at the end of the bridge, the way we had come. He looked okay.

I stood on the sill, holding the gun by the barrel, and let the air fill my lungs, let the cramp in my forearm relax. Lynch had a nice pistol, a Wilson Combat.

Someone was coming from farther up the bridge. I took the gun by the grip. A man approached, walking down the center of our lane.

I aimed the pistol at his head. It was Jack. He approached the van.

'Hands, Jack,' I said.

'Are you okay?'

'You're suddenly concerned about my safety? Hands, or I kill you. And you will absolutely deserve it.'

He raised them. I didn't see any obvious signs that he was carrying. Bloom had been driving well ahead of us, but she must have seen something. She was now parked facing us at the end of the bridge, the direction Jack had approached from. I imagined there was plenty of hardware in her truck.

'I'm sorry, Mike. I had no choice.'

'I don't care why. I'm done with you. Step back.'

'At the end of the day, I knew they would kill me and you wouldn't. It's as simple as that. I'm your brother, and you're a good guy. Good guys don't kill people.'

That last bit was actually a matter of some debate between Annie and me.

'Stop pretending you're going to shoot me,' Jack said, and came toward the driver's side door. I ducked down, to have a clear shot through the van.

He started to lower his hand.

'I'm going to open this door, Mike.'

'I'll do anything to keep her safe. Don't test me, Jack. I *will* shoot.'

'You're a good guy, Mike. Now come out before you get hurt.'

He opened the door, leaned toward me, and filled his face with kindness.

I knew every line he might use, every gesture, every subtlety of speech to draw me back in. I'd seen them all before, whenever Jack made one of his offers. How many times had he leaned his head toward me with a sly look, a tightening of the eyes, a little roll of the fingers as he tried to pull me into the con?

I knew them because they were my father's expressions, because they were my own. But now there was something awfully strange about his face, about those eyes the same green as mine. Probably because it was my first time seeing them down the barrel of a gun.

I centered the sights on his face. He was my brother, sure. But how many times do you turn the other cheek? Where would it end if not now? He had ruined my life once before, left me to take the fall for the job that had nearly landed me in prison so many years ago. After all the suffering Jack had put me through, how much, really, did I care whether he lived or died?

'Last chance,' I said.

He moved closer. 'Come on, Mike—'

I tightened my hand. And Jack, for once, realized he had read me wrong. I saw the fear in him. I pulled the trigger. The gun jumped. My brother cried out in pain.

Chapter Forty-Eight

The driver's side window blew out. Jack dropped beside the van, hands to his face. I crossed over to the driver's seat. The door was still open. Jack lay on the ground.

He was screaming at me, a long string of curses, as he brought his hand down, then felt around his cheeks and eyes.

He must have thought I'd shot him in the face. And I could understand how he might take that the wrong way. I hoped Bloom would have the same impression, because I needed time.

'Stop being a baby,' I said as I reached down, covered by the open door, and pressed the gun to his head. There was a small cut on his cheek. 'I shot the window. It's a scratch from the glass. Now give me your cell phone.'

'What?'

'Your cell phone. I know they didn't have you locked down. Where is it? I have to make some calls.'

He pointed to his pocket. I pulled out the phone, then patted his waist.

'Where's your gun?' I asked.

'My back.'

'Roll on your face.'

He complied. I pulled a baby Glock out of an inside-the-waistband holster.

'You don't know me, Jack. And you're not as good at this as you think you are.' I gave him a light slap on the cheek. 'I win.'

I climbed into the van, slammed the door shut, and stomped the gas. My head pressed against the seat as I shot toward Bloom's truck. I veered left, across the double-yellow, then curved back at her truck.

I took a last look as Bloom stepped from the driver's side door and raised her pistol, then I dropped behind the dash. I could hear the shots plinking the hood of the van.

My face smashed into the steering wheel on impact. The van skidded to the side. Red and white lights filled my vision.

The van was still running. I'd spun around 180 degrees. Bloom's truck was halfway up the end of the parapet. I pressed down on the gas, more controlled this time, as I tasted the blood coming from my lip where it had hit the wheel.

I crunched into her rear bumper and hung her truck up on the railing, two wheels lifted in the air. Even with its high clearance, there was no easy way down from that, and I prayed this would buy me enough time to get away.

Bloom came up shooting from the brush. I reversed down the highway, botched a J-turn, and had to go up and over the curb to finish my turnaround.

The back windows and the passenger's side mirror exploded as I pulled away, but I was putting distance between us fast. I pulled some quick turns through the houses on the edge of town, then raced downhill toward a road along the river.

As I sped away, I lifted up Jack's cell phone. I needed to warn Annie.

Her phone rang and rang, then went to voicemail. I left the number, told her to call me immediately, that she was in danger.

I swerved down the country road, trying to figure out how to reach Annie and my father, how to get back to our house in Alexandria in time.

I tried our landline. No answer. I needed to reach her at work, but first I had to start another ball rolling. I called 911.

'What is your emergency?'

'I need the nearest Secret Service field office.'

'What is your situation?'

'I need the Secret Service. There's a threat. Or just give me the number and I'll call myself.'

'I'll connect you.'

The Secret Service has 150 field offices throughout the country. You can find them in the emergency pages of the phone book. I remembered what Cartwright had said: the Secret Service does computer and bank fraud. As soon as Jack and I stepped into the Fed, we were the Secret Service's problem, and could sidestep Lynch's pull at the FBI. Before the job I didn't have enough evidence to take down Bloom and Lynch and their master, but now I had them cold.

'Secret Service,' a dispatcher answered.

'I need to report a serious crime.'

'When did it happen?'

'It's happening now.'

'Where?'

'The Federal Reserve Bank of New York.'

'And who are you?'

'I'm the guy who robbed it. I need to talk to a senior agent or an SAIC.'

'What is the nature of the crime?'

'We stole the directive, the decision from the open markets committee in DC. It's not public until two fifteen, and we're going to inside trade on it. You have no reason to believe me; I understand. But you can call the Fed. Confirm they have a breach. It's probably on the news by now. There's a camera hidden behind the senior vice president's desk in a baseball stand he received as a gift.'

'Hold please.' I heard a click. The Service deals with more than their fair share of cranks, so I expected some screening.

A moment later they connected me with a new voice, an agent.

'Did you hear what I said to the operator?' I asked.

'Yes. I'm going to connect you to New York, and they can check this out.'

'Don't. I'm already in Virginia. All of the culprits are. I'm going to give you some more info so you can check my story. Are you ready?'

'Go ahead.'

'There's a virus we planted on the computer in workspace 923. And the PIN code to the secure fax on the trading desk is 46195019.'

I heard him typing, taking it down.

'And there's a note,' I went on, 'in the office of the SOMA desk manager, the executive vice president.'

'A note?'

'Yeah. It says, "I just stole the directive."'

'Seriously? You expect me to—'

'Just call New York and confirm.'

'Who are you?'

'No names,' I said. 'But I'll give you my address.'

He took it down. I told him to write down the trades to watch for, to confirm the insider information. And then I hung up.

I figured the Secret Service might have people not far from the address I had given them. There's a secure site called Mount Weather in the Blue Ridge Mountains, a little over an hour from DC. It's a bunker built into the mountainside, set to serve as the seat of government in case of an emergency. It's where they kept stashing Dick Cheney after the September 11 attacks.

Next I called 411. I had almost forgotten it existed. I asked for Annie's office. They put me through. The receptionist at her firm connected to her desk, but there was no answer.

Where was she? I called again, and asked for a friend of hers in the same practice group. She picked up.

'It's Mike Ford. I'm sorry to bother you at work, but I need to find Annie. She's in danger.'

'I don't think she wants to talk to you, Mike.'

'Do you know where she is?' It's never a good situation when you are consciously trying not to sound like a stalker.

'I can't tell you. But she said she's going someplace safe. I have to go. I'm sorry, but I can't get in the middle of—' she started to beg off.

I hung up. *Someplace safe.* I knew where she was going. I'd told her to go there myself. And right now it was the most dangerous place she could be. It was the address I had just given the Secret Service.

I slowed, palmed the wheel, and pulled a U-turn across the double-yellow.

All I wanted to do was get away, to take her and my father and run from the violence coming for us.

But now I had run into the fire.

Chapter Forty-Nine

I tore down the byways at seventy miles an hour. The roads were mostly empty as I navigated from memory: the farm stand, the gun shop, the country store. I'd been here many times.

It was almost two p.m. The announcement was at two fifteen. I would be at ground zero when it all fell apart.

I pulled off the road about fifty feet from the entrance to the estate and came to a stop surrounded by shrubs and towering oaks. On the hill where the main mansion stood, I could see the circular driveway. Annie wasn't here yet. I could catch her before they did. I had a decent view of the road. I would wait and flag her down, jump out in front of her car and hope she was still fond enough of me to stop.

I chewed the nail of my thumb while I watched the clock count down.

After ten minutes, I leaned over to check the cell phone.

'Hands!' someone barked.

Lynch came from the passenger side, where I was blind since Bloom had blown the side mirror off.

I dropped, grabbed the pistol, and rolled out the driver's side door. I circled toward the front of the van. We aimed straight for each other's heads. He had scratched the side of his face up pretty bad when I had thrown him into the brush, and I gathered he was looking forward to revenge.

'Boys and their guns.' I turned to see Bloom cross the

road, her pistol aimed at me. My chances in this fight plummeted.

'Finger off the trigger, Mike. Hold it by the barrel. Place it on the ground and back away,' Bloom said. 'I'd prefer not to kill you here.'

I stood there, figuring my odds and my outs. They weren't good. Before I could say or do anything, I heard another car, and then caught a glimpse of Annie's Accord curving down the hill, coming from the opposite direction.

'I've got him covered,' Bloom said to Lynch. 'Why don't you go say hi to Annie? I don't think she'd be very happy to see me.'

Lynch started off. Bloom reminded him to keep his radio on as he jogged past the entrance to the driveway. The road curved slightly, but through the brush I could see Lynch as he stepped into the roadway in front of Annie's car.

The Accord came screeching to a halt.

Bloom held a radio in one hand and kept her gun on me.

'You may believe that *you* are some kind of martyr, Mike, but I don't see you letting Annie die. So please, stop with the drama and put the gun down, and we can sort this out like grown-ups.'

'I don't think so.'

She seemed surprised. 'You see Annie?' she asked.

I peered around the car. I could barely make her out, but I could hear her cursing at Lynch, clearly shaken up after he had stepped in front of her car. She was leaning out the driver's side window. Lynch stood in the road, turned slightly to conceal the gun he was holding next to his right thigh.

Bloom lifted the radio. 'Put it down, Mike, and play nice, or I'll let him kill her. Just between us, I'm starting to have my worries about him. I think he gets off on it.'

If they'd just come after me, I don't know what would have

happened. I was high on adrenaline and pain, in the mood to burn everything down to the ground. But with Annie at the point of the gun, the game was over.

Or that's what they assumed. And my only strength in all this was that they really had no idea who they were dealing with. Annie thought she knew me. So did Jack. So did Bloom.

But they had a lot to learn.

'Now, Mike. Or she dies.' Bloom spoke so confidently.

'Please.'

For once, she was rattled.

'Sorry?'

'Go ahead,' I said.

She swallowed and pressed the button on the radio. I could hear the faint static on the open channel. 'We'll kill her.'

'Will you?'

I could see the muscles tense in her forearm, the doubt creep into her eyes, but that was it. No command. No shot.

'You want her to die?' Bloom shouted.

'I see right through you, through all this.'

She lowered the radio.

'Good,' I said. 'I'll take that as confirmation of who you're working for.'

'Annie, run!' I yelled. 'He's got a gun!'

I stepped toward Bloom, steadied my gun with both hands. She spoke into the radio to Lynch: 'Forget the woman. Get back here.'

Now that she had lost her leverage on me and we were in a fair fight, Bloom didn't seem so excited about our standoff.

Lynch ran away from Annie's car, toward me and Bloom.

'Hey! You broke my—' I heard Annie shout after him. She followed him slowly in her car. 'What are you doing in the middle of the road? Are you all right?'

As she moved closer, my face-off with Bloom came into full view. Annie stepped out of the car.

'Mike? Is that – what the hell is *she* doing here? Is that a gun?'

'Run!' I shouted.

She paused, then jumped back into her car. I saw Lynch hesitate as she started the engine, unsure whether to cover Bloom or keep Annie under control. I moved toward him, training my gun at his head.

'I'm the one you want,' I said.

He turned back to me. That gave Annie a chance to hit the gas and throw the car through a U-turn. The wheels spun out in the dirt on the side of the road and kicked gravel our way. She straightened out the car and the engine revved high as she shot away.

Lynch and Bloom had me covered. I didn't like the new math.

'Now put the gun down, Mike. It's really a pain in the ass to kill you in the middle of a public roadway. Play along and we'll take it easy on you.'

I watched Annie disappear around the curve. Of course I wanted her to get away. I was happy to give myself up to save her. But I could have used a half-second of hesitation, a wistful backward glance, maybe even an 'I won't forget you' before she left me behind with the killers. Just something for old times' sake.

'Okay.' I pulled my finger out of the trigger guard, grabbed the barrel of the gun with my left hand, and raised both arms.

'On the ground,' Bloom said. 'Then step away from it.'

I complied.

'Hands on top of your head. This way.'

They walked me back down the road, Lynch in close with the gun and Bloom covering me at a distance. I could see her truck hidden in the woods on the opposite side of the road.

'It's a shame, Mike. I was really starting to enjoy all this cat-and—'

The blasé tone she was aiming for lost some of its punch as the tail end of her remarks were swallowed up by the sound of an engine with the throttle wide open. It was a solid 3.5-liter V6 that I kept in good shape. Annie had gone for the six-speed manual in the Accord. She liked driving. The car didn't look like much, but it roared like a jet as it bore down on us.

The impending crash distracted Bloom and Lynch. I had time to take two giant steps toward the side of the road.

They could have shot her, but that would have left them with no time to get out of her way, so they dove off the road on Annie's passenger side and landed in a ditch choked with weeds. I threw myself onto the asphalt on the driver's side.

Annie skidded to a halt just past us. Bloom and Lynch started climbing out of the ditch, guns in their hands. I sprinted for Annie's rear door, threw it open, and jumped in.

She had a Kabuki look: face white, eyes wide, breath coming fast.

'Go go go!' I yelled.

I could see she was pretty tuned up. She slammed it into reverse and flew back past the entrance to the estate. I could hear glass tinkling, then something shatter as she hit the brakes hard and turned up the drive toward the house. Shards littered the floor mats. I recognized Annie's centerpieces. They must have crashed when she stopped short for Lynch.

'Not that way.'

She looked at me in the rearview.

'You're not giving orders. Understood?'

I sat on the center of the rear bench, leaning forward, my arm resting on the passenger seat. Halfway up the winding driveway, Annie stopped the car. She looked in the rearview. There was no sign of Lynch and Bloom in pursuit.

Maybe they were scared of the small army of security guards that roamed the estate, but I didn't think so.

'Thanks for coming back,' I said.

'I didn't come back for you. I came back for those two.' She gestured with her head toward the roadway where she'd left Bloom and Lynch. 'They fucked with the wrong woman.'

She turned and looked at me, saw the blood staining my shirt, my eye scratched and red from Lynch's gouging. I thought maybe she would finally see that I had done all of this to hold off the threats against her. She grabbed the sides of my head, pulled me forward, and gave me a long desperate kiss, then let me go. I started to smile, almost in tears with relief, and then she struck me, hard, across the face.

I fell back.

At least she hadn't left me for dead. It wasn't forgiveness, but it was a start.

Chapter Fifty

It was 2:13.

'We've got to get out of here. Annie, it's—'

'One more word and I'm handing you back to your girl-friend,' she said as we wound up the driveway. Attack dogs bounded alongside the car.

I had started to suspect it at the shower, but only since this morning had I been certain. Who was rich enough to bet tens of millions of dollars on the directive, to afford a mercenary like Bloom, to orchestrate all this? Who hated me that much? Who would be so hell-bent on setting me up as a criminal, on driving me away from Annie?

We pulled to a stop near the columned entrance.

'We're going inside.' Annie killed the engine and then stepped out. 'The security people will take care of whoever that was back there.'

I followed her along the white stone of the driveway, asking her to come back, to reconsider.

The dogs, silent except for their panting, shot toward me.

'Hutz!' Annie yelled. They sat, ten feet away with their black eyes fixed on me, slowly opening and closing their jaws and drooling. Two security guards stepped out from side entrances and flanked us.

Annie climbed the steps.

'Annie, don't,' I said. 'You're in danger. That's the only reason

I left with her that morning at the house. If I hadn't, they were going to kill you. They've been trying to set me up as a fall guy. They forced me. It was all against my will.'

'Enough, Mike. I'm so tired of it.'

'They shot me, Annie.' I lifted my shirt to show the rust-stained gauze on my lower back. 'That's why I was out all night.'

'God.'

'I was trying to protect you,' I said. 'We need to go. The man behind everything, the man who set me up—'

The front door opened before I could finish. Lawrence Clark stepped onto the porch, crossed his arms over his chest, and planted his thick legs like Atlas.

'It's your father, Annie,' I said. 'He's a killer.'

I held out my hand to her. 'Let's go.'

'Annie,' Clark said and moved toward her. 'Come inside, dear. Jesus Christ. Does he have a gun?'

I still had the 1911 in my belt. 'Wait,' I said.

'He's behind that murder on the Mall, Annie.'

'It wasn't me. It was all your father. He's stealing the Fed decision before it goes public. He's trading on it. That man on the Mall found out, so he was killed.'

'How do you know all this, Mike?' Annie asked.

'Because I stole it for him. Today, in New York. He was working through middlemen, coercing me, threatening Jack and me. It was all so he could have the numbers and I would take the fall. He was trying to keep us apart.'

'What are you talking about?' Annie asked.

Clark let out a laugh. 'He sounds very trustworthy. Now, Annie, come inside before this man hurts you.'

Every room in that house had a TV, all constantly tuned to Bloomberg News. Clark never had a conversation without half his attention directed toward the markets.

It was 2:15.

He glanced back inside to look at the TV just off the main foyer. The volume was way up, as you might expect when you had a few hundred million riding on the day's headlines.

'And we're hearing from the lockup that the FOMC statement might be a few minutes late,' the broadcaster said. 'I don't recall this ever happening before. Let's go to Jonathan Maurer in Washington.'

Standing just inside the door, Clark turned back toward us, then nodded to his guards. They pulled their sidearms and closed in.

I drew mine.

'Are you going to shoot me too, Mike?' He shook his head in disgust. 'This is the man you were about to marry,' he told Annie. 'Take a good look at him.'

She did. She'd seen me kill before. It had always felt like a bad dream remembered, an airless space, a break in our real lives. Yet here I was again, on the doorstep of her family home, drawing a gun on her father.

Reflected in the glass beside the doorway, I could see my haunted face, see the blood staining my teeth. Clark was winning. I looked every bit the killer Annie feared.

'Come inside, dear.' He held out his hand to her.

He wouldn't get rid of me in front of her, but if she went inside and left me alone with his guards, I was done. They would take me and hand me over to Lynch. Bloom would spin the story until all that was left were lies: that I had killed Sacks, that I was nothing more than a criminal.

Annie took a step toward him, then hesitated, looking back and forth between her father and me.

One day I had asked her if she would still love me if it meant losing everything. 'Of course,' she'd said.

Things change. She moved toward her father. Then she spoke. She wasn't seeking protection. She was looking for answers.

'Who were you arguing with on the phone, Dad?'

'What?'

'Last week in your office. You were shouting at someone. I'd never heard you sound so afraid. Who was it?'

'I don't remember that, Annie. There's no time. Please, love, come over here.'

'Tell me about Barnsbury,' she said.

'What?'

'Tell me how you built a billion-dollar fund so quickly when the markets had seized up.'

'Please, Annie.'

I kept my mouth shut, let her mind work. I must have planted the seed with the accusations at the shower, reinforcing some of her lingering suspicions.

'Tell me why we had to leave London so quickly when I was young,' she said.

I didn't need to convince Annie of anything, and I probably couldn't have if I tried. She made up her own mind, and clearly, she had done some homework.

'Mom said she'd tell me one day. But she never had the chance. So please, just tell me the truth.'

'Annie, I swear to you. He's lying. Look at him, for God's sake.'

The guards wavered. They wouldn't do it with her present. Her doubts were the only thing keeping me alive.

'Mike,' she told me, 'put the gun down.'

'That's right, dear,' Clark said.

I took my finger off the trigger, held the pistol in the air. Her father grinned. He was going to win.

'I'm not leaving him,' she said to Clark.

'Now, Annie, listen!' he said, but then the news broke through on the TV.

Chapter Fifty-One

'The Federal Open Market Committee has released its statement. Despite the growing dissent on the board, the Fed has recommitted to measures to stimulate the economy—'

Clark walked over to the TV. 'That's not right,' he said. Annie was stunned as she watched him walk away from her fate and an armed standoff to check his stocks.

He changed the channel to Fox Business.

'—decided on more of the same at what was certainly a contentious Fed meeting today—'

CNBC: '—keep the money flowing. They're not taking away the punch bowl anytime soon.'

'They have it wrong,' he said.

Annie looked toward me.

'I told you, Annie.'

The reality sank in. Clark knew I had beaten him. He came roaring back across the foyer.

'I'll fucking *kill* you,' he growled. 'What did you do?'

In the distance, I could see Black Suburbans speeding down the road toward the house.

'What's wrong?' I asked. 'Bad tip?'

'What's going on, Mike?' Annie asked.

'Why don't you tell her?' I said to her father.

Clark stepped toward me, fists balled at his side, ready to

300

strike. It would have been worth taking a knockout shot to demonstrate to Annie who the real lowlife was here.

'Annie,' I said, 'you should go. This could get bad.'

'They had you covered,' Clark said. 'You couldn't have switched it.'

I had absolute faith in Jack in one important respect: that he was absolutely untrustworthy. This was valuable in its way, like knowing a man who can always pick the losing team. Once you account for it, you're home free.

I knew that Lynch wouldn't let me pull the job without having his own man watching me to make sure I didn't screw them over. That was Jack. I knew he would betray me just as surely as I knew the three-card-monte man back in New York was going to switch in the losing card if I picked the ace. Jack had pretended to lose his nerve before the heist in order to get me to confess my plan. Once I'd given him the papers I needed to accomplish the switch, Lynch and Bloom could relax. They had me covered, had foiled my attempt to make this blow back in their faces.

But I erred on the side of caution when pulling the job, always have. I had two copies of the forged directives. I hid the second set in the take-out menus as Lynch's men searched me. When I let Jack in on the switch, I was playing him back at Bloom and Lynch. After Jack refused to help me swap the papers, they believed the directive I was carrying was the real thing.

But it was a forgery I had switched in. I shredded the true directive and replaced it with a copy saying the Fed would do exactly the opposite of its real plans. Clark had bet one hundred percent wrong.

'It's gone,' Clark said, and started rubbing the back of his neck. 'It's all gone. I'm a dead man.'

'What are you talking about, Dad?'

'I'm fine. I'll be fine.'

He walked in a small circle, eyes fixed on the stock ticker running along the bottom of the TV screen. Clark was an apex predator. He lived for these sorts of risks. He had the will to make instant decisions that could bankrupt him or earn him billions, the spine to double down when his bets started to turn against him so he could fight back from the brink.

He looked into the empty space of the grand foyer as he calculated. He stepped over to a narrow marble table, lifted a two-foot-high bronze sculpture of a horse, and with one arm heaved it at a tall mirror. Broken glass rained onto the floor.

He rested his hands on the table and looked down.

'Get out of here, Annie,' he said. 'Leave me with him.'

'No, Dad. What do you mean, you're a dead man?'

'Get out,' he said.

I looked back outside. The Suburbans had pulled into the end of the driveway. From the antennas, I took them for government-issue. The Secret Service was coming for us.

'That wasn't your money, was it, Dad?'

He didn't answer.

'Whose is it?' Her voice seemed to calm him down a little. I didn't say anything, just stood by, ready to jump Clark if he tried anything.

'Bad people,' he said. 'Very bad people.'

'Who?'

'The fund had a few tough years. Everyone did. But the men who gave me their money didn't care. I had to make it back or they would kill me. I needed a sure thing. We were lever-aged twelve to one. But now it's gone. All of it. The last eighty million. We were all in.'

'What are you talking about?' Annie asked.

'They're going to kill me. You think I would do this for fun? I was going to lose everything. The house. Your trust. My life. I had no other choice.'

I watched as more black trucks arrived. We were surrounded.

'Who, Lawrence?' I asked. He was always traveling in the Middle East, in South America. He'd grown his fund far faster than any honest man could have with honest money.

'Bad people.'

'Who?'

'Cartels,' he said. 'Certain Iranian gentlemen. If this had worked, if I could have made it to the third quarter, I could have been back on top. The strategy was fine. It was the fucking execution.'

He massaged his cheek and cast a strange, unfocused gaze on me. I didn't know if he was going to break down or, now that he'd lost it all, go for broke and kill me on the spot.

The law was coming, and my hands weren't clean, no matter what my intentions had been.

I thought I saw a way out with Clark, but even if I managed that hurdle, Bloom and Lynch might still kill me pro bono, for their own reasons. I knew too much about them. The Suburbans rolled up the driveway, closing in on the house.

'There's a way,' I said.

'What are you talking about?'

'We can make this win-win.' I thought back to Bloom's words after she'd kidnapped me from the shower.

'The cops are after all of us,' I said to Clark. 'Bloom's after me and will probably be after you once she finds out money is you bet wrong. Your clients are going to kill you once they realize their money's gone.'

'What's the point?' Annie asked.

'It's good,' I said. 'I can work with it. The cartels. Bad guys. We need a bargaining chip. That's great.'

'Great?' Clark started toward me, his rage breaking through. Annie stepped between us.

Larry was a banker. Bankers don't go to jail anymore, and I could use that. What we needed was a deal.

'These clients. You want protection from them?'

'There's no protection from them. Nowhere in the world. You'd need—'

'An army,' I said. 'The US has a pretty good one.'

I thought for a minute. 'There are two ways this can go. You can run or you can try to fight the feds. If the law doesn't get you, the killers will. But there's a third way. You know about billions in dirty money. You know about bigger fish. Take that leverage. Make a deal. They'll protect you.'

The Secret Service trucks fanned through the circular driveway. Clark's security strode out to stall the agents.

'That's the Secret Service,' I said. 'I tipped them off. They were watching your trades. They know all they need to know. Cut a deal.'

'What do you want out of it?'

'Call off Bloom and her goon.'

'I can't stop them. This has gone far beyond anything I asked for. They're off leash.'

'Where are they?' I asked. 'Can you call them?'

'In the garage,' he said.

'Which one?'

He pointed toward the east wing of the house. They must have been waiting for Clark's guards to hand me over. Security didn't need to deliver me to Lynch to die. I was going to do it myself.

Chapter Fifty-Two

'Where are you going, Mike?' Annie asked as I walked down a side hall.

I looked out the window and saw the Secret Service agents in their raid jackets moving toward the house.

'Go to the police,' I said.

'I'm coming with you.'

'It's safer—'

'I'm coming with you.'

We walked toward Clark's garage, although that term might give the wrong impression. Picture a luxury car showroom. I looked through the window in the door that led to the garage. Past the Aston Martin V8 Vantage, past the 1955 Mercedes 300SL Gullwing, past the 1940 Plymouth Super Deluxe, sat Bloom's old Land Cruiser with deep gashes in the metal from our run-in at the bridge.

'Wait here,' I said to Annie. 'Please. No arguments. I'm just going to talk to them. If anything happens, run to the agents. You'll be safe there.'

'Fine.' I opened the door and stepped inside. Lynch had been waiting. He raised his pistol as soon as I set foot in the garage. I lifted my hands as Bloom walked toward me, her gun at her side. This wasn't in their playbook: me walking in here on my own, unguarded.

'I want to talk,' I said. 'I have an offer I think you'll like.'

305

'This isn't a negotiation, Mike,' Bloom said.

To appease her, I needed Larry Clark to cooperate with the authorities. We could take down his very bad people. By cutting Bloom in and letting her take credit for busting Clark's clients, I could give her enough to leave me alone. I could taste bile rising in my throat as I contemplated the compromise, but it was the only way to buy my safety.

This plan had sounded a lot smarter in my head by the front door than it did out loud here in the garage as I stared down two guns, my shirt damp with sweat.

'You've heard the news?' I asked.

'I did.'

'Then we have a lot to talk about.'

'You blew up our position. You wrecked my car. You knocked me into a ditch. I'm unhappy. Lynch is *very* unhappy.'

'We're all screwed,' I said. 'I tipped the Secret Service. They're here. Clark can't pay you. He's talking with the agents now, and I have to say he's looking squishy. I think he's going to cut a deal. Do you want to be the first out of this clusterfuck or the last?'

Rule number one in crime, as in politics, is to always be the first to move when everyone starts selling everyone else out.

'I'm not too worried about that,' Bloom said. 'You can't take me down, Mike.'

I thought through the interested parties: the FBI, DC Metro, Virginia State Troopers, the Secret Service, Fed Police, the SEC, the DEA, the US Attorney for DC, and the District Attorney for New York. Not to mention the Foreign Service and intelligence people who would take an interest in the clients laundering money through Clark's funds. It was a long list of very ambitious people, all out to make their careers with a case like this.

Bloom would face a lot of heat. She knew the game, but this was beyond her. That's why I'd had to go through with the heist, to catch Bloom and Clark red-handed, to create such an intractable mess that no one, not even Bloom, could clean it up.

'No, I probably can't take you down,' I said. 'But this has gone bad enough that I can at least take your knees out. It's the prisoner's dilemma. We all make nice, or we all hang. You'd at the very least end up having to give up all your extra-curriculars, to go straight, on your best behavior, begging for pats on the head from all those patronizing old men on your board.'

I could see that got under her skin.

'Say what you have to say,' she said.

I moved closer to her. Lynch barked at me to stop. After I let him search me, I moved forward, stood whispering-close to Bloom.

'The whole thing's going south. Do you know who Clark's investors are? Why he was bankrolling this insane job?'

'I have some ideas.'

'He's going to flip to the Secret Service. I'll do you a favor. Say the whole heist was some undercover job. Say you were investigating him. You were after his clients, the dirty money he was laundering. It's cartels, it's foreign intelligence, Iran, sanction money. It'll be a goddamn field day for you. They'll carry you down Pennsylvania Avenue on their shoulders, and you'll be able to get away with anything you want from now on. You need me. I'll say what you need me to say. Broker this thing between Clark and the feds. You be the hero. I don't give a shit, so long as we have a truce and you leave my family alone.'

She turned her head slightly and thought about it. 'We could have that conversation,' she said. 'Grow the pie.'

I put my hand on her shoulder, my lips to her ear.

'One condition. Nonnegotiable. Lynch goes down for the murder on the Mall.'

'That's a tough sell,' she whispered.

307

She tapped her fingers on the truck as she thought through it.

'I like how you played this, Mike,' she said. 'Very creative. Tell you what. I won't kill you right this second. I'll put out a few feelers. Are the feds here?'

'Out front. The driveways are covered.'

She nodded. 'We're not too far apart. I'll have a few words with the agents on my way out.'

'Do we have a deal?'

'You'll know soon.'

She walked past Lynch and said something I couldn't hear. He lowered his gun and looked as downcast as if she'd taken away his ball. They climbed in the truck, circled around, and drove out an open bay of the garage.

The door back to the house opened.

'Mike!' Annie said. 'They're coming!'

I walked back into the house. The agents were already inside.

A man and a woman in Secret Service windbreakers strode up the hall toward us.

'I'm the one who called,' I said and lifted my hands over my head. 'She had nothing to do with this.'

The agent cocked her head at me. 'What is your name?'

'Michael Ford,' I said.

'Michael Ford?'

'That's right.'

She conferred with the other agent. I heard 'Holy shit' and something about the Fed.

'Are you armed?' she asked.

'No,' I said.

'Lie on your stomach. Slowly. Spread your arms away from your body.'

I dropped a knee, then lay on the floor.

'Now cross your ankles and turn your wrists so your palms face the ceiling.'

This procedure is called a felony stop, reserved for the most dangerous suspects. When it comes to getting taken in by the police, it's the royal treatment.

She circled to my side while the other agent covered me.

'Lift your left hand off the ground,' she said. I raised it, awkwardly, six inches off the floor. In one sudden movement, she swept down, turned my wrist, wrenched my arm back, knelt on my shoulder and snapped the cuffs on. She pulled my right arm behind me and finished the job.

They dragged me to my feet and started walking me between the marble columns of Clark's hall. I kept my head up. I'd never looked more like a guilty criminal, because I had finally done the honest thing.

I gave Annie a half smile. 'I've got them right where I want them,' I said.

'I'll talk to my father. He'll turn.'

She walked with me to the driveway. Other agents were questioning Clark as he stood beside a truck. I met his eyes, and he gave me a slow nod.

They shoved me into the back of another Suburban. 'I love you, Annie,' I said. 'Don't worry about me.'

'Love you.'

We rolled down the long driveway. Out my window I could see Bloom and Lynch. She had her arms crossed, talking to a captain as if she were just another cop. And Lynch, the FBI man, was in his element, leaning back against a truck.

As I passed, Bloom turned, looked to me, and held an index finger across her lips.

Chapter Fifty-Three

They took me to the Secret Service headquarters in downtown DC. It's a beautiful building of sand-colored bricks and sweeping lines of glass, and fits in among all the new construction around Mount Vernon Square. Passersby would think the HQ was just a high-end office building or condos. There are no identifying signs.

I knew dozens of lawyers, but when it came to a complex criminal defense, I drew a blank. I knew a bunch of public defenders from my pro bono stuff, but they're usually bleeding-heart types. I didn't hang out with any of the big-money criminal defense guns. They tend to be bitter after too many instances of helping guilty men buy their freedom, and they were just the sort I needed right now.

When the agents let me make my phone call, I left a message for a friend from my section at Harvard Law who was working at Steptoe & Johnson.

A special agent led me into a conference room that was a lot nicer than the FBI's. I was getting to be a connoisseur of interrogation boxes. Another agent sat in the corner and said nothing.

The lead man undid my cuffs, opened a file folder on the table, and sat down as I rubbed my wrists.

'Take a seat,' he said, and pointed to the chair opposite.

I pulled up to the table.

He read out the Miranda warning. I acknowledged my rights.

'You're an attorney?'

'I am,' I said.

'Then you know you're looking at a lot of time. Frankly, I can't believe you called us.'

'It was time to start telling the truth.'

'You want anything? Coffee? Food?'

'I *am* a little hungry.'

'Chinese?'

They were really doing this cop thing right. I almost laughed. Next they would pull out those blue-and-white Greek diner coffee cups. 'Chicken lo mein would be great.'

'Start at the beginning,' he said, which was smart. No hardball, not even the question of whether I would talk, just silence and a sympathetic ear. I thought back to New York, to the insane impulse to walk down that alley to the three-card-monte game. I thought of that first night at Jack's, that sickening moment when I realized, or thought I realized, that he was in serious trouble.

Where to begin?

The agent waited.

'Well . . .' I looked at the far corner and leaned back like a man settling into a favorite story. 'I'm really looking forward to the lo mein.'

The agent let out an annoyed breath.

'You know ninety-seven percent of cases end in a plea, Michael. Juries and judges don't matter. Your fate's in our hands, so make it easy on yourself. Your brother flipped. Clark flipped. They all pegged you as the ringleader.'

Law enforcement is allowed, even encouraged, to lie during an interrogation. I didn't bite. He closed the folder, then walked around the table to tower over me. Before he could speak again, the door opened. It was a supervisor, looking pissed.

'Mr Ford's lawyer is here,' he said. A man shoved his way

in the door. It took me a minute to recognize him. It was Bloom's assistant, Sebastian.

He crouched next to me and whispered in my ear. 'Did you say anything?'

'Not yet. But I will. What do you have for me?'

'She's on board.'

'The big boss?'

He nodded.

'Deal,' I said.

Sebastian turned to the two lawmen. 'We'll be going, then.'

The lead agent stepped in front of him. 'This guy's under arrest for a dozen felonies and counting. He's not leaving until after arraignment and bond, and probably not even then.'

'Call your boss,' Sebastian said.

The agent looked at the supervisor. 'Don't even tell me this is true.'

He just nodded his head.

Sebastian escorted me out. They gave me back my personal effects in an envelope at the front desk.

I pulled my belt back through the loops and was buckling it as we exited the lobby. Bloom was waiting downstairs, sitting on the hood of her truck.

'You left a fucking note?' she said.

'I did.'

'You're a nightmare. You have fun in there?' she asked, and nodded toward the headquarters.

'Time of my life. So what now?'

'I'll give you the full brief later,' she said, and handed me an ID badge.

BLOOM SECURITY

MICHAEL FORD

SPECIAL INVESTIGATOR

Underneath it was a plastic-and-metal card. I flipped it over and saw a button on the back. It was the same security token I had found at that dinner at Jack's a week ago, at the beginning of all this.

'I'm not working for you.'

'Unofficially, you can do whatever you want. But officially, you'll want to rethink that. Because as a member of Bloom Security's penetration testing division, you performed admirably in our red team audit of the physical access controls at the Federal Reserve Bank of New York.'

'You're fucking kidding me.'

'That's the story,' she said. 'And there's a whole bit about an undercover sting to take down Clark's clients. Or you can give that card back and try your luck with the agents upstairs. And SEC. FBI. MPD. NYPD. Who am I forgetting?'

'Maybe I *will* hang on to it for a little while,' I said, and put it in my pocket. 'They really bought it?'

'Of course. The only scandals you ever hear about are the fringe cases, buffoon congressmen who can't keep their pants on, who get too greedy. Those guys are isolated. There are interest groups on the side you can use as cutouts. The damage is contained. But you'll never get to something like this, the real corruption, the endemic stuff. Everyone in DC has to play by those rules, like it or not. Everyone's complicit, because everyone gets paid.'

'I'll back up your story. But no one touches Annie or my father.'

'Of course. There's no point in it now. It was all bluster anyway.'

'And Lynch, or whatever his real name is, pays for the murder of Sacks.'

'Agreed,' she said. 'He was getting a little hard to handle anyway. Something happened when his wife passed. He really went off the deep end.'

313

'But how do you prosecute a dirty FBI agent? He knows everything. He won't go down without a fight.'

'These things have a way of working themselves out. He'll get what he deserves. I guarantee it. So we have a deal?'

It was ugly, but it was a lot better than my options nine hours ago. 'Yes we do.'

'Welcome aboard, Mike. And if you're looking for some excitement, we might consider extending your contract. Call me anytime.'

'I'm done with excitement,' I said. 'I just want to go home. Do you have my car? I left it back at the river.'

'It's in the garage in Georgetown. You want a lift?'

'I'll walk. Do you have a cell phone you could lend me?'

She gestured Sebastian over, and he offered me one of his.

'Anything else?' she asked.

I patted my pockets. 'Do you have a dime?'

She reached into the console and offered me a quarter.

'No dime?'

Sebastian searched his jacket, then laid one in my palm.

'Thanks,' I said.

Chapter Fifty-Four

I tried Annie on my way over to Georgetown. No answer. But there was no reception at her father's place.

My Jeep was in the garage next to Bloom's office.

The dime just fit the screws on the rear license plate. I eased out the top two and pulled out the spare key I had taped behind the stamped metal.

I drove home. I tried the landline at her dad's house, but they tended to ignore my calls when Annie was there. I was starting to get the impression the in-laws weren't very fond of me.

Annie had e-mailed. Everything was fine. I wrote back, let her know I was out already, and then crashed onto the couch. Her family had already started coming in from England for the wedding, and they were staying in a guest house at the estate. She was trying to talk them all down, including her grand-mother, and my presence was not going to help matters.

I was starving and restless, and couldn't stand another second in that empty house. I drove over to the end of King Street, the heart of Old Town, right next to the water. It's all cobblestone streets, eighteenth-century taverns, and preserved colonial row houses.

I grabbed takeout at an Irish fish-and-chips place and walked along the river as I ate. The sun went down as I passed through a dirt parking lot where the historic buildings gave way to dingy garages and boats up on blocks.

It was probably just the paranoia and fatigue I'd been fighting for days, but I felt as if someone was watching me. I passed a marine repair shack, hid around a corner, and waited. I looked back. There was no one.

When I turned to start walking again, I crashed into a man's chest. I shoved him back, came up ready to fight.

'Mike, it's me,' he said. It was my brother. Did he think that would make me want to punch him *less*? I moved toward him, fists raised. He jumped back, stepping on my dinner where I had dropped it.

'What do you want?' I asked

'Just making sure you're okay.'

'I'm fine,' I said. 'But what do you *want*?'

'What makes you think I want something?'

'Because every word out of your mouth is a calculated ploy meant to ruin my life.'

'I guess I should start by saying thank you for not shooting me back at the bridge.'

He was trying for levity.

'Don't thank me,' I said. 'I missed.'

Jack looked toward the open water. 'What are we going to do?'

'*We?*'

'I'm sorry, Mike.' He paused and took on a grave expression. 'I'm so fucking sorry. You weren't going to get hurt. That's what they told me. Bloom just wanted to bring you in. I tried to stop it once I saw what was going on, I tried to warn you, but by then they had me. They were going to kill me. Mike, I know you can't forgive me, but . . .'

He went on with apologies and pleas for a while, talking himself into the role. The lower lip trembled. The voice hitched. His face twisted with despair.

It was a move I'd learned from him and had used once or twice myself to great effect. When you're in trouble, you respond with remorse so over the top that the person you've wronged just wants the embarrassment to end, wants to make sure you don't off yourself. By the end of the performance, the victim is telling you not to be so hard on yourself and rubbing your back, the original transgression forgotten.

'Just stop,' I said.

'We can run, Mike. Get a little distance, a little time to think. Let's just go.'

'I'm not running, Jack. I never want to see you again.'

'What do you mean? Did you get cover for the job?'

'I'll be all right.'

'Can you fix me up, too?'

'You're serious?' I asked.

He nodded. 'You're unbelievable,' I said. 'I won't dime you out. I should, but I won't. I'm not putting myself on the line for you, either. I'm done cleaning up your mistakes.'

'But Bloom has it worked out?'

'I think so. I don't know where you land in that equation.'

'That's good.' He tried to be casual for a moment. I could tell he was up to something.

'Goddamn it, Jack, just say what's on your mind.'

'Well, you always split aces, right?'

I groaned.

'And you always bet a sure thing,' he went on.

I searched his expression for a moment. 'You ran with the tip, the fake directive?' I asked.

'Yeah. I mean, of course. A sure thing. How many times do you get a sure thing?'

'So what the hell do you want?'

'Well . . . it didn't go too well, as you can imagine,' he said. 'And seeing how it's sort of, not exactly your fault, but . . . Anyway, I thought maybe you could help me get it squared away.'

'Get what?'

'Well, I borrowed a little. I mean, a sure thing. And these dudes are serious, Mike. I know it's asking a lot, but—'

I shook my head. I was right on the line between righteous anger and sheer admiration for the balls on this guy.

'You're not asking me for money. Tell me you're not asking me for money.'

'Not necessarily, but there are—'

'Stop,' I said.

'But these guys, I mean *these* guys are serious, Mike.'

I started walking down a dock. Half the boards were rotted out, and a thirty-year-old cabin cruiser squeaked against the pilings at the end.

'Where are you going?' he asked. I put one hand on the gunwale and vaulted into the boat.

'I'm sorry, Mike. What else can I say?'

I pulled open a panel to the right of the steering podium.

He stepped onto the boat.

'The life you're living, Jack,' I said. 'Trash the whole thing. Start fresh.'

'I get it, Mike, I understand. This is on me. I'm going to get myself sorted out. But I don't know if I can, man . . .' His voice broke, but he held it together. 'They might get me for the Fed job. And then there are these guys I owe the money to. I need help.'

'Anything I owe you as my brother has been paid in full, many times over. All I can give you is a head start.'

I pointed at the controls beside the wheel. 'First, put the throttle forward, and then, inside the panel, run the black to the solenoid. It'll start. Turn right into the channel. Keep the green buoys on your right. You can pick up the Intracoastal Waterway in Norfolk. That'll take you all the way to Key West without hitting blue water, and from there it's up to you. I don't care. But this whole thing may not break your way, so I suggest you never set foot in the US again.'

'This is just who I am, Mike. I can't help it. People don't change. Once a crook, man—'

'I know firsthand that is bullshit. The brother I knew is dead, and good riddance. I love you, Jack. One more word and I'll kill you, but I still love you. Start over. Change your life.'

I stepped off the boat.

He held out the knife Bloom had taken from me at the shower, the knife from New York. He must have stolen it back.

I shook my head – no more – then turned and walked up the planks.

He didn't say anything. He let me go.

I didn't look back until I was a quarter mile away, walking along the docks. Jack had killed the running lights. I could barely see him as the boat slid across the black water and disappeared in the distance.

Chapter Fifty-Five

I expected the full spectacle of the Washington scandal to swallow me up. The press vans would swarm my house. The FBI would fan out, rounding up every corrupt official, pulling all the hard drives and files from Bloom's offices, slowly working its way up from her goons to the paymasters in high places who had helped her get away with it all. I pictured the resignations and press conference denials; pictured photographers kneeling on the Senate floor as the investigation reached its peak; pictured the perp walks as justice was served.

But there was none of that. Instead, at an afternoon press conference, Emily Bloom stood flanked by an assistant attorney general, a US Attorney, and a Secret Service agent as they announced their success in one of the largest money-laundering cases in the history of the Department of Justice. It was a shining example of the effectiveness and efficiency of private-public partnerships in law enforcement.

That was the price I paid for my life, for Annie's, for my father's. I managed not to be sick when I watched it on TV. For months, as I watched this all unfold, witnessed Bloom work her magic as she papered over the truth, I couldn't shake that unclean feeling, like oil on my skin.

There were questions and rumors and hints at deeper secrets, of course, but soon it was election season. There were more important stories: the president's dog passed away. The usual obsession with political tactics, one-upmanship, and winning the day filled the papers. The press moved on.

Clark was sentenced to two years in a prison without fences, which destroyed his reputation. I didn't know you could bet completely wrong on the markets and still be convicted of insider trading. It didn't speak well to his skills as an investor, but given everything I knew about Wall Street, I assumed it would be about six years before people once again started handing him their money.

I tended to avoid Bloom on the dinner party circuit, but I kept up the threat. Lynch had to answer for the murder on the Mall or else I would take us all down. She told me she had it taken care of.

Lynch retired from the Bureau right after the Fed job and moved to New Mexico. There had been an investigation of him at Justice, supposedly. Asking around, I learned that his case had been 'sent to Florida' – handed off to an agent or assistant US Attorney who was due to retire in a year or two. He'd be told something like: *Here's the folder, don't kill yourself on it. One call a week and memo it to the file. If anyone asks, 'We don't comment on ongoing investigations.'* That bought them time for everyone to forget what had happened.

I wouldn't let up. Then Bloom sent me the clipping. Lynch had been shot and killed during a robbery at a gas station around the corner from his house. There were no suspects and no leads. His passing was very convenient for her, but as she had once told me, these things have a way of working themselves out.

I didn't ask.

This was politics, the efficient alignment of power and interests, and it was a terrifying thing to see up close.

I knew that victory in the real world could feel like defeat. I would do what I always did: put my head down and get back to long hours of hard work, doing what good I could do.

Chapter Fifty-Six

That would all come later. That first day of freedom after the heist, after dealing with Jack on the waterfront in Alexandria, all I felt was relief. I had pulled a job I had initially thought was impossible. I'd survived, escaped the fall they'd laid out for me, and turned the trap back on Lynch and Bloom and Clark. And I was prouder than I care to admit that I had gone head-to-head with Jack and outconned him. My family was safe. I was out. All I wanted was to return to sweet, boring workaday life, exploring the finer points of QuickBooks with my accountant neighbor, dragging my trash cans to the curb, and holding Annie on the couch as she fell asleep during a movie.

But after sending Jack off at the docks, I had one more job to do.

I drove fast and made it there by ten. I circled along the fence to the side gate near the creek. The latch wasn't much trouble. I reached through the bars and shimmed it from the inside. The owner probably wasn't too concerned about people getting through, because it was a lethal place for trespassers.

I picked my way through the woods around the property, waiting for them to strike. They made no noise. I had to hope I could catch their glowing eyes before they closed their jaws on my throat.

But I had a secret this time. I walked past the outbuildings.

It was familiar ground. I was on the open lawn, near the pools and tennis courts. I had never consciously cased the property, but old habits die hard, so in my mind I had a ready map of the security lights and motion sensors. I worked a circuitous route through the blind spots.

First I heard the panting breath of the dogs, then the fast drumbeat of their feet on the ground. A hundred pounds of sleek muscle and teeth shot toward me. Their eyes flashed like coins in the night.

'Hutz!' I commanded.

In an instant they sat, waited for me to approach, then licked my fingers like family dogs. I continued on, and they loped beside me in a silent pack as I neared the house. I guess that day I had spent hanging out with Jürgen the dog trainer hadn't been such a waste of time after all.

There were only a few lights on in the massive house. I saw figures moving, but they weren't who I was after. The place was a fortress, alarmed and secured with Medeco cylinders all around. I didn't have tools, but that didn't matter. I had an inside man.

I circled to the rear of the house, bounced a few pebbles off a high window, then tinked a few more.

The light came on. A black silhouette appeared.

'Annie,' I said.

The window was closed. She couldn't hear me. I found an inside corner near the spa room. I stepped onto a window ledge, then grabbed a lantern and hoisted myself up, then onto a first-story roof. I climbed across the tiles and dormers, and from there it was an easy haul to Annie's window.

I tapped on the glass three times. 'It's Mike.'

The window opened. And there was my bride, with a cricket bat over her shoulder, ready to strike.

'It's me, hon,' I said. 'Sorry I surprised you.'

She leaned the bat against a vanity, reached out and hugged me hard for a minute, then eased up and pressed her face against mine.

I took her hand and led her onto the roof. We sat side by side. She leaned against me, laced her fingers between mine.

'You know we have a front door, right?'

'Your grandma's been intercepting my calls.'

'I could strangle her.'

'There's been enough of that sort of thing. I couldn't deal with her right now, so I came around the back.' Armed guards, gold vaults, and psycho killers, no problem, but I couldn't face down Vanessa.

'Probably a good idea. Between today and your performance at the shower, you're non grata. I'm not in much better shape. She couldn't believe it about Dad. I had to give her some tough love.'

'How'd she take it?'

'Shock, cunning retreat. She's probably planning her revenge.'

'Your Dad okay?'

'Do you want him to be okay?'

'I don't want the bastard to get killed.'

'He's taking a deal.'

I nodded. 'That's good. There's going to be a lot of compromises, but we can make some real good come from all this, bring your father's clients to justice.'

We were silent for a moment, tracing the constellations over the black contours of the Blue Ridge. I'd never gotten over how many stars you could see out here.

'Annie, I kept you in the dark. You were right about Jack. I thought I could bring everyone together. I thought if I worked hard enough, somehow I could fix everything, fix the past, fix our families, fix Jack.'

'You were doing what you thought you needed to do. And it's a good thing that you try, that you have that hope.'

'I wanted to talk to you about everything. It's stupid, but I was worried I would disappoint you or scare you off. Everything that happened, the violence with our old boss, it got so out of control. I never wanted you to see me like that. I never wanted to be like that. It's not me. It's not my nature.'

'I know. You don't scare me, Mike. Just let me in next time. I can handle it. It's what I want, what I signed up for. All of you. You don't have to protect me.'

'I've noticed. You're pretty good behind the wheel. Thanks for saving my ass.'

'Don't worry about it. I'm sorry about my father. Jesus, I don't even know where to begin. Is that why he was being nice to you recently?'

'Yes. I knew something was up. It was misdirection. He could finally relax because he'd figured out how to destroy me.'

'You're lucky you signed that prenup,' she said. 'The Clarks are broke.'

I laughed with her, pulled her in close and pressed my lips to her temple. She put her hand in mine.

'What are you thinking?' she asked.

'What I've been thinking since the first time I met you. I nearly blurted it out in the middle of the conference room. "I love you. Let's get married. Run away with me."'

'Yes,' she said.

I looked at her.

'Thanks. I was worried about whether this whole thing was still a go. You can take your time. I'm just glad you're talking to me.'

'No. I'm saying let's go. Right now. We'll drive through the mountains, find a place to stay, look up a justice of the peace or a chapel in the morning.'

'Are you serious?'

She punched me in the arm. 'You're going to sneak up to a girl's window like that and not elope with her? Have some class, for God's sake.'

'You asked for it,' I said.

She gave me a suspicious look. 'So this wasn't your plan when you came out here?'

I ducked it. She could see right through me.

'What about the wedding?' I asked.

'We can still do something like that if we want. There'll be time to sort it out. But this will just be you and me. Our thing.'

I stood and helped her to her feet. 'I love it. Let's go.'

She smiled, then leaned in for a long kiss. 'You're in for it,' she said. 'And if you think I'm going to take it easy on you just because of a little gunshot wound, you'd better think again.'

Maybe I wouldn't make it out of this alive. I led her from the roof to the gable, then guided her steps as we climbed down the windows. I caught her as she jumped down, then held her to me, my co-conspirator.

We ran across the lawns and through the thick stands of trees, headed for the river and my Jeep. For a moment, I lost her in the shadows. Then she took my hand and pulled me into the night.

Acknowledgments

Thanks to my wife, Heather, a continual inspiration who stayed up late many nights fleshing out the plot with me and gamely helped act out the fight scenes. And to our families for their enthusiasm and support. I'm particularly indebted to my mother, Ellen, who was my second set of eyes on every draft.

For help and encouragement along the way, I'm grateful to Jeff Abbot, Marc Ambinder, Allen Appel, Arianne Cohen, Zoë Ferraris, Joseph Finder, Annie Lowrey, Justin Manask, Sommer Mathis, Mike Melia, Ben Mezrich, Peter Nichols, Roger Pardo-Maurer, James Patterson, Pradeep Ramamurthy, Cullen Roche, Kevin Rubino, Dan Wagner, Daniel H. Wilson, Matt Yglesias, Rafael Yglesias, International Thriller Writers, and Mystery Writers of America.

Steven Davis and Evan Macosko guided me on medical details. The advice and work of Deviant Ollam, Wil Allsopp, Kevin Mitnick, Marc Weber Tobias, Bruce Schneier, and Chris Gates at Lares Consulting were invaluable for the Fed break-in plot and the finer points of physical security. Gary Cohen and Doug Frantz helped with background on private intelligence and corporate espionage. John Dearie, Mike Derham, and several others who asked not to be named were kind enough to talk to me about Federal Reserve operations. I took a few liberties: the foil trick is slightly more complicated in practice; DC has a new evidence warehouse; and I changed the particulars of how the Board of Governors transmits the directive to the Fed's New York trading desk.

I'm honored to have the backing of an absolutely first-rate team at Little, Brown and Hachette Book Group: Heather Fain, Miriam Parker, Amanda Lang, Tracy Williams, and everyone who helped get these books into readers' hands. I would especially like to thank Wes Miller for his excellent revisions, Peggy Freudenthal and Chris Jerome for a great copyedit, and Marlena Bittner for her humor and the unbelievable job she did spreading the word about Mike Ford. I'm indebted to the foreign editors and translators on this series and the booksellers and readers who make this work possible.

My agent Shawn Coyne has been an essential partner, at my side from the first notion to the last page. My editor, Reagan Arthur, saved the day on this one with her patience and unerring judgment. This book wouldn't have been possible without their guidance, and I'm incredibly lucky to have them in my corner.

About the Author

Matthew Quirk studied history and literature at Harvard College. After graduation, he joined *The Atlantic* and spent five years at the magazine reporting on a variety of subjects including crime, private military contractors, the opium trade, terrorism prosecutions, and international gangs. He is the author of *The 500*. He lives in Washington, DC.